MICHAEL MOORCOCK

An All-New Novel of Elric

The Fortress of the Pearl

ACE BOOKS, NEW YORK

THE FORTRESS OF THE PEARL

An Ace Book
Published by The Berkley Publishing Group
200 Madison Avenue, New York, New York 10016

Book design by Sheree Goodman

You can join the Michael Moorcock fan club! Write to: *Nomads of the
Time Streams*, The International Michael Moorcock Appreciation So-
ciety, PO Box 451048, Atlanta, GA 30345-1048.

First Edition: October 1989

Library of Congress Cataloging-in-Publication Data
Moorcock, Michael, 1939–
    The fortress of the pearl.
I. Title.
PR6063.059F6   1989   823'.914   89-6838
ISBN 0-441-19123-1

Printed in the United States of America

10 9 8 7 6 5 4 3 2 1

For
Shane and Leslie,
Ed and Paul
—the first Nomads . . .

And when Elric had told his three lies to Cymoril, his betrothed, and had set his ambitious cousin Yyrkoon as Regent on the Ruby Throne of Melniboné, and when he had taken leave of Rackhir the Red Archer, he set off into lands unknown, to seek knowledge which he believed would help him rule Melniboné as she had never been ruled before.

But Elric had not reckoned with a destiny already determining that he should learn and experience certain things which would have a profound effect upon him. Even before he encountered the blind captain and the Ship Which Sailed the Seas of Fate, he was to find his life, his soul and all his idealism in jeopardy.

In Ufych-Sormeer he was delayed over a matter involving a misunderstanding between four unworldly wizards who amiably and inadvertently threatened the destruction of the Young Kingdoms before they had served the Balance's ultimate purpose; and in Filkhar he experienced an affair of the heart which he would never again speak about; he was learning, at some cost, the power and the pain of bearing the Black Sword.

But it was in the desert city of Quarzhasaat that he began the adventure which was to help set the course of his weird for years to come . . .

The Chronicle of the Black Sword

PART ONE

Is there a madman with a brain
To turn the stuff of nightmare sane
And demons crush and Chaos tame,
Who'll leave his realm, forsake his bride
And, tossed by contradictory tides,
Give up his pride for pain?

The Chronicle of the Black Sword

PART ONE

1

A Doomed Lord Dying

It was in lonely Quarzhasaat, destination of many caravans but terminus of few, that Elric, hereditary Emperor of Melniboné, last of a bloodline more than ten thousand years old, sometime conjuror of terrible resource, lay ready for death. The drugs and herbs which usually sustained him had been used in the final days of his long journey across the southern edge of the Sighing Desert and he had been able to acquire no replacements for them in this fortress city which was more famous for its treasure than for its sufficiency of life.

Slowly and feebly the albino prince stretched his bone-coloured fingers to the light and brought to vividness the bloody jewel in the Ring of Kings, the last traditional symbol of his ancient responsibilities; then he let the hand fall. It was as if he had briefly hoped the Actorios would revive him, but the stone was useless while he lacked energy to command its powers. Besides, he had no great desire to summon demons here. His own folly had brought him to Quarzhasaat; he owed her citizens no vengeance. They, indeed, had cause to hate him, had they but known his origins.

Once Quarzhasaat had ruled a land of rivers and lovely valleys, its forests verdant, its plains abundant with crops, but that had been before the casting of certain incautious spells in a war with threatening Melniboné more than two thousand years earlier. Quarzhasaat's empire had been lost to both sides. It had been engulfed by a vast mass of sand which swept over it like a tide, leaving only the capital and her traditions which in time became the prime reason for her continuing existence. Because Quarzhasaat had always stood there, she must be sustained, her citizens believed, at any cost throughout eternity. Though she had no purpose or function, still her masters felt a heavy obligation to continue her existence by whichever means they found expedient. Fourteen times had armies attempted to cross the Sighing Desert to loot fabulous Quarzhasaat. Fourteen times had the desert itself defeated them.

Meanwhile the city's chief obsessions (some would say her chief industry) were the elaborate intrigues amongst her rulers. A republic, albeit in name only, and hub of a vast inland empire, albeit entirely covered by sand, Quarzhasaat was ruled by her Council of Seven, whimsically known as the Six and One Other, who controlled the greater part of the city's wealth and most of her affairs. Certain other potent men and women, who chose not to serve in this septocracy, wielded considerable influence while displaying none of the trappings of power. One of these, Elric had learned, was Narfis, Baroness of Kuwai'r, who dwelled in a simple yet beautiful villa at the city's southern extreme and gave most of her attention to her notorious rival, the old Duke Ral, patron of Quarzhasaat's finest artists, whose own palace on the northern heights was as unostentatious as it was lovely. These two, Elric was told, had elected three members each to the Council, while the seventh, always nameless and simply called the Sexocrat (who ruled the Six), maintained a balance, able to sway any vote one way or the other. The ear of the Sexocrat was most profoundly desired by all the many rivals in the city, even by Baroness Narfis and Duke Ral.

Uninterested in Quarzhasaat's ornate politics as he was in

his own, Elric's reason for being here was curiosity and the fact that Quarzhasaat was clearly the only haven in a great wasteland lying north of the nameless mountains dividing the Sighing Desert from the Weeping Waste.

Moving his exhausted bones on the thin straw of his pallet, Elric wondered sardonically if he would be buried here without the people ever knowing that the hereditary ruler of their nation's greatest enemies had died amongst them. He wondered if this had after all been the fate his gods had in store for him: nothing as grandiose as he had dreamed of and yet it had its attractions.

When he had left Filkhar in haste and some confusion, he had taken the first ship out of Raschil and it had brought him to Jadmar, where he had chosen wilfully to trust an old Ilmioran drunkard who had sold him a map showing fabled Tanelorn. As the albino had half-guessed, the map proved a deception, leading him far from any kind of human habitation. He had considered crossing the mountains to make for Karlaak by the Weeping Waste but on consulting his own map, of more reliable Melnibonéan manufacture, he had discovered Quarzhasaat to be significantly closer. Riding north on a steed already half-dead from heat and starvation, he had found only dried river-beds and exhausted oases, for in his wisdom he had chosen to cross the desert in a time of drought. He had failed to find fabled Tanelorn and, it seemed, would not even catch sight of a city which, in his people's histories, was almost as fabulous.

As was usual for them, Melnibonéan chroniclers showed only a passing interest in defeated rivals, but Elric remembered that Quarzhasaat's own sorcery was said to have contributed to her extinction as a threat to her half-human enemies: A misplaced rune, he understood, uttered by Fophean Dals, the Sorcerer Duke, ancestor to the present Duke Ral, in a spell meant to flood the Melnibonéan army with sand and build a bulwark about the entire nation. Elric was still to discover how this accident was explained in Quarzhasaat now. Had they created myths and legends to rationalise the city's ill-luck entirely as a result of evil emanating from the Dragon Isle?

Elric reflected how his own obsession with myth had brought him to almost inevitable destruction. "In my miscalculations," he murmured, turning dull crimson eyes again towards the Actorios, "I have shown that I share something in common with these people's ancestors." Some forty miles from his dead horse, Elric had been discovered by a boy out searching for the jewels and precious artefacts occasionally flung up by those sandstorms which constantly came and went over this part of the desert and were partially responsible for the city's survival as well as for the astonishing height of Quarzhasaat's magnificent walls. They were also the origin of the desert's melancholy name.

In better health Elric would have relished the city's monumental beauty. It was a beauty derived from an aesthetic refined over centuries and bearing no signs of outside influence. Though so many of the curving ziggurats and palaces were of gigantic proportions there was nothing vulgar or ugly about them; they had an airy quality, a peculiar lightness of style which made them seem, in their terra-cotta reds and glittering silver granite, their whitewashed stucco, their rich blues and greens, as if they had been magicked out of the very air. Their luscious gardens filled marvellously complex terraces, their fountains and water-courses, drawn from deep-sunk wells, gave tranquil sound and wonderful perfume to her old cobbled ways and wide tree-lined avenues, yet all this water, which might have been diverted to growing crops, was used to maintain the appearance of Quarzhasaat as she had been at the height of her imperial power and was more valuable than jewels, its use rationed and its theft punishable by the severest of laws.

Elric's own lodgings were in no way magnificent, consisting as they did of a truckle bed, straw-strewn flagstones, a single high window, a plain earthenware jug and a basin containing a little brackish water which had cost him his last emerald. Water permits were not available to foreigners and the only water on general sale was Quarzhasaat's single most expensive commodity. Elric's water had almost certainly been stolen from a public fountain. The statutory penalties for such thefts were rarely discussed, even in private.

Elric required rare herbs to sustain his deficient blood, but their cost, even had they been available, would have proven far beyond his present means which had been reduced to a few gold coins; a fortune in Karlaak but of virtually no worth in a city where gold was so common it was used to line the city's aqueducts and sewers. His expeditions into the streets had been exhausting and depressing.

Once a day the boy, who had found Elric in the desert and brought him to this room, paid the albino a visit, staring at him as if at a curious insect or captured rodent. The boy's name was Anigh and, though he spoke the Melnibonéan-derived *lingua franca* of the Young Kingdoms, his accent was so thick it was sometimes impossible to understand all he said.

Once more Elric tried to lift his arm only to let it fall. That morning he had reconciled himself to the fact that he would never again see his beloved Cymoril and would never sit upon the Ruby Throne. He knew regret, but it was of a distant kind, for his illness made him oddly euphoric.

"I had hoped to sell you."

Elric peered, blinking, into the shadows of the room on the far side of a single ray of sunlight. He recognised the voice but could make out little more than a silhouette near the door.

"But now it seems all I have to offer in next week's market will be your corpse and your remaining possessions." It was Anigh, almost as depressed as Elric at the prospect of his prize's death. "You are still a rarity, of course. Your features are those of our ancient enemies but whiter than bone and those eyes I have never seen before in a man."

"I'm sorry to disappoint your expectations." Elric rose weakly on his elbow. He had deemed it imprudent to reveal his origins but instead had said he was a mercenary from Nad-sokor, the Beggar City, which sheltered all manner of freakish inhabitants.

"Then I had hoped you might be a wizard and reward me with

some bit of arcane lore which would set me on the path to becoming a wealthy man and perhaps a member of the Six. Or you might have been a desert spirit who could confer on me some useful power. But I have wasted my waters, it seems. You are merely an impoverished mercenary. Have you no wealth left at all? Some curio which might prove of value, for instance?'' And the boy's eyes went towards a bundle which, long and slender, rested against the wall near Elric's head.

"That's no treasure, lad," Elric informed him grimly. "He who possesses it could be said to bear a curse impossible to exorcise." He smiled at the thought of the boy trying to find a buyer for the Black Sword which, wrapped in a torn cassock of red silk, occasionally gave out a murmur, like a senile old man attempting to recall the power of speech.

"It's a weapon, is it not?" said Anigh, his thin, tanned features making his vivid blue eyes seem large.

"Aye," Elric agreed. "A sword."

"An antique?" The boy reached under his striped brown djellabah and picked at the scab on his shoulder.

"That's a fair description." Elric was amused but found even this brief conversation tiring.

"How old?" Now Anigh took a step forward so that he was entirely illuminated by the ray of sunlight. He had the perfect look of a creature adapted to dwell amongst the tawny rocks and the dusky sands of the Sighing Desert.

"Perhaps ten thousand years." Elric found that the boy's startled expression helped him forget, momentarily, his almost certain fate. "But probably more than that . . ."

"Then it's a rarity, indeed! Rarities are prized by Quarzha-saat's lords and ladies. There are those amongst the Six, even, who collect such things. His honour the Master of Unicht Shlur, for instance, has the armour of a whole Ilmioran army, each piece arranged on the mummified corpses of the original warriors. And my Lady Talith possesses a collection of war-instruments numbering several thousands, each one different. Let me take that, Sir Mercenary, and I'll discover a buyer. Then I'll seek the herbs you need."

"Whereupon I'll be fit enough for you to sell me, eh?" Elric's amusement increased.

Anigh's face became exquisitely innocent. "Oh, no, sir. Then you will be strong enough to resist me. I shall merely take a commission on your first engagement."

Elric felt affection for the boy. He paused, gathering strength before he spoke again. "You expect I'll interest an employer, here in Quarzhasaat?"

"Naturally," Anigh grinned. "You could become a bodyguard to one of the Six, perhaps, or at least one of their supporters. Your unusual appearance makes you immediately employable! I have already told you what great rivals and plotters our masters are."

"It is encouraging"—Elric paused for breath—"to know that I can look forward to a life of worth and fulfillment here in Quarzhasaat." He tried to stare directly into Anigh's brilliant eyes, but the boy's head turned out of the sunlight so that only part of his body was exposed. "However, I understood from you that the herbs I described grew only in distant Kwan, days from here—in the foothills of the Ragged Pillars. I will be dead before even a fit messenger could be half-way to Kwan. Do you try to comfort me, boy? Or are your motives less noble?"

"I told you, sir, where the herbs grew. But what if there are some who have already gathered Kwan's harvest and returned?"

"You know of such an apothecary? But what would one charge me for such valuable medicines? And why did you not mention this before?"

"Because I did not know if it before." Anigh seated himself in the relative cool of the doorway. "I have made enquiries since our last conversation. I am a humble boy, your worship, not a learned man, nor yet an oracle. Yet I know how to banish my ignorance and replace it with knowledge. I am ignorant, good sir, but not a fool."

"I share your opinion of yourself, Master Anigh."

"Then shall I take the sword and find a buyer for you?"

He came again into the light, hand reaching towards the bundle.

Elric fell back, shaking his head and smiling a little. "I, too, young Anigh, have much ignorance. But, unlike you, I think I might also be a fool."

"Knowledge brings power," said Anigh. "Power shall take me into the entourage of the Baroness Narfis, perhaps. I could become a captain in her guard. Maybe a noble!"

"Oh, one day you'll surely be more than either." Elric drew in stale air, his frame shuddering, his lungs enflamed. "Do what you will, though I doubt the sword will go willingly."

"May I see it?"

"Aye." With painful awkward movements Elric rolled to the bed's edge and plucked the wrappings free of the huge sword. Carved with runes which seemed to flicker unsteadily upon the blade of black, glowing metal, decorated with ancient and elaborate work, some of mysterious design, some depicting dragons and demons intertwined as if in battle, Stormbringer was clearly no mundane weapon.

The boy gasped and drew back, almost as if regretting his suggested bargain. "Is it alive?"

Elric contemplated his sword with a mixture of loathing and something akin to sensuality. "Some would say it possessed both a mind and a will. Others would claim it to be a demon in disguise. Some believe it composed of the vestigial souls of all damned mortals, trapped within as once, in legend, a great dragon was said to dwell inside another pommel than that which the sword now bears." To his own faint distaste, he found that he was taking a certain pleasure in the boy's growing dismay. "Have you never looked upon an artefact of Chaos before, Master Anigh? Or one who is wedded to such a thing? Its slave, perhaps?" He let his long, white hand descend into the dirty water and raised it to wet his lips. His red eyes flickered like dying embers. "During my travels I have heard this blade described as Arioch's own battlesword, able to slice down the walls between the very Realms. Others, as they die upon it, believe it to be a living creature. There is a theory that it is but one member of an entire race, living in our dimension but capable, should it desire, of summoning a million brothers. Can you hear it speaking, Master Anigh? Will that voice delight and charm the casual buyers in your market?'' And a sound came from the pale lips that was not a laugh yet contained a desolate kind of humour.

Anigh withdrew hastily into the sunlight again. He cleared his throat. ''You called the thing by a name?''

''I called the sword *Stormbringer* but the peoples of the Young Kingdoms sometimes have another name, both for myself and for the blade. The name is *Soulstealer*. It has drunk many souls.''

''You're a dreamthief!'' Anigh's eyes remained on the blade. ''Why are you not employed?''

''I do not know the term and I do not know who would employ a 'dreamthief.' '' Elric looked to the boy for further explanation.

But Anigh's gaze did not leave the sword. ''Would it drink my soul, master?''

''If I chose. To restore my energy for a while, all I would have to do is let Stormbringer kill you and perhaps a few more and then she'll pass her energy on to me. Then, doubtless, I could find a steed and ride away from here, possibly to Kwan.''

Now the Black Sword's voice grew more tuneful, as if approving of this notion.

''Oh, Gamek Idianit!'' Anigh got to his feet, ready to flee if necessary. ''This is like that story on Mass'aboon's walls. This is what those who brought about our isolation were said to wield. Aye, the leaders bore identical swords to these. The teachers at the school tell of it. I was there. Oh, what did they say!'' And he frowned deeply, an object lesson to anyone wishing to point a moral concerning the benefits of attending at classes.

Elric regretted frightening the boy. ''I am not disposed, young Anigh, to maintain my own life at the expense of others who have offered me no harm. That is partly the reason why I find myself in this specific predicament. You saved my life, child. I would not kill you.''

''Oh, master. Thou art dangerous!'' In his panic he spoke

a tongue more ancient than Melnibonéan, and Elric, who had learned such things to aid his studies, recognised it.

"Where came you by that language, by that Opish?" the albino asked.

Even in his terror the boy was surprised. "They call it the gutter cant, here in Quarzhasaat. The thieves' secret. But I suppose it is common enough to hear it in Nadsokor."

"Aye, indeed. In Nadsokor, true." Elric was again intrigued by this minor turn of events. He reached towards the boy, to reassure him.

The motion caused Anigh to jerk up his head and make a noise in his throat. Clearly he set no store by Elric's attempt to regain his confidence. Without further remark, he left the room, his bare feet pattering down the long corridor and the steps into the narrow street.

Convinced that Anigh was now gone for good, Elric knew a sudden pang of sadness. He regretted only one thing now, that he would never be reunited with Cymoril and return to Melniboné to keep his promise to wed her. He understood that he had always been and probably would always be reluctant to ascend the Ruby Throne again, yet he knew it was his duty to do so. Had he deliberately chosen this fate for himself, to avoid that responsibility?

Elric knew that though his blood was tainted by his strange disease, it was still the blood of his ancestors and it would not have been easy to deny his birthright or his destiny. He had hoped he might, by his rule, turn Melniboné from the introverted, cruel and decadent vestige of a hated empire into a reinvigorated nation capable of bringing peace and justice to the world, of presenting an example of enlightenment which others might use to their own advantage.

For a chance to return to Cymoril he would more than willingly trade the Black Sword. Yet secretly he had little hope that this was possible. The Black Sword was more than a source of sustenance, a weapon against his enemies. The Black Sword bound him to his race's ancient loyalties, to Chaos, and he could not see Lord Arioch willingly allowing him to break that particular bond. When he considered these matters, these hints at a greater destiny, he found his mind growing confused and he preferred to ignore the questions whenever possible.

"Well, perhaps in folly and in death, I shall break that bond and thwart Melniboné's bad old friends."

The breath in his lungs seemed to grow thin and no longer burned. Indeed, it felt cool. His blood moved more sluggishly in his veins as he tried to rise and stagger to the rough wooden table where his few provisions lay. But he could only stare at the stale bread, the vinegary wine, the wizened pieces of dried meat whose origins were best not speculated upon. He could not get up; he could not summon the will to move. He had accepted his dying if not with equanimity then at least with a degree of dignity. Falling into a languorous reverie, he recalled his deciding to leave Melniboné, his cousin Cymoril's trepidation, his ambitious cousin Yyrkoon's secret glee, his pronouncements made to Rackhir the Warrior Priest of Phum, who had also sought Tanelorn.

Elric wondered if Rackhir the Red Archer had been any more successful in his quest or whether he lay somewhere in another part of this vast desert, his scarlet costume reduced to rags by the forever sighing wind, his flesh drying on his bones. Elric hoped with all his heart that Rackhir had succeeded in discovering the mythical city and the peace it promised. Then he found that his longing for Cymoril was growing and he believed that he wept.

Earlier he had considered calling upon Arioch, his patron Duke of Chaos, to save him, yet had continued to feel a deep reluctance even to contemplate the possibility. He feared that by employing Arioch's help once more he would lose far more than his life. Each time that powerful supernatural agreed to help, it further strengthened an agreement both implicit and mysterious. Not that the debate was anything more than notional, Elric reflected ironically. Of late Arioch had shown a distinct reluctance to come to his aid. Possibly Yyrkoon had superseded him in every way . . .

This thought brought Elric back to pain, to his longing for

Cymoril. Again he tried to rise. The sun's position had changed. He thought he saw Cymoril standing before him. Then she became an aspect of Arioch. Was the Duke of Chaos playing with him, even now?

Elric moved his gaze to contemplate the sword which seemed to shift in its loose silk wrappings and whisper some kind of warning, or possibly a threat.

Elric turned his head away. "Cymoril?" He peered into the shaft of sunlight, following it until he looked through the window at the intense desert sky. Now he believed he saw shapes moving there, shadows that were almost the forms of men, of beasts and demons. As these shapes grew more distinct they came to resemble his friends. Cymoril was there again. Elric moaned in despair. "My love!"

He saw Rackhir, Dyvim Tvar, even Yyrkoon. He called out to them all.

At the sound of his own cracked speech he realised he had grown feverish, that his remaining energy was being dissipated by his fantasies, that his body was feeding on itself and that death must be close.

Elric reached to touch his own brow, feeling the sweat pour from it. He wondered how much each bead might fetch on the open market. He found it amusing to speculate on this. Could he sweat enough to buy himself more water, or at least a little wine? Or was this production of liquid in itself against Quarzhasaat's bizarre water laws?

He looked again beyond the sunlight, thinking he saw men there, perhaps the city's guard come to inspect his premises and demand to see his licence to perspire.

Now it seemed that the desert wind, which was never very far away, came sliding through the room, bringing with it some elemental gathering, perhaps a force which was to bear his soul to its ultimate destination. He felt relief. He smiled. He was glad in several ways that his struggle was over. Perhaps Cymoril would join him soon?

Soon? What could Time mean in that intemporal Realm? Perhaps he must wait for Eternity before they could be together? Or a mere passing moment? Or would he never see her? Was all that lay ahead for him an absence, a nothingness? Or would his soul enter some other body, perhaps equally as sickly as his present one, and be faced again with the same impossible dilemmas, the same terrible moral and physical challenges which had plagued him since his emergence into adulthood?

Elric's mind drifted further and further from logic, like a drowning mouse swept away from the shore, spinning ever more crazily before death brought oblivion. He chuckled, he wept; he raved and occasionally slept as his life dissipated its last with the vapours now pouring from his strange, bone-white flesh. Any uninformed onlooker would have seen that some misborn diseased beast, not a man at all, lay in its final and doubtless felicitous agonies upon that rough bed.

Darkness came and with it a brilliant panoply of people from the albino's past. He saw again the wizards who had educated him in all the arts of sorcery; he saw the strange mother he had never known, and a stranger father; the cruel friends of his childhood with whom, bit by bit, he could no longer enjoy the luscious, terrible sports of Melniboné; the caverns and secret glades of the Dragon Isle, the slim towers and hauntingly intricate palaces of his unhuman people, whose ancestors were only partially of this world and who had arisen as beautiful monsters to conquer and rule before, with a deep weariness which he could appreciate all the better now, declining into self-examination and morbid fantasies. And he cried out, for in his mind he saw Cymoril, her body as wasted as his own while Yyrkoon, giggling with horrible pleasure, practised upon it the foulest of abominations. And then, again, he wanted to live, to return to Melniboné, to save the woman he loved so deeply that often he refused to let himself be conscious of the intensity of his passion. But he could not. He knew, as the visions passed and he saw only the dark blue sky through his window, that soon he would be dead and there would be nobody to save the woman he had sworn to marry.

By morning the fever was gone and Elric knew he was but a short hour or two from the end. He opened misted eyes to see the shaft of sunlight, soft and golden now, no longer glaring directly in as it had the previous day, but reflected from the glittering walls of the palace beside which his hovel had been built.

Feeling something suddenly cool upon his cracked lips, he jerked his head away and tried to reach for his sword, for he feared that steel was being positioned against him, perhaps to cut his throat.

"Stormbringer . . ."

His voice was feeble and his hand was too weak to leave his side, let alone grip his murmuring blade. He coughed and realised that liquid was being dripped into his mouth. It was not the filthy stuff he had bought with his emerald but something fresh and clean. He drank, trying hard to focus his eyes. Immediately before him was an ornamental silver flask, a golden, soft hand, an arm clothed in exquisitely delicate brocade, a humorous face which he did not recognise. He coughed again. The liquid was more than ordinary water. Had the boy found some sympathetic apothecary? The potion was like one of his own sustaining distillations. He drew a ragged, grateful breath and stared in wary curiosity at the man who had resurrected him, however briefly. Smiling, his temporary saviour moved with studied elegance in his heavy, unseasonable robes.

"Good morning to you, Sir Thief. I trust I'm not insulting you. I gather you're a citizen of Nadsokor, where all kinds of robbery are practised with pride?"

Elric, conscious of the delicacy of his situation, saw fit not to contradict him. The albino prince nodded slowly. His bones still ached.

The tall, clean-shaven man slipped a stopper into his flask. "The boy Anigh tells me you have a sword to sell?"

"Perhaps." Certain now that his recovery was only temporary, Elric continued to exercise caution. "Though I would guess 'tis the kind of purchase most would regret making . . ."

"But your sword is not representative of your main trade, eh? You have lost your crooked staff, no doubt. Sold for water?" A knowing expression.

Elric chose to humour the man. He allowed himself to hope

for life again. The liquid had revived him enough to bring back his wits, together with a proportion of his usual strength. "Aye," he said, appraising his visitor. "Maybe."

"So ho? What? Do you advertise your own incompetence? Is this the way of the Nadsokor Thieves' Company? Thou art a subtler felon than thy guise suggests, eh?" This last was delivered in the same canting tongue Anigh had used on the previous day.

Now Elric realised that this wealthy person had formed an opinion of his status and powers which, while at odds with any actuality, could provide him with a means of escape from his immediate predicament. Elric grew more alert. "You'd buy my services, is that it? My special prowess? That of myself and possibly my sword?"

The man affected carelessness. "If you like." But it was clear he suppressed some urgency. "I have been told to inform you that the Blood Moon must soon burn over the Bronze Tent."

"I see." Elric pretended to be impressed by what to him was pure gibberish. "Then we must move swiftly, I suppose."

"So my master believes. The words mean nothing to me, but they have significance for you. I was told to offer you a second draft if you appeared to respond positively to that knowledge. Here." And smiling more broadly, he held out the silver flask, which Elric accepted, drinking sparingly and feeling still more strength return, his aches gradually dissipating.

"Your master would commission a thief? What does he wish stolen that the thieves of Quarzhasaat cannot steal for him?"

"Aha, sir, you affect a literal-mindedness I cannot believe in now." He took back the flask. "I am Raafi as-Keeme and I serve a great man of this empire. He has, I believe, a commission for you. We have heard much of the Nadsokorian skills and for some while have been hoping one of your folk might wander this way. Did you plan to steal from us? None is ever successful. Better to steal *for* us, I think."

"Wise advice, I would guess." Elric rose in his bed and put his feet upon the flagging. Already the liquid's strength was ebbing. "Perhaps you would outline the nature of the task you

have for me, sir?'' He reached for the flask but it was with-
drawn into Raafi as-Keeme's sleeve.

"By all means, sir," said the newcomer, "when we have
discussed a little of your background. You steal more than
jewels, the boy says. Souls, I hear."

Elric felt some alarm and looked suspiciously at the man whose
expression remained bland. "In a manner of speaking . . ."

"Good. My master wishes to make use of your services. If
you're successful you'll have a cask of this elixir to carry you
back to the Young Kingdoms or anywhere else you desire to go."

"You are offering me my life, sir," said Elric slowly, "and
I am willing to pay only so much for that."

"Ah, sir, you have a streak of the merchant's bartering instinct, I see. I am sure a good bargain can be struck. Will you
come with me now to a certain palace?"

Smiling, Elric took Stormbringer in his two hands and flung
himself back across the bed, his shoulders against the wall and
the source of the sunlight. Placing the sword upon his lap, he
waved his hand in mockery of lordly hospitality. "Would you
not prefer to stay and sample what I have to offer, Sir Raafi
as-Keeme?"

The richly clad man shook his head deliberately. "I think
not. You have doubtless become used to this stink and to the
stink of your own body, but I can assure you it is not pleasant
to one who is unfamiliar with it."

Elric laughed as he accepted this. He rose to his feet, hook-
ing his scabbard to his belt and slipping the murmuring runesword into the black leather. "Then lead on, sir. I must admit
I'm curious to discover what considerable risks I am to take
that would make one of your own thieves refuse the kind of
rewards a lord of Quarzhasaat can offer."

And in his mind he had already made a bargain: that he
would not allow his life to slip away so easily a second time.
He owed that much, he had decided, to Cymoril.

2

"The Pearl at the Heart of the World"

In a room through which mellow sunlight slanted in dusty bands from a massive grille set deep into the ornately painted roof of a place called Goshasiz whose complicated architecture was stained by something more sinister than time, Lord Gho Fhaazi entertained his guest to further drafts of the mysterious elixir and food which, in Quarzhasaat, was at least as valuable as the furnishings.

Bathed and wearing fresh robes, Elric possessed a new vitality, the dark blues and greens of his silks emphasising the whiteness of his skin and long, fine hair. The scabbarded runesword leaned against the carved arm of his chair and he was prepared to draw it and use it should this audience prove an elaborate trap.

Lord Gho Fhaazi was modishly coiffed and clad. His black hair and beard were teased into symmetrical ringlets, the long moustachios were waxed and pointed, the heavy brows bleached blond above pale green eyes and a skin artificially whitened until it resembled Elric's own. The lips were painted a vivid red. He sat at the far end of a table which slanted down

subtly towards his guest, his back to the light so that he almost
resembled a magistrate sitting in judgement on a felon.

Elric recognised the deliberateness of the arrangement and
was not put out by it. Lord Gho was still relatively young, in
his early thirties, and had a pleasant, slightly high-pitched
voice. He waved plump fingers at the plates of figs and dates
in mint leaves, of honeyed locusts, which lay between them,
pushed the silver flask of elixir in Elric's direction with an
awkward display of hospitality, his movements revealing that
he performed tasks he would usually have reserved for his servants.

"My dear fellow. More. Have more." He was unsure of
Elric, almost wary of him, and it grew clear to the albino that
there was some urgency involved in the matter, which Lord
Gho had not yet proposed, nor revealed through the courier
he had sent to the hovel. "Is there perhaps some favourite food
we have not provided?"

Elric raised yellow linen to his lips. "I'm obliged to you,
Lord Gho. I have not eaten so well since I left the lands of the
Young Kingdoms."

"Aha, just so. Food is plentiful there, I hear."

"As plentiful as diamonds in Quarzhasaat. You have visited
the Young Kingdoms?"

"We of Quarzhasaat have no need to travel." Lord Gho
spoke in some surprise. "What is there abroad that we could
possibly desire?"

Elric reflected that Lord Gho's people had a good deal in
common with his own. He reached and took another fig from
the nearest dish and as he chewed it slowly, savouring its sweet
succulence, he stared frankly at Lord Gho. "How came you
to learn of Nadsokor?"

"We do not travel ourselves—but, naturally, travellers come
to us. Some of them have taken caravans to Karlaak and elsewhere. They bring back the occasional slave. They tell us such
astonishing lies!" He laughed tolerantly. "But there's a grain
of truth, no doubt, in some of what they say. While dreamthieves, for instance, are secretive and circumspect about their

origins, we have heard that thieves of every kind are welcomed in Nadsokor. It takes little intelligence to draw the obvious conclusion . . .''

"Especially if one is blessed with only the barest information concerning other lands and peoples." Elric smiled.

Lord Gho Fhaazi did not recognise the albino's sarcasm, or perhaps he ignored it. "Is Nadsokor your home city or did you adopt it?" he asked.

"A temporary home at best," Elric told him truthfully.

"You have superficial looks in common with the people of Melniboné, whose greed led us to our present situation," Lord Gho informed him. "Is there Melnibonéan blood in your ancestry, perhaps?"

"I have no doubt of it." Elric wondered why Lord Gho failed to draw the most obvious conclusion. "Are the folk of the Dragon Isle still hated for what they did?"

"Their attempt upon our empire, you mean? I suppose so. But the Dragon Isle has long since sunk beneath the waves, a victim of our sorcerous revenge, and her puny empire with her. Why should we give much thought to a dead race which was duly punished for its infamy?"

"Indeed." Elric realised that so thoroughly had Quarzhasaat explained away her defeat and provided for herself a reason for taking no action, that she had consigned his entire people to oblivion in her legends. He could not therefore be a Melnibonéan, for Melniboné no longer existed. On that score, at least, he could know some peace of mind. Moreover, so uninterested were these people in the rest of the world and its denizens that Lord Gho Fhaazi had no further curiosity about him. The Quarzhasaatim had decided who and what Elric was and were satisfied. The albino reflected on the power of the human mind to build a fantasy and then defend it with complete determination as a reality.

Elric's chief dilemma now lay in the fact that he had no clear notion at all of the profession he was thought to practise or of the task Lord Gho wished him to perform.

The Quarzhasaati nobleman lowered his hands into a bowl

of scented water and washed his beard, ostentatiously letting the liquid fall upon the geometrical mosaics of the floor.

"My servant tells me you understood his references," he said, drying himself upon a gauzy towel. Again it was clear he usually employed slaves for this task but had chosen to dine alone with Elric, perhaps for fear of his secrets being overheard. "The actual words of the prophecy are a little different. You know them?"

"No," said Elric with immediate frankness. He wondered what would happen if Lord Gho realised that he was here under false pretences.

"When the Blood Moon makes fire of the Bronze Tent, then the Path to the Pearl will be opened."

"Aha," said Elric. "Just so."

"And the nomads tell us that the Blood Moon will appear over the mountains in little less than a week. And will shine upon the Waters of the Pearl."

"Exactly," said Elric.

"And so the path to the Fortress shall, of course, be revealed."

Elric nodded with gravity and as if in confirmation.

"And a man such as yourself, with a knowledge at once supernatural and not supernatural, who can tread between reality and unreality, who knows the ways along the borders of dreams and waking, may break through the defences, overwhelm the guardians and steal the Pearl!" Lord Gho's voice was a mixture of lasciviousness, venality and hot excitement.

"Indeed," said the Emperor of Melniboné.

Lord Gho took Elric's reticence for discretion. "Would you steal that Pearl for me, Sir Thief?"

Elric gave the matter apparent consideration before he spoke. "There is considerable danger in the stealing, I would guess."

"Of course. Of course. Our people are now convinced that none but one of your craft is able even to enter the Fortress, let alone reach the Pearl itself!"

"And where lies this Fortress of the Pearl?"

"I suppose at the Heart of the World."

Elric frowned.

"After all," said Lord Gho with some impatience, "the jewel is known as the Pearl at the Heart of the World, is it not?"

"I follow your reasoning," said Elric, and resisted an urge to scratch the back of his head. Instead he considered a further draft of the marvellous elixir, although he was growing increasingly disturbed, both by Lord Gho's conversation and the fact that the pale liquid was so delicious to him. "But surely there is some other clue . . . ?"

"I had thought such things your sphere, Sir Thief. You must go, of course, to the Silver Flower Oasis. It is the time when the nomads hold one of their gatherings. Some significance, no doubt, concerning the Blood Moon. It is most likely that at the Silver Flower Oasis the path will be opened to you. You have heard of the oasis, naturally."

"I have no map, I fear," Elric informed him, a little lamely.

"That will be provided. You have never travelled the Red Road?"

"As I've explained. I'm a stranger to your empire, Lord Gho."

"But your geographies and histories must concern themselves with us!"

"I fear we are a little ignorant, my lord. We of the Young Kingdoms, so long in the shadow of wicked Melniboné, had not the opportunity to discover the joys of learning."

Lord Gho raised his unnatural eyebrows. "Yes," he said, "that would be the case, of course. Well, well, Sir Thief, we'll provide you with a map. But the Red Road's easy enough to follow since it leads from Quarzhasaat to the Silver Flower Oasis and beyond are only the mountains the nomads call the Ragged Pillars. They're of no interest to you, I think. Unless the Path of the Pearl takes you through them. That's a more mysterious road and not, you'll appreciate, marked on any conventional map at least. None that we possess. And our libraries are the most sophisticated in the world."

So determined was Elric to get the best from his reprieve that he was prepared to continue with this farce until he was clear of Quarzhasaat and riding for the Young Kingdoms again. "And a steed, I hope. You'll give me a mount."

"The finest. Will you need to redeem your crooked staff? Or is that merely a kind of sign of your calling?"

"I can find another."

Lord Gho put his hand to his peculiar beard. "Just as you say, Sir Thief."

Elric determined to change the subject. "You have said little about the nature of my fee." He drained his goblet and clumsily Lord Gho filled it again.

"What would you usually ask?" said the Quarzhasaati.

"Well, this is an unusual commission." Elric grew amused again at the situation. "You understand that there are very few of my skill or indeed standing, even in the Young Kingdoms, and fewer still who come to Quarzhasaat . . ."

"If you bring me that specific Pearl, Sir Thief, you will have all manner of wealth. At least enough to make you one of the most powerful men in the Young Kingdoms. I would furnish you with an entire nobleman's household. Clothes, jewels, a palace, slaves. Or, if you wished to continue your travels, a caravan capable of purchasing a whole nation in the Young Kingdoms. You could become a prince there, possibly even a king!"

"A heady prospect," said the albino sardonically.

"Add to that what I have already paid and shall be paying and I think you'll judge the reward handsome enough."

"Aye. Generous, no doubt." Elric frowned, glancing around the great room, with its hangings, its rich gem-work, its mosaics of precious stones, its elaborately ornamental cornices and pillars. He had it in mind to bargain further, because he guessed it was expected of him. "But if I have a notion of the Pearl's worth to you, Lord Gho—what it will purchase for you here—you'll admit that the price you offer is not necessarily a large one."

Lord Gho Fhaazi grew amused in turn. "The Pearl will buy me the place on the Council of Six which shall shortly be vacated. The Nameless Seventh has given the Pearl as her price.

It is why I must have it so soon. It is already promised. You have guessed this. There are rivals, but none who has offered so much.''

"And do these rivals know of your offer?''

"Doubtless there are rumours. But I would warn you to keep silent on the nature of your task . . .''

"You do not fear that I could look for a better bargain elsewhere in your city?''

"Oh, there will be those who would offer you more, if you were so greedy and so disloyal. But they could not offer you what I offer, Sir Thief.'' And Lord Gho Fhaazi let his mouth form a terrible grin.

"Why so?'' Elric felt suddenly trapped and his instinct was to reach for Stormbringer.

"They do not possess it.'' Lord Gho pushed the flask towards the albino and Elric was a little surprised to see that he had already drunk another goblet of the elixir. He filled his cup once more and drank thoughtfully. Some of the truth was coming to him and he feared it.

"What can be as rare as the Pearl?'' The albino put down his goblet. He believed he had an idea of the answer.

Lord Gho was staring at him intently. "You understand, I think.'' Lord Gho smiled again.

"Aye.'' Elric felt his spirits drop and he knew a frisson of deep terror mixed with a growing anger. "The elixir, I suppose . . .''

"Oh, that's relatively easy to make. It is, of course, a poison—a drug which feeds off its user, giving him only an appearance of vitality. Eventually there is nothing left for the drug to feed upon and the death which results is almost always unpleasant. What a wretch the stuff makes of men and women who only a week or so earlier believed themselves powerful enough to rule the world!'' Lord Gho began to laugh, his little ringlets bobbing at his face and on his head. "Yet, dying, they will beg and beg for the thing which has killed them. Is that not an irony, Sir Thief? What's so rare as the Pearl? you ask.

Why, the answer must be clear to you now, eh? An individual's life, is it not?''

"So I am dying. Why then should I serve you?"

"Because there is, of course, an antidote. Something which replaces everything the other drug steals, which does not cause a craving in the one who drinks it, which restores the user to full health in a matter of days and drives out the need for the original drug. So you see, Sir Thief, my offer to you was by no means an empty one. I can give you enough of the elixir to let you complete your task and, so long as you return here in good time, I can give you the antidote. You'll have gained much, eh?''

Elric straightened himself in his chair and put his hand upon the pommel of the Black Sword. "I have already informed your courier that my life has only limited worth to me. There are certain things I value more.''

"I understood as much," said Lord Gho Fhaazi with cruel joviality, "and I respect you for your principles, Sir Thief. Your point's well put. But there's another life to consider, is there not? That of your accomplice?''

"I have no accomplice, sir."

"Have you not? Have you not, Sir Thief? Would you come with me?''

Elric, mistrustful of the man, still saw no reason not to follow him when he strode arrogantly through the huge, curving doorway of the hall. At his belt once more Stormbringer grumbled and stirred like a suspicious hound.

The passages of the palace, lined in green, brown and yellow marble to give the feeling of a cool forest, scented with the most exquisite flowering shrubs, led them past rooms of retainers, menageries, tanks of fish and reptiles, a seraglio and an armoury, until Lord Gho arrived at a wooden door guarded by two soldiers in the impractically baroque armour of Quarzhasaat, their own beards oiled and forked into fantastically exaggerated shapes. They presented their engraved halberds as Lord Gho approached.

"Open this," he ordered. And one took a massive key from within his breastplate, inserting it into the lock.

The door opened upon a small courtyard containing a defunct fountain, a little cloister and a set of living quarters on the far side.

"Where are you? Where are you, my little one? Show yourself! Quickly now!" Lord Gho was impatient.

There was a clink of metal and a figure emerged from the doorway. It had a piece of fruit in one hand, a loop or two of chain in the other, and it walked with difficulty for the links were attached to a metal band riveted around its waist. "Ah, master," it said to Elric, "you have not served me as I would have hoped."

Elric's smile was grim. "But maybe as you deserve, eh, Anigh?" He let his anger show. "I did not imprison you, boy. I think the choice, in reality, was probably your own. You tried to deal with a power which clearly recognises no decencies."

Lord Gho was unmoved. "He approached Raafi as-Keeme's manservant," he said, staring at the boy with a certain interest, "and offered your services. He said he was acting as your agent."

"Well, so he was," agreed Elric, his smile more sympathetic in view of Anigh's evident discomfiture. "But that surely is not against your laws?"

"Certainly not. He showed excellent enterprise."

"Then why is he imprisoned?"

"That's a matter of expediency. You appreciate that, Sir Thief?"

"In other circumstances I would suspect some minor infamy," said Elric carefully. "But I know you, Lord Gho, to be a nobleman. You would not hold this boy in order to threaten me. It would be beneath you."

"I hope I am a nobleman, sir. Yet in such time as as these not all nobles in this city are bound by the old codes of honour. Not when such stakes are played for. You appreciate that even though you are not yourself a nobleman. Or even, I suppose, a gentleman."

"In Nadsokor I am thought one," said Elric quietly.

"Oh, but of course. In Nadsokor." Lord Gho pointed at Anigh, who smiled uncertainly from one to the other, not following this exchange at all. "And in Nadsokor, I am sure, they would hold a convenient hostage if they could."

"But this is unfair, sir." Elric's voice was trembling with rage and he had to control himself not to reach his right hand towards the Black Sword on his left hip. "If I am killed in pursuit of my goal, the boy dies, just as if I had made my escape."

"Well, yes, that is true, dear thief. But I expect you to return, you see. If not—well, the boy will still be useful to me, both alive and dead."

Anigh no longer smiled. Terror came slowly into his eyes. "Oh, masters!"

"He'll not be harmed." Lord Gho placed a cold, powdered hand on Elric's shoulders. "For you will return with the Pearl at the Heart of the World, will you not?"

Elric breathed deeply, controlling himself. He felt a need deep within him; a need he could not readily identify. Was it bloodlust? Did he want to draw the Black Sword and suck the soul from this scheming degenerate? He spoke evenly. "My lord, if you would release the boy, I will assure you of my best efforts . . . I will swear . . ."

"Good thief, Quarzhasaat is full of men and women who give the most fulsome reassurances and who, I am sure, are sincere when they do so. They will swear great, important oaths upon all that is most holy to them. Yet should circumstances change, they forget those oaths. Some security, I find, is always useful to remind them of obligations undertaken. We are, you will appreciate, playing for the very highest stakes. There are really none higher in the whole world. A seat upon the Council." This last sentence was emphasised without mockery. Clearly Lord Gho Fhaazi could see no greater goal.

Disgusted by the man's sophistry and contemptuous of his provincialism, Elric turned his back on Lord Gho. He addressed the lad. "You'll observe, Anigh, that little luck befalls those who league themselves with me. I warned you of this. Yet still I shall endeavour to return and save you." His next sentence was uttered in the thievish cant. "Meanwhile do not trust this filthy creature and make every sensible effort to escape on your own."

"No gutter patois here!" cried Lord Gho, suddenly alarmed, "or you both die at once!" Evidently he did not understand the cant as his courier had done.

"Best not to threaten me, Lord Gho." Elric returned his hand to the hilt of his sword.

The nobleman laughed. "What? Such belligerence! Understand you not, Sir Thief, that the elixir you drink is already killing you? You have three weeks before only the antidote will save you! Do you not feel the gnawing need for the drug? If such an elixir were harmless, why, sir, we should all use it and become gods!"

Elric could not be sure if it was his mind or his body which felt the pangs. He realised that even as his instincts drove him to kill the Quarzhasaati nobleman his craving for the drug threatened to dominate him. Even close to death when his own drugs failed him he had never craved anything so much. He stood with his whole body trembling as he sought to master it again. His voice was icy. "This is more than minor infamy, Lord Gho. I congratulate you. You are a man of the cruellest and most unpleasant cunning. Are all those who serve upon the Council as corrupt as yourself?"

Lord Gho grew still more genial. "This is unworthy of you, Sir Thief. All I am doing is assuring myself that you'll follow my interests for a while." Again he chuckled. "I have assured myself, in fact, that for this period of time your interests become mine. What is so wrong with that? I would not think it befitting in a self-confessed thief, to insult a noble of Quarzhasaat merely because he knows how to strike a good bargain!"

Elric's hatred for the man, who originally he had only disliked, still threatened to consume him. But a new, colder mood took him as his hold over his own emotions returned. "So you are saying that I am your slave, Lord Gho."

"If you wish to put it so. At least until you bring me back the Pearl at the Heart of the World."

"And should I find this Pearl for you, how do I know you will supply me with the poison's antidote?"

Lord Gho shrugged. "That is for you to determine. You are an intelligent man for an outlander, and have survived this long, I'm sure, on your wits. But make no mistake. This potion is brewed for me alone and you'll not find the identical recipe anywhere else. Best hold to our bargain, Sir Thief, and depart from here ultimately a rich man. With your little friend all in one piece."

Elric's mood had changed to one of grim humour. With his strength returned, no matter how artificially, he could wreak considerable destruction to Lord Gho and, indeed, the whole city if he chose. As if reading his mind, Stormbringer seemed to stir against his hip and Lord Gho permitted himself a small, nervous glance towards the great runesword.

Yet Elric did not want to die and neither did he desire Anigh's death. He decided to bide his time, to pretend, at least, to serve Lord Gho until he discovered more about the man and his ambitions, and found out more, if possible, of the nature of the drug he so longed for. Possibly the elixir did not kill. Possibly it was a potion common to Quarzhasaat and many possessed the antidote. But he had no friends here, other than Anigh, not even temporary allies serving interests prepared to help him against Lord Gho as a common enemy.

"Perhaps," said Elric, "I do not care what becomes of the boy."

"Oh, I think I read your character well enough, Sir Thief. You are like the nomads. And the nomads are like the people of the Young Kingdoms. They place unnaturally high values on the lives of those with whom they associate. They have a weakness for sentimental loyalties."

Elric could not help considering the irony of this, for Melnibonéans thought themselves equally above such loyalties and he was one of the few who cared what happened to those not of his own immediate family. It was the reason he was here now. Fate, he reflected, was teaching him some strange lessons. He sighed. He hoped they did not kill him.

"If the boy is harmed when I return, Lord Gho—if he is harmed in any way—you will suffer a fate a thousand times worse than any you bestow on him. Or, I'll add, on me!" He turned blazing red eyes upon the aristocrat. It seemed that the fires of Hell raged inside that skull.

Lord Gho shuddered, then smiled to hide his fear. "No, no, no!" His unnatural brow clouded. "It is not for you to threaten me! I have explained the terms. I am unused to this, Sir Thief, I warn you."

Elric laughed and the fire in his eyes did not fade. "I will make you used to everything you have accustomed others to, Lord Gho. Whatever happens. Do you follow me? This boy will not be harmed!"

"I have told you . . ."

"And I have warned you." Elric's lids fell over his terrible eyes, as if he closed a door on a Realm of Chaos, yet still Lord Gho took a step backward. Elric's voice was a cold whisper. "By all the power I command, I will be revenged upon you. Nothing will stop that vengeance. Not all your wealth. Not death itself."

This time when Lord Gho made to smile he failed.

Anigh grinned suddenly, like the happy child he had been before these events. Evidently he believed Elric's words.

The albino prince moved like a hungry tiger towards Lord Gho. Then he staggered a little and drew a sharp breath. Clearly the elixir was losing its strength, or demanding more of him, he could not tell. He had experienced nothing like this before. He longed for another draft. He felt pains in his belly and chest, as if rats chewed him from within. He gasped.

Now Lord Gho found a vestige of his former humour. "Refuse to serve me and your death's inevitable. I would caution you to greater politeness, Sir Thief."

Elric drew himself up with some dignity. "You should know this, Lord Gho Fhaazi. If you betray any part of our bargain I will keep my oath and bring such destruction upon you and your city you will regret you ever heard my name. And you will only hear who I am, Lord Gho Fhaazi, before you die, your city and all its degenerate inhabitants dying with you.''

The Quarzhasaati made to reply then bit back his words, saying only: "You have three weeks."

With his remaining strength, Elric dragged Stormbringer from its scabbard. The black metal pulsed, black light pouring from it while the runes carved upon the blade twisted and danced and a hideous, anticipatory song began to sound in that courtyard, echoing through all the old towers and minarets of Quarzhasaat. "This sword drinks souls, Lord Gho. It could drink yours now and give me more strength than any potion. But you have a minor advantage over me for the moment. I'll agree to your bargain. But if you lie . . .''

"I do not lie!" Lord Gho had retreated to the other side of the barren fountain. "No, Sir Thief, I do not lie! You must do as I say. Bring me the Pearl at the Heart of the World and I will repay you with all the wealth I promised, with your own life and that of the boy!''

The Black Sword growled, clearly demanding the nobleman's soul there and then.

With a yelp, Anigh disappeared into the little room.

"I'll leave in the morning." Reluctantly Elric sheathed the sword. "You must tell me which of the city's gates I must use to travel upon the Red Road to the Silver Flower Oasis. And I will want your honest advice on how best to ration that poisoned elixir.''

"Come." Lord Gho spoke with nervous eagerness. "There is more in the hall. It awaits you. I had no wish to spoil our encounter with bad manners . . .''

Elric licked lips already growing unpleasantly dry. He paused, looking towards the doorway from which the boy's face could just be seen.

"Come, Sir Thief." Lord Gho's hand again went to Elric's arm. "In the hall. More elixir. Even now. You long for it, do you not?''

He spoke the truth, but Elric let his hatred control his lust for the potion. He called: "Anigh! Young Anigh!"

Slowly the boy emerged. "Aye, master."

"I swear you'll suffer no harm from any action of mine. And this foul degenerate now understands that if he hurts you in any way while I am gone he will die in the most terrible torment. And yet, boy, you must remember all I've said, for I know not where this adventure will lead me." And Elric added in the cant: "Perhaps to death."

"I hear you," said Anigh in the same tongue. "But I would beg you, master, not to die yourself. I have some interest in your remaining alive."

"No more!" Lord Gho strode across the courtyard signalling for Elric to accompany him. "Come. I'll supply you with all you need to find the Fortress of the Pearl."

"And I would be most grateful if you did not let me die. I would be a most grateful boy, master," said Anigh from behind them as the door closed.

3

On the Red Road

So it was that next morning Elric of Melniboné left ancient Quarzhasaat not knowing what he sought or where to find it; knowing only that he must take the Red Road to the Silver Flower Oasis and there find the Bronze Tent where he would learn how he might continue on the Path to the Pearl at the Heart of the World. And if he failed in this numinous quest, his own life at very least would be forfeit.

Lord Gho Fhaazi had offered no further illumination and it was evident the ambitious politician knew no more than he had repeated.

"The Blood Moon must make fire of the Bronze Tent before the Pathway to the Pearl shall be revealed."

Knowing nothing of Quarzhasaat's legends or history and very little of her geography, Elric had decided to follow the map he had been given to the oasis. It was simple enough. It showed a trail stretching for at least a hundred miles between Quarzhasaat and the oddly named oasis. Beyond this were the Ragged Pillars, a range of low mountains. The Bronze Tent was not named and neither was there any reference to the Pearl.

Lord Gho believed the nomads to be better informed but had not been able to guarantee that they would be prepared to talk to Elric. He hoped that, once they understood who he was, and with a little of Lord Gho's gold to reassure them, they would be friendly, but he knew nothing of the Sighing Desert's interland, nor its people. He knew only that Lord Gho despised the nomads as primitives and resented occasionally admitting them into the city to trade. Elric hoped the nomads would be better mannered than those who still believed this whole continent to be under their rule.

The Red Road was well-named, dark as half-dried blood, cutting through the desert between high banks which suggested it had once been the river on whose sides originally Quarzhasaat had been built. Every few miles the banks descended to reveal the great desert in all directions—a sea of rolling dunes which stirred in a breeze whose voice was faint here but still resembled the sighing of some imprisoned lover.

The sun climbed slowly into a glaring indigo sky as still as an actor's backdrop and Elric was grateful for the local costume provided him by Raafi as-Keeme before he left, a white cowl, loose white jerkin and breeches, white linen shoes to the knee and a visor which protected his eyes. His horse, a bulky, graceful beast capable of great speed and endurance, was similarly clothed in linen, to protect it from both the sun and the sand which blew in constant gentle drifts across the landscape. Clearly some effort was made to keep the Red Road free of the drifts which gathered against its banks and gradually built them into walls.

Elric had lost none of his hatred either of his situation or of Lord Gho Fhaazi; neither had he lost his determination to remain alive and rescue Anigh, return to Melniboné and be reunited with Cymoril. Lord Gho's elixir had proved as addictive as he had claimed and Elric carried two flasks of it in his saddle-bags. Now he truly believed it must indeed kill him eventually and that only Lord Gho possessed an antidote. This belief reinforced his determination to be revenged upon that nobleman at the earliest possible opportunity.

The Red Road seemed endless. The sky shivered with heat as the sun climbed higher. And Elric, who disapproved of useless regret, found himself wishing he had never been foolish enough to buy the map from the Ilmioran sailor or to venture so badly prepared into the desert.

"To summon supernaturals to aid me now would compound the folly," he said aloud to the wilderness. "What's more, I might need that aid when I reach the Fortress of the Pearl." He knew that his self-disgust had not merely caused him to commit further foolishness, but still dictated his actions. Without it, his thoughts might have been clearer and he might better have anticipated Lord Gho's trickery.

Even now he doubted his own instincts. For the past hour he had guessed that he was being followed but had seen no one behind him on the Red Road. He had taken to glancing back suddenly, to stopping without warning, to riding back a few yards. But he was apparently as alone now as he had been when he began the journey.

"Perhaps that damned elixir addles my senses also," he said, patting the dusty cloth of his horse's neck. The great bulwarks of the road were falling away here, becoming little more than mounds on either side of him. He reined in the horse, for he fancied he could see movement that was more than drifting sand. Little figures ran here and there on long legs, upright like so many tiny manikins. He peered hard at them but then they were gone. Other, larger creatures, moving with far slower speeds, seemed to creep just below the surface of the sand while a cloud of something black hovered over them, following them as they made their ponderous way across the desert.

Elric was learning that, in this part of the Sighing Desert at least, what appeared to be a lifeless wilderness was actually no such thing. He hoped that the large creatures he detected did not regard man as a worthwhile prey.

Again he received a sense of something behind him and turning suddenly thought he glimpsed a flash of yellow, perhaps a cloak, but it had disappeared in a slight bend behind him. His temptation was to stop, to rest for an hour or two before continuing, but he was anxious to reach the Silver Flower Oasis as soon as possible. There was little time to achieve his goal and return with the Pearl to Quarzhasaat.

He sniffed the air. The breeze brought a new smell. If he had not known better he would have thought someone was burning kitchen waste; it was the same acrid stink. Then he peered into the middle-distance and detected a faint plume of smoke. Were there nomads so close to Quarzhasaat? He had understood that they did not like coming within a hundred miles or more of the city unless they had specific reasons to do so. And if people were camped here, why did they not set their tents closer to the road? Nothing had been said of bandits, so he did not fear attack, but he remained curious, continuing his journey with a certain caution.

The walls rose up again and blocked his view of the desert, but the stink of burning grew stronger and stronger until it was almost unbearable. He felt the stuff clogging his lungs. His eyes began to stream. It was a most noxious smell, almost as if someone were burning putrefying corpses.

Again the walls sank a little until he could see over them. Less than a mile away, as best he could judge, he saw about twenty plumes of smoke, darker now, while other clouds danced and zig-zagged about them. He began to suspect that he had come upon a tribe who kept their cooking fires alight as they travelled in waggons of some kind. Yet it was hard to know what kind of waggons would easily cross the deep drifts. And again he wondered why they were not on the Red Road.

Tempted to investigate he knew he would be a fool to leave the road. He might again become lost and be in even worse condition than when Anigh had found him all those days ago on the far side of Quarzhasaat.

He was about to dismount and rest his mind and eyes, if not his body, for an hour, when the wall nearest him began to heave and quake and large cracks appeared in it. The terrible smell of burning was even closer now and he cleared his throat, coughing to rid himself of the stench while his horse began to whinny and refuse the rein as he tried to drive him forward.

Suddenly a flock of creatures ran directly across his path, bursting from the newly made holes in the walls. These were what he had mistaken for tiny men. Now that he saw them more closely he realised they were some kind of rat, but a rat which ran on long hind-legs, its forelegs short and held up high against its chest, its long, grey face full of sharp little teeth, its huge ears making it seem almost like some flying creature attempting to leave the ground.

There came a great rumbling and cracking. Black smoke blinded Elric and his horse reared. He saw a shape moving out of the broken banks—a massive, flesh-coloured body on a dozen legs, its mandibles clattering as it chased the rats which were clearly its natural prey. Elric let the horse have its head and looked back to get a clearer view of a creature he had thought existed only in ancient times. He had read of such beasts but had believed them extinct. They were called firebeetles. By some trick of biology the gigantic beetles secreted oily pools in their heavy carapaces. These pools, exposed to the sunlight and the flames already burning on other backs, would catch fire so that sometimes as many as twenty spots on the beetles' impervious backs would be burning at any one time and would only be extinguished when a beast dug its way deep underground during its breeding season. This was what he had seen in the distance.

The firebeetles were hunting.

They moved with awful speed now. At least a dozen of the gigantic insects were closing in on the road and Elric realised to his horror that he and his horse were about to be trapped in a sweep designed to catch the man-rats. He knew that the firebeetles would not discriminate where flesh was concerned and he could well be eaten by purest accident by a beast which was not known for making prey of men. The horse continued to rear and snort and only put all hooves on the ground when Elric forced it under his control, drawing Stormbringer and considering how useless even that sorcerous sword would be against the pink-grey carapaces from which flames now leapt and guttered. Stormbringer drew scant energy from natural creatures like these. He could only hope for a lucky blow, splitting a back, perhaps, and breaking through the tightening circle before he was completely trapped.

He swung the great black battle-blade down and severed a waving appendage. The beetle hardly noticed and did not pause for a second in its progress. Elric yelled and swung again and fire scattered. Hot oil was flung into the air as he struck the firebeetle's back and again failed to do it any significant harm. The shrieking of the horse and the wailing of the blade now mingled and Elric found himself yelling as he turned the horse this way and that in search of escape while all around his horse's feet the man-rats scurried in terror, unable to burrow easily into the hard clay of that much-travelled road. Blood spattered against Elric's legs and arms, against the linen which clad his horse to below its knees. Little spots of flaming oil flared on cloth and burned holes. The beetles were feasting, moving more slowly as they ate. There was nowhere in the circle a gap large enough for horse and rider to escape.

Elric considered trying to ride the horse over the backs of the great beetles, though it seemed their shells would be too slippery for purchase. There was no other hope. He was about to force the horse forward when he heard a peculiar humming in the air around him, saw the air suddenly fill with flies and knew that these were the scavengers which always followed the firebeetles, feeding off whatever scraps they left and upon the dung they scattered as they travelled. Now they were beginning to settle on him and his horse, adding to his horror. He slapped at the things, but they formed a thick coat, crawling on every part of him, their noise both sickening and deafening, their bodies half-blinding him.

The horse cried out again and stumbled. Elric desperately tried to see ahead. The smoke and the flies were too much for both himself and his horse. Flies filled his mouth and nostrils. He gagged, trying to brush them from him, spitting them down to where the little man-rats squealed and died.

Another sound came dimly to him, and miraculously the flies began to rise. Through watering eyes he saw the beetles start to move all in one direction, leaving a space through which he might ride. Without another thought he spurred his horse towards the gap, dragging great gasps of air into his lungs, still unsure if he had escaped or whether he had merely moved into a wider circle of firebeetles, for the smoke and the noise were still confusing him.

Spitting more flies from his mouth, he adjusted his visor and peered ahead. The beetles were no longer in sight, though he could hear them behind him. There were new shapes in the dust and smoke.

There were riders, moving on either side of the Red Road, driving the beetles back with long spears which they hooked under the carapaces and used as goads, doing the creatures no real harm but giving them enough pain to make them move, where Elric's blade had failed. The riders wore flowing yellow robes which were caught by the breeze of their own movement and lifted about them like wings as, systematically, they herded the firebeetles away from the road and out into the desert while the remainder of the man-rats, perhaps grateful for this unexpected salvation, scattered and found burrows in the sand.

Elric did not sheath Stormbringer. He knew enough to understand that these warriors might well be saving him only incidentally and might even blame him for being in their way. The other possibility, which was stronger, was that these men had been following him for some time and did not wish the firebeetles to cheat them of their prey.

Now one of the yellow-clad riders detached himself from the throng and galloped up to Elric, hailing him with spear raised.

"I thank you mightily," the albino said. "You have saved my life, sir. I trust I did not disrupt your hunt too much."

The rider was taller than Elric, very thin, with a gaunt dark face and black eyes. His head was shaved and both his lips were decorated, apparently with tiny tattoos, as if he wore a mask of fine, multicoloured lace across his mouth. The spear was not sheathed and Elric prepared to defend himself, knowing that his chances against even so many human beings were greater than they had been against the firebeetles.

The man frowned at Elric's statement, puzzled for a moment. Then his brow cleared. "We did not hunt the firebeetles. We saw what was happening and realised that you did not know enough to get out of the creatures' way. We came as quickly as we could. I am Manag Iss of the Yellow Sect, kinsman to Councillor Iss. I am of the Sorcerer Adventurers."

Elric had heard of these sects, who had been the chief warrior caste of Quarzhasaat and had been largely responsible for the spells which inundated the Empire with sand. Had Lord Gho, not trusting him completely, set them to following him? Or were they assassins instructed to kill him?

"I thank you, nonetheless, Manag Iss, for your intervention. I owe you my life. I am honoured to meet one of your sect. I am Elric of Nadsokor in the Young Kingdoms."

"Aye, we know of you. We were trailing you, waiting until we were far enough from the city to speak to you safely."

"Safely? You're in no danger from me, Master Sorcerer Adventurer."

Manag Iss was evidently not a man who smiled often and when he smiled now it was a strange contortion of the face. Behind them, other members of the sect were beginning to ride back, rehousing their long spears in the scabbards attached to their saddles. "I did not think we were, Master Elric. We come to you in peace and we are your friends, if you will have us. My kinswoman sends her greetings. She is the wife of Councillor Iss. Iss remains, however, our family name. We all tend to marry the same blood, our clan."

"I am glad to make your acquaintance." Elric waited for the man to speak further.

Manag Iss waved a long, brown hand whose nails had been removed and replaced with the same tattoos as those on his mouth. "Would you dismount and talk, for we come with messages and the offer of gifts."

Elric slipped Stormbringer back into the scabbard and swung his leg over his saddle, sliding to the dust of the Red Road.

He watched as the beetles lurched slowly away, perhaps in search of more man-rats, their smoking backs reminding him of the fires of the leper camps on the outskirts of Jadmar.

"My kinswoman wishes you to know that she, as well as the Yellow Sect, is at your service, Master Elric. We are prepared to give you whatever aid you require in seeking out the Pearl at the Heart of the World."

Now Elric felt a certain amusement. "I fear you have me at a disadvantage, Sir Manag Iss. Do you journey in quest of treasure?"

Manag Iss let an expression of mild impatience cross his strange face. "It is known that your patron Lord Gho Fhaazi has promised the Pearl at the Heart of the World to the Nameless Seventh and she, in turn, has promised him the new place on the Council in return. We have discovered enough to know that only an exceptional thief could have been commissioned to this task. And Nadsokor is famous for her exceptional thieves. It is a task which, I am sure you know, all Sorcerer Adventurers have failed in completing. For centuries members of every sect have tried to find the Pearl at the Heart of the World, whenever the Blood Moon rises. Those few who ever survived to return to Quarzhasaat were raving mad and died soon after. Only recently have we received some little knowledge and evidence that the Pearl does actually exist. We know, therefore, that you are a dreamthief, though you disguise your profession by not carrying your hooked staff, for we now know that only a dreamthief of the greatest skill could reach the Pearl and bring it back."

"You tell me more than I knew, Manag Iss," said Elric seriously. "And it is true that I am commissioned by Lord Gho Fhaazi. But know you this also—I go upon this journey reluctantly." And Elric trusted his instincts enough to reveal to Manag Iss the hold that Lord Gho had over him.

Manag Iss plainly believed him. His tattooed fingertips brushed lightly over the tattoos of his lips as he considered this information. "That elixir is well-known to the Sorcerer Adventurers. We have distilled it for millennia. It is true that it feeds the very substance of the user back to him. The antidote is much harder to prepare. I am surprised that Lord Gho claims to possess it. Only certain sects of the Sorcerer Adventurers own small quantities. If you would return with us to Quarzhasaat we shall, I know, be able to administer the antidote to you within a day at the most.''

Elric considered this carefully. Manag Iss was employed by one of Lord Gho's rivals. This made him suspicious of any offer, no matter how generous it seemed. Councillor Iss, or the Lady Iss, or whoever it was desired to place their own candidate upon the Council, would no doubt be prepared to stop at nothing to achieve that end. For all Elric knew, Manag Iss's offer might merely be a means of lulling him out of his wariness so that he might be the more easily murdered.

''You'll forgive me if I am blunt,'' said the albino, ''but I have no means of trusting you, Manag Iss. I know already that Quarzhasaat is a city whose chief sport is intrigue and I have no wish to be involved in that game of plots and counterplots which your fellow citizens seem to enjoy so thoroughly. If the antidote to the elixir exists, as you say, I would be better disposed to consider your claims if, for instance, you were to meet me at the Silver Flower Oasis in, say, six days from today. I have enough elixir to last me three weeks, which is the time of the Blood Moon plus the time of my journey from and to your city. This will convince me of your altruism.''

''I shall also be frank,'' said Manag Iss, his voice cool. ''I am commissioned and bound by my blood oath, my sect contract and my honour as a member of our holy guild. That commission is to convince you, by any means, either to relinquish your quest or to sell the Pearl. If you will not relinquish the quest, then I will agree to purchase the Pearl from you at any price save, of course, a position on our Council. Therefore, I will match Lord Gho's offer and add to it anything else you desire.''

Elric spoke with some regret. ''You cannot match his offer, Manag Iss. There is the matter of the boy whom he will kill.''

''The boy is of little importance, surely.''

"Not, doubtless, in the great scheme of things as they are played out in Quarzhasaat." Elric grew weary.

Realising he had made a tactical mistake, Manag Iss said hastily: "We'll rescue the boy. Tell us how to find him."

"I think I'll keep to my original bargain," said Elric. "There seems little to choose between the offers."

"What if Lord Gho was assassinated?"

Elric shrugged and made to remount. "I'm grateful for your intervention, Manag Iss. I'll consider your offer as I ride. You'll appreciate I have little time to find the Fortress of the Pearl."

"Master Thief, I would warn you—" At this Manag Iss broke off. He looked behind him, along the Red Road. There was a faint cloud of dust to be seen. Out of it emerged dim shapes, their robes pale green and flowing behind them as they rode. Manag Iss cursed. But he was smiling his peculiar smile as the leaders galloped up.

It was clear to Elric, from their garb, that these men were also members of the Sorcerer Adventurers. They, too, had tattoos, but upon the eyelids and the wrists, and their billowing surcoats, which reached to their ankles, bore an embroidered flower upon them while the trimming of sleeves had the same design in miniature. The leader of these newcomers jumped from his horse and approached Manag Iss. He was a short man, handsome and clean-shaven save for a tiny goatee which was oiled in the fashion of Quarzhasaat and drawn to an exaggerated point. Unlike the Yellow Sect members, he carried a sword, unscabbarded in a simple leather harness. He made a sign which Manag Iss imitated.

"Greetings, Oled Alesham, and peace upon you. The Yellow Sect wishes great successes to the Foxglove Sect and is curious as to why you travel so far along the Red Road." All this was spoken rapidly, a formality. Manag Iss doubtless was as aware as Elric why Oled Alesham and his men followed.

"We ride to give protection to this thief," said the leader of the Foxglove Sect with a nod of acknowledgement to Elric.

"He is a stranger to our land and we would offer him help, as is our ancient custom."

Elric himself smiled openly at this. "And are you, Master Oled Alesham, related, by any chance, to some member of the Six and One Other?"

Oled Alesham's sense of humour was better developed than that of Manag Iss. "Oh, we are all related to everyone in Quarzhasaat, Sir Thief. We are on our way to the Silver Flower Oasis and thought you might require assistance with your quest."

"He has no quest," said Manag Iss, then instantly regretted the stupidity of the lie. "No quest, that is, save the one he shares with his friends of the Yellow Sect."

"Since we are bound by our guild loyalties not to fight, we are not, I hope, going to quarrel over who is to escort our guest to the Silver Flower Oasis," said Oled Alesham with a chuckle. He was greatly amused by the situation. "Are we all to journey together, perhaps? And each receive a little piece of the Pearl?"

"There is no Pearl," said Elric, "and shall not be if I am further hindered in my journey. I thank you, gentlemen, for your concern, and I bid you all good afternoon."

This caused some consternation amongst the two rival sects and they were attempting to decide what to do when over the rubble created by the firebeetles there rode about a dozen black-clad, heavily veiled and cowled warriors, their swords already drawn.

Elric, guessing these to mean him no good, withdrew so that Manag Iss and Oled Alesham and their men were surrounding him. "More of your kind, gentlemen?" he asked, his hand on the hilt of his own sword.

"They are the Moth Brotherhood," said Oled Alesham, "and they are assassins. They do nothing but kill, Sir Thief. You would best throw in with us. Evidently someone has determined that you should be murdered before you even see the Blood Moon rising."

"Will you help me defend myself?" said the albino, getting ready to fight.

"We cannot," said Manag Iss, and he sounded genuinely regretful. "We cannot do battle with our own kind. But they will not kill us if we surround you. You would be best advised to accept our offer, Sir Thief."

Then the impatient rage which was a mark of his ancient blood took hold of Elric and he drew Stormbringer without further ado. "I am tired of these little bargains," he said. "I would ask you to stand aside from me, Manag Iss, for I mean to do battle."

"There are too many!" Oled Alesham was shocked. "You'll be butchered. These are skilled killers!"

"Oh, so am I, Master Sorcerer Adventurer. So am I!" And with that Elric drove his horse forward, through the startled ranks of Yellow and Foxglove Sects, directly at the leader of the Moth Brotherhood.

The runesword began to howl in unison with its master and the white-face glowed with the energy of the damned while the red eyes blazed and the Sorcerer Adventurers realised for the first time that an extraordinary creature had come amongst them and that they had underestimated him.

Stormbringer rose in Elric's gloved hand, its black metal catching the rays of the glaring sun and seeming to absorb them. The black blade fell, almost as if by accident, and split the skull of the Moth Brotherhood's leader, clove him to his breastbone and howled as it sucked the man's soul from him in the very split second of his dying. Elric turned in his saddle, the sword swinging to bury its edge in the side of the assassin riding up on his left. The man shrieked. "It has me! Ah, no!" And he, too, died.

Now the other veiled riders were warier, circling the albino at some distance while they determined their strategy. They had thought they would need none, that all they must do was ride a Young Kingdom thief down and destroy him. There were five of the black riders left. They were calling on their fellow guild members for aid, but neither Manag Iss nor Oled

Alesham was ready to give orders to their own people which could result in the unholy death they had already witnessed.

Elric showed no such prudence. He rode directly at the next assassin, who parried with great cleverness and even struck under Elric's guard for a second before his arm was severed and he fell back in his saddle, blood gouting from the stump. Another graceful movement, half Elric's, half his sword's, and that man, too, had his soul drawn from him. Now the others fell back amongst the yellow and green robes of their brothers. There was panic in their eyes. They recognised sorcery even if this was something more powerful than they had ever anticipated.

"Hold! Hold!" cried Manag Iss. "There is no need for any more of us to die! We are here to make the thief an offer. Did old Duke Ral send you here?"

"He wants no more intrigue around the Pearl," growled one of the veiled men. "He said clean death was the best solution. But these deaths are not clean for us."

"Those who commission us have set the pattern," said Oled Alesham. "Thief! Put up your sword. We do not wish to fight you!"

"I believe that." Elric was grim. The bloodlust was still upon him and he fought to control it. "I believe you merely wish to slay me without a fight. You are fools all. I have already warned Lord Gho of this. I have the power to destroy you. It is your good fortune that I am sworn to myself not to use my power merely to make others perform my will to my own selfish ends. But I am not sworn to let myself die at the hands of hired slaughterers! Go back! Go back to Quarzhasaat!"

This last was almost screamed and the sword echoed it as he lifted the great black blade into the sky, to warn them of what would befall them if they did not obey.

Manag Iss said softly to Elric: "We cannot, Sir Thief. We can only pursue our commissions. It is the way of our guild, of all the Sorcerer Adventurers. Once we have agreed to perform a task, then the task must be performed. Death is the only excuse for failure."

"Then I must kill you all," said Elric simply. "Or you must kill me."

"We can still make the bargain I spoke of," said Manag Iss. "I was not deceiving you, Sir Thief."

"My offer, too, is sound," said Oled Alesham.

"But the Moth Brotherhood is sworn to kill me," Elric pointed out, almost amused, "and you cannot defend me against them. Nor, I would guess, can you do anything but aid them against me."

Manag Iss was trying to draw back from the black-robed assassins but it was clear they were determined to retain the safety of their guild ranks.

Then Oled Alesham murmured something to the leader of the Yellow Sect which made Manag Iss thoughtful. He nodded and signed to the remaining members of the Moth Brotherhood. For a few moments they were in conference, then Manag Iss looked up and addressed Elric.

"Sir Thief, we have found a formula which will leave you in peace and allow us to return with honour to Quarzhasaat. If we retreat now, will you promise not to follow us?"

"If I have your word you'll not let those Moths attack me again." Elric was calmer now. He laid the crooning runeblade across his arm.

"Put away your swords, brothers!" cried Oled Alesham, and the Moths obeyed at once.

Next Elric sheathed Stormbringer. The unholy energy which he had drawn from those who sought to slay him was filling him now and he felt all the old heightened sensibility of his race, all the arrogance and all the power of his ancient blood. He laughed at his enemies. "Know you not whom you would kill, gentlemen?"

Oled Alesham scowled a little. "I am beginning to guess a little of your origins, Sir Thief. 'Tis said that the lords of the Bright Empire carried such blades as yours once, in a time before this time. In a time before history. 'Tis said those blades are living things, a race allied to your own. You have the look of our long-lost enemies. Does this mean that Melniboné did not drown?''

''I'll leave that for you to think on, Master Oled Alesham.'' Elric suspected that they plotted some trick but was almost careless. ''If your people spent less time maintaining their own devalued myths about themselves and more upon studying the world as it is, I think your city would have a greater chance of surviving. As it is, the place is crumbling beneath the weight of its own degraded fictions. The legends which offer a race their sense of pride and history eventually become putrid. If Melniboné drowns, Master Sorcerer Adventurer, it will be as Quarzhasaat drowns now . . .''

''We are unconcerned with matters of philosophy,'' Manag Iss said with evident poor temper. ''We do not question the motives or the ideas of those who employ us. That is written in our charters.''

''And must therefore be obeyed!'' Elric smiled. ''Thus you celebrate your decadence and resist reality.''

''Go now,'' said Oled Alesham. ''It is not your business to instruct us in moral matters and not ours to listen. We have left our student days behind.''

Elric accepted this mild rebuke and turned his tiring horse again towards the Silver Flower Oasis. He did not look back once at the Sorcerer Adventurers but guessed them to be deeper than ever in conversation. He began to whistle as the Red Road stretched before him and the stolen energy of his enemies filled him with euphoria. His thoughts were on Cymoril and his return to Melniboné, where he hoped to ensure his nation's survival by bringing about in her the very changes he had spoken of to the Sorcerer Adventurers. At this moment, his goal seemed a little closer, his mind clearer than it had been for several months.

Night seemed to come swiftly and with it a rapid descent in temperature which left the albino shivering and robbed him of some of his good humour. He drew heavier robes from his saddle-bags and donned them as he tethered his horse and prepared to build a fire. The elixir on which he had depended had not been touched since his encounter with the Sorcerer Adventurers and he was beginning to understand its nature a little better. The craving had faded, although he was still conscious of it, and he could now hope to free himself of his dependency without need of further bargaining with Lord Gho.

"All I have to do," he said to himself as he ate sparingly of the food provided him, "is to make sure that I am attacked at least once a day by members of the Moth Brotherhood . . ." And with that he put away his figs and bread, wrapped himself in the night-cloak and prepared to sleep.

His dreams were formal and familiar. He was in Imrryr, the Dreaming City, and Cymoril sat beside him as he lay back upon the Ruby Throne, contemplating his court. Yet this was not the court which the emperors of Melniboné had kept for the thousands of years of their rule. This was a court to which had come men and women of all nations, from each of the Young Kingdoms, from Elwher and the Unmapped East, from Phum, from Quarzhasaat even. Here information and philosophies were exchanged, together with all manner of goods. This was a court whose energies were not devoted to maintaining itself unchanged for eternity, but to every kind of new idea and lively, humane discussion, which welcomed fresh thought not as a threat to its existence but as a very necessity to its continued well-being, whose wealth was devoted to experiment in the arts and sciences, to supporting those who were needy, to aiding thinkers and scholars. The Bright Empire brightness would come no longer from the glow of putrefaction but from the light of reason and good will.

This was Elric's dream, more coherent now than it had ever been. This was his dream and it was why he travelled the world, why he refused the power which was his, why he risked his life, his mind, his love and everything else he valued, for he believed that there was no life worth living that was not risked in pursuit of knowledge and justice. And this was why his fellow countrymen feared him. Justice was obtained, he believed, not by administration but by experience. One must know what it was to suffer humiliation and powerlessness, at

least to some degree, before one could entirely appreciate its
effect. One must give up power if one was to achieve true
justice. This was not the logic of Empire, but it was the logic
of one who truly loved the world and desired to see an age
dawn when all people would be free to pursue their ambitions
in dignity and self-respect.

"Ah, Elric," said Yyrkoon, crawling like a serpent from
behind the Ruby Throne, "thou art an enemy of your own
race, an enemy of her gods and an enemy of all I worship and
desire. That is why you must be destroyed and why I must
possess all you own. All . . ."

At this, Elric woke up. His skin was clammy. He reached
for his sword. He had dreamed of Yyrkoon as a serpent and
now he could swear he heard something slithering over the
sand not far off. The horse smelled it and grunted, displaying
increasing agitation. Elric rose, the night-cloak falling from
him. The horse's breath was steaming in the air. There was a
moon overhead casting a faintly blue light over the desert.

The slithering came closer. Elric peered at the high banks of
the road but could make out nothing. He was sure that the
firebeetles had not returned. And what he heard next confirmed this certainty. It was a great outpouring of foetid breath,
a rushing sound, almost a shriek, and he knew some gigantic
beast was nearby.

Elric knew also that the beast was not of this desert, nor
indeed of this world. He could sniff the stink of something
supernatural, something which had been raised from the pits
of Hell, summoned to serve his enemies, and he knew suddenly
why the Sorcerer Adventurers had called off their attack so
readily, what they had planned when they had let him go.

Cursing his own euphoria, Elric drew Stormbringer and
crept back into the darkness, away from the horse.

The roar came from behind him. He whirled and there it was!

It was a huge catlike thing, save that its body resembled that
of a baboon with an arching tail and there were spines along
its back. Its claws were extended and it reared up, reaching
for him as he yelled and jumped to one side, slashing at it.

The thing flickered with peculiar colours and lights, as if not quite of the material world. He was in no doubt of its origin. Such things had been summoned more than once by the sorcerers of Melniboné to help them against those they sought to destroy. He searched his mind for some spell, something which would drive it back to the regions from which it had been summoned, but it had been too long since he had practised any kind of sorcery himself.

The thing had got his scent now and was moving in pursuit as he ran rapidly and erratically away from it across the desert, attempting to put as much space between himself and the creature as possible.

The beast screamed. It was hungry for more than Elric's flesh. Those who had summoned it had promised it his soul at very least. It was the usual reward to a supernatural beast of that kind. He felt its claws whistle in the air behind him as it again attempted to seize him and he turned, slashing at the creature's forepaws with his sword. Stormbringer caught one of the pads and drew something like blood. Elric felt a sickening wave of energy pour into him. He stabbed this time and the beast shrieked, opening a red mouth in which rainbow-coloured teeth glittered.

"By Arioch," gasped Elric, "you're an ugly creature. 'Tis almost a duty to send you back to Hell . . ." And Stormbringer leapt out again, slashing at the same wounded paw. But this time the cat-thing saved itself and began to gather itself for a spring which Elric knew he had little chance of surviving. A supernatural beast was not as easily slain as the warriors of the Moth Brotherhood.

It was then he heard a yell and turning saw an apparition moving towards him in the moonlight. It was manlike, riding on an oddly humped animal which galloped more rapidly than any horse.

The cat-creature paused uncertainly and turned, spitting and growling, to deal with this distraction before finishing the albino.

Realising that this was not a further threat but some passing traveller attempting to come to his assistance, Elric shouted: "Best save yourself, sir. That beast is supernatural and cannot easily be killed by familiar means!''

The voice which replied was deep and vibrant, full of good humour. "I'm aware of that, sir, and would be obliged if you could deal with the thing while I draw its attention to myself.'' Whereupon the rider turned his odd mount and began to ride at a reduced pace in the opposite direction. The supernatural creature was not, however, deceived. Clearly those who had raised it had instructed it as to its prey. It scented at the air, seeking out Elric again.

The albino lay behind a dune, gathering his strength. He remembered a minor spell which, given the extra energy he had drawn already from the demon, he might be able to employ. He began to sing in the old, beautiful, musical language they called High Melnibonéan, and as he did so he took up a handful of sand and passed it through the air with strange, graceful movements. Gradually, from the grains of the dunes, a spiral of sand began to move upward, whistling as it spun faster and faster in the oddly coloured moonlight.

The cat-beast growled and rushed forward. But Elric stood between it and the whirling spiral. Then, at the last moment, he moved aside. The spiral's voice rose still higher. It was no more than a simple trick taught to young sorcerers by way of encouragement, but it had the effect of blinding the cat-thing long enough for Elric to charge and with his sword duck under the claws to plunge the blade deep into the beast's vitals.

At once the energy began to drain into the blade and from the blade into Elric. The albino screamed and raved as the stuff filled him. Demon-energy was not unfamiliar to him, but it threatened to make a demon of him, too, for it was all but impossible to control.

"Aah! It is too much. Too much!'' He writhed in agony while the demonic life-essence poured into him and the cat-thing roared and died.

Then it was gone and Elric lay gasping on the sand as the beast's corpse gradually faded into nothingness, returning to the realm from which it had been summoned. For a few seconds Elric wanted to follow the thing into its home regions, for the stolen energy threatened to spill out of his body, burst its way from his blood and his bones, but old habits fought to control this lust until at last he once again had a rein upon himself. He began slowly to rise from the ground only to hear the approach of hooves.

He whirled, the sword ready, but saw it was the traveller who had earlier sought to help him. Stormbringer felt no sentiment in the matter and stirred in his hand, ready to take the soul of this friend as readily as it had stolen the souls of Elric's enemies.

"No!" The albino forced the blade back into its scabbard. He felt almost sick with the energy leeched from the demon but he made himself take a grave bow as the rider joined him. "I thank you for your help, stranger. I had not expected to find a friend this close to Quarzhasaat."

The young man regarded him with some sympathy and good will. He had startlingly handsome features with dark, humorous eyes in his gleaming black flesh. On his short, curly hair he wore a skull cap decorated with peacock feathers and his jacket and breeches seemed to be of black velvet stitched with gold thread, over which was thrown a pale-coloured hooded cloak of the pattern usually worn by desert peoples in these parts. He rode up slowly on the loping, bovine mount which had cloven hooves and a broad head, a massive hump above its shoulders, like that of certain cattle Elric had seen in scrolls depicting the Southern Continent.

At the young man's belt was a richly carved stick of some kind with a crooked handle, about half his height, and on his other hip he wore a simple flat-hilted sword.

"I had not expected to find an emperor of Melniboné in these parts, either!" said the man with some amusement. "Greetings, Prince Elric. I am honoured to make your acquaintance."

"We have not met? How do you know my name?"

"Oh, such tricks are nothing to one of my craft, Prince Elric. My name is Alnac Kreb and I am making my way to the oasis they call the Silver Flower. Shall we return to your camp and your horse? I am glad to say he is unharmed. What powerful enemies you have, to send such a foul demon against you. Have you given offence to the Sorcerer Adventurers of Quarzhasaat?''

"It would seem so.'' Elric walked beside the newcomer as they made their way back towards the Red Road. "I am grateful to you, Master Alnac Kreb. Without your help, I should now be absorbed body and soul in that creature and borne back to whatever hell gave birth to it. But I must warn you, there is some danger that I shall be attacked again by those who sent it.''

"I think not, Prince Elric. They were doubtless confident of their success and, what's more, wanted no further business with you, once they realised that you were no ordinary mortal. I saw a pack of them—from three separate sects of that unpleasant guild—riding rapidly back to Quarzhasaat not an hour since. Curious as to what they fled from, I came this way. And so found you. I was glad to be of some minor service.''

"I, too, am riding for the Silver Flower Oasis, though I know not what to expect there.'' Elric had taken a strong liking to this young man. "I would be glad of your company on the journey.''

"Honoured, sir. Honoured!'' Smiling, Alnac Kreb dismounted from his odd beast and tethered it close to Elric's horse, which was yet to recover from its terror, though was now quieter.

"I will not ask you to weary yourself further tonight, sir,'' Elric added, "but I'm mightily curious to know how you guessed my name and my race. You spoke of a trick of your craft. What would that trade be, may I ask?''

"Why, sir,'' said Alnac Kreb, dusting sand from his velvet breeches. "I'd thought you guessed. I am a dreamthief.''

4

A Funeral
at the Oasis

"The Silver Flower Oasis is rather more than a simple clearing in the desert, as you'll discover," said Alnac Kreb, dabbing delicately at his beautiful face with a kerchief trimmed with glittering lace. "It is a great meeting place for all the nomad nations, and much wealth comes to it to be traded. It is frequented by kings and princes. Marriages are arranged and often take place there, as do other ceremonies. Great political decisions are made. Alliances are maintained and fresh ones struck. News is exchanged. Every manner of thing is bartered. Not everything is conventional, not every desire is material. It is a vital place, unlike Quarzhasaat, which the nomads visit reluctantly only when necessity—or greed—demands."

"Why have we seen none of these nomads, friend Alnac?" Elric asked.

"They avoid Quarzhasaat. For them the place and its people are the equivalent of Hell. Some even believe that the souls of the damned are sent to Quarzhasaat. The city represents everything they fear and everything that is at odds with what they most value."

"I'd be inclined to see eye to eye with those nomads." Elric allowed himself a smile. Still free of the elixir, his body was again craving it. The energy his sword had given him would normally have sustained him for a considerably longer time. This was further proof that the elixir, as explained by Manag Iss, fed off his very life-force to give him temporary physical strength. He was beginning to suspect that he was feeding the elixir as well as his own vitality. The distillation had come almost to represent a sentient creature, like the sword. Yet the Black Sword had never given him the same sense of being invaded. He kept his mind free of such thoughts as much as he could. "I feel a certain kinship with them already," he added.

"Your hope, Prince Elric, is that they find you acceptable!" And Alnac laughed. "Though an ancient enemy of the Lords of Quarzhasaat must have certain credentials. I have acquaintances amongst some of the clans. You must let me introduce you, when the time comes."

"Willingly," said Elric, "though you have yet to explain how you came to know me."

Alnac nodded as if he had forgotten the matter. "It is not complicated and yet it is remarkably complex, if you do not understand the fundamental workings of the multiverse. As I told you, I'm a dreamthief. I know more than most because I am familiar with so many dreams. Let's merely say that I heard of you in a dream and that it is sometimes my destiny to be your companion—though not for long, I'd guess, in my present guise."

"In a dream? You have yet to tell me what a dreamthief does."

"Why, steal dreams, of course. Twice a year we take our booty to a certain market to trade, just as the nomads trade."

"You trade in dreams?" Elric was disbelieving.

Alnac enjoyed his astonishment. "There are dealers at the market who'll pay well for certain dreams. In turn they sell them to those unfortunates who either cannot dream or have such banal dreams they desire something better."

Elric shook his head. "You speak in parables, surely?"

"No, Prince Elric, I speak the exact truth." He dragged the oddly hooked staff from his belt. It reminded Elric of a shepherd's crook, though it was shorter. "One does not acquire this without having studied the basic skills of the dreamthief's craft. I am not the best in my trade, nor am I likely ever to be, but in this realm, in this time, this is my destiny. There are few in this realm, for reasons you shall no doubt learn, and only the nomads and the folk of Elwher recognise our craft. We are not known, save to a few wise people, in the Young Kingdoms."

"Why do you not venture there?"

"We are not asked to do so. Have you ever heard of anyone seeking the services of a dreamthief in the Young Kingdoms?"

"Never. But why should that be?"

"Perhaps because Chaos has so much influence in the West and South. There, the most terrible nightmares can readily become reality."

"You fear Chaos?"

"What rational being does not? I fear the dreams of those who serve her." Alnac Kreb looked away towards the desert. "Elwher and what you call the Unmapped East have in the main less complicated inhabitants. Melniboné's influence was never so strong. Nor was it, of course, in the Sighing Desert."

"So it is my folk whom you fear?"

"I fear any race which gives itself over to Chaos; which makes pacts with the most powerful of supernaturals; with the very Dukes of Chaos; with the Sword Rulers themselves! I do not regard such dealings as wholesome or sane. I am opposed to Chaos."

"You serve Law?"

"I serve myself. I serve, I suppose, the Balance. I believe that one can live and let live and celebrate the world's variety."

"Such philosophy is enviable, Master Alnac. I aspire to it myself, though I suppose you do not believe me."

"Aye, I believe you, Prince Elric. I am party to many

dreams and you occur in some of them. And dreams are reality and vice versa in other realms.'' The dreamthief glanced sympathetically at the albino. ''It must be hard for one who has known millennia of power to attempt a relinquishing of such power.''

''You understand me well, Sir Dreamthief.''

''Oh, my understanding is only ever of the broadest kind in such matters.'' Alnac Kreb shrugged and made a self-deprecating gesture.

''I have spent much time in seeking the meaning of justice, in visiting lands where it is said to exist, in trying to discover how best it may be accomplished, how it may be established so that all the world shall benefit. Have you heard of Tanelorn, Alnac Kreb? There justice is said to rule. There the Grey Lords, those who keep charge of the world's equilibrium, are said to have their greatest influence.''

''Tanelorn exists,'' said the dreamthief quietly. ''And it has many names. Yet in some realms, I fear, it is no more than an idea of perfection. Such ideas are what maintain us in hope and fuel our urge to make reality of dreams. Sometimes we are successful.''

''Justice exists?''

''Of course it does. But it is not an abstraction. It must be worked for. Justice is your demon, I think, Prince Elric, more than any Lord of Chaos. You have chosen a cruel and an unhappy road.'' He smiled delicately as he stared ahead of them at the long, red trail stretching out to the horizon. ''Crueller, I think, than the Red Road to Silver Flower Oasis.''

''You're not encouraging, Master Alnac.''

''You must know yourself that there's precious little justice in the world that is not hard fought for, hard won and hard held. It is in our mortal nature to make such a burden the responsibility of others or, indeed, to seek out the strongest forces and hope that by allying themselves with power they will somehow survive better. Experience frequently proves them right, in the short term at least. Yet poor creatures like yourself continue to try to relinquish power while acquiring more and more responsibility. Some would say that it is admirable to do as you do, that it builds character and strength of purpose, that it reaches towards a higher form of sanity . . .''

"Aye. And some would say it is the purest form of madness, at odds with all natural impulses. I do not know what it is I long for, Sir Dreamthief, but I know I hope for a world where the strong do not prey on the weak like mindless insects, where mortal creatures may attain their greatest possible fulfillment, where all are dignified and healthy, never victims of a few stronger than themselves . . .''

"Then you serve the wrong masters in Chaos, Prince. For the only justice recognised by the Dukes of Hell is the justice of their own unchallenged existence. They are like fresh-born babes in this. They are opposed to your every ideal.''

Elric grew disturbed and spoke softly when he replied. ''But can one not use such forces to defeat them—or at least challenge their power and adjust the Balance?''

"Only the Balance gives you the power you desire. And it is a subtle, sometimes exceptionally delicate power.''

"Not strong enough in my world, I fear.''

"Strong only when sufficient numbers believe in it. Then it is stronger than Chaos and Law combined.''

"Well, I shall work for that day when the power of the Balance holds sway, Master Alnac Kreb, but I am not sure I will live to see it.''

"If you live," said Alnac quietly, "I suspect it will not come. But it will be many years before you are called upon to blow Roland's horn.''

"A horn? What horn is that?'' But Elric's question was casual. He believed that the dreamthief was making another allegorical allusion.

"Look!'' Alnac pointed ahead. "See in the far distance? There is the first sign of the Silver Flower Oasis.''

To their left the sun was going down. It cast deep shadows across the dunes and the high banks of the Red Road while the sky was darkening to a deep amber on the horizon. Yet almost at the limit of his vision Elric made out another shape, something that was neither a shadow nor a sand-dune but which might have been a group of rocks.

"What is it? What do you recognise?"

"The nomads call it *kashbeh*. In our common tongue we would say it was a castle, perhaps, or a fortified village. We have no exact word for such a place, for we have no need of them. Here, in the desert, it is a necessity. The Kashbeh Moulor Ka Riiz was built long before the extinction of the Quarzhasaatin Empire and is named for a wise king, founder of the Aloum'rit dynasty which still holds the place in charge for the nomad clans and is respected above all other peoples of the desert. It is a kashbeh sheltering anyone in need. Anyone who is a fugitive may seek shelter there and be assured of a fair trial."

"So justice exists in this desert, if nowhere else?"

"Such places exist, as I said, throughout the realms of the multiverse. They are maintained by men and women of the purest and most humane principles . . ."

"Then is this kashbeh not Tanelorn, whose legend brought me to the Sighing Desert?"

"It is not Tanelorn, for Tanelorn is eternal. The Kashbeh Moulour Ka Riiz must be maintained through constant vigilance. It is the antithesis of Quarzhasaat, and that city's lords have made many attempts to destroy it."

Elric felt the pangs of craving and he resisted reaching for one of his silver flasks. "Is that also called the Fortress of the Pearl?"

At this, Alnac Kreb laughed suddenly. "Oh, my good prince, clearly you have only the haziest notion of the place and the thing you seek. Let me now say that the Fortress of the Pearl may well exist within that kashbeh and that the kashbeh could also have an existence within the Fortress. But they are in no way the same!"

"Please, Master Alnac, do not confuse me further! I pretended to know something of this, first because I wished to extend my own life and then because I needed to purchase the life of another. I would be grateful for some illumination. Lord

Gho Fhazzi thought me a dreamthief, after all, which supposes that a dreamthief would know of the Blood Moon, the Bronze Tent and the location of the Place of the Pearl.''

"Aye, well. Some dreamthieves are better informed than others. And if a dreamthief is required for this task, Prince, if, as you've told me, Quarzhasaat's Sorcerer Adventurers cannot achieve it, then I would guess the Fortress of the Pearl is more than mere stones and mortar. It has to do with realms familiar only to a trained dreamthief—but one probably more sophisticated than myself.''

"Know you, Master Alnac, that I have already travelled to strange realms in pursuit of my various goals. I am not completely unsophisticated in such matters . . .''

"These realms are denied to most." Alnac seemed reluctant to say more but Elric pressed him.

"Where lie these realms?" He stared ahead, straining his eyes to see more of the Kashbeh Moulor Ka Riiz but failing, for the sun was now almost below the horizon. "In the East? Beyond Elwher? Or in another part of the multiverse altogether?''

Alnac Kreb was regretful. "We are sworn to speak as little as we can of our knowledge, save in the most crucial and specific of circumstances. But I should inform you that those realms are at once closer and more distant than Elwher. I promise you that I will not mystify you any more than I have done so already. And if I can illuminate you and help you in your quest, that I will do also." He made to laugh, to lighten his own mood. "Best ready yourself for company, Prince. We shall have a great deal of it by nightfall, if I'm not mistaken.''

The moon had risen before the last rays of the sun had vanished and its silver bore a pinkish sheen, like that of a rare pearl itself, as they reached a rise in the Red Road and looked down now upon a thousand fires. Silhouetted against them were as many tall tents, settled on the sand so as to resemble gigantic winged insects stretched out to catch the last warmth from above. Within these tents burned lamps while men, women and children wandered in and out. A delicious smell of mingled herbs, spices, vegetables and meats drifted up towards them and the soft smoke of the fires rose and curled into the sky above the great rocks on which perched the Kashbeh Moulor Ka Riiz, a massive tower about which had grown a collection of buildings, some of wonderfully imaginative architecture, the whole surrounded by a crenellated wall of irregular but equally monumental proportions, all of the same red rock so that it seemed to grow out of the very earth and sand that surrounded it.

At intervals around those battlements great torches blazed, revealing men who were evidently guards patrolling the walls and roofs, while through tall gates a steady stream of traffic came and went across a bridge carved from the living rock.

This was, as Alnac Kreb had warned him, not the simple resting place of primitive caravans Elric had expected to find on the Red Road.

They were not challenged as they descended towards the wide sheet of water around which blossomed a rich variety of palms, cypresses, poplars, fig trees and cactus, but many looked at them with open curiosity. And not all the curious eyes were friendly.

Their horses were of a similar build to Elric's own, while others of the nomads rode the bovine creatures favoured by Alnac. The sounds of bellowing, grunting and spitting rose from every quarter and Elric could see that beyond the field of tents lay corrals in which riding beasts as well as sheep, goats and other creatures were penned.

But the sight which dominated this extraordinary scene was that of some hundred or more torches blazing in a semi-circle at the water's edge.

Each torch was held by a cloaked and cowled figure and each burned with a bright, white steady flame which cast the same strong light upon a dais of carved wood at the very centre of the gathering.

Elric and his companion reined in their mounts to watch, as fascinated by this vision as the scores of other nomads who walked slowly to the edge of the semi-circle to witness what was clearly a ceremony of some magnitude. The witnesses stood in attitudes of respect, their various robes and costumes identifying their clan. The nomads were of a variety of colours, some as black as Alnac Kreb, some almost as white-skinned as Elric, with every shade in between, yet in features they were similar, with strong-boned faces and deep-set eyes. Both men and women were tall and bore themselves with considerable grace. Elric had never seen so many handsome people and he was as impressed by their natural dignity as he had been disgusted by the extremes of arrogance and degredation he had witnessed in Quarzhasaat.

Now a procession approached down the hill and Elric saw that six men bore a large, domed chest on their shoulders, proceeding with grave slowness until they came to the dais.

The white light showed every detail of the scene. The men were drawn from different clans, though all of the same height and all of middle age. A single drum began to sound, its beat sharp and clear in the night air. Then another joined it, then another, until at least twenty drums were echoing across the waters of the oasis and the rooftops of Kashbeh Moulor Ka Riiz, their voices at once slow and obeying complicated rhythmic patterns whose subtlety Elric gradually came to marvel at.

"Is it a funeral?" the albino asked his new friend.

Alnac nodded. "But I know not who they bury." He pointed to a series of symmetrical mounds in the distance beyond the trees. "Those are the nomad burial grounds."

Now another, older man, his beard and brows grey beneath his cowl, stepped forward and began to read from a scroll he produced from his sleeve, while two others opened the lid of the elaborate coffin and, to Elric's astonishment, spat into it.

Now Alnac gasped. He stood on his toes and peered, for the brands clearly illuminated the coffin's contents. He turned, still more mystified, to Elric. " 'Tis empty, Prince Elric. Or else the corpse is invisible."

The rhythm of the drums increased in tempo and complexity. Voices began to chant, rising and falling like waves in an ocean. Elric had never heard such music before. He found that it was moving him to obscure emotions. He felt rage. He felt sorrow. He found that he was close to weeping. And still the music continued, growing in intensity. He longed to join in, but could understand nothing of the language they used. It seemed to him that the words were older by far than the speech of Melniboné, which was the oldest in the Young Kingdoms.

And then, suddenly, the singing and the drumming ended.

The six men took the coffin from the dais and began to march away with it, towards the mounds, and the men with the torches followed, the light casting strange shadows amongst the trees, illuminating sudden patches of shining whiteness which Elric could not identify.

As suddenly as it had stopped, the drumming and the chanting began again, but this time it had a celebratory, triumphant note to it. Slowly the crowd lifted its heads and from several hundred throats came a high-pitched ululation, clearly a traditional response.

Then the nomads began to drift back towards their tents. Alnac stopped one, a woman wearing richly decorated green and gold robes, and pointed to the disappearing procession. "What is this funeral, sister? I saw no corpse."

"The corpse is not here," she said, and she was smiling at his confusion. "It is a ceremony of revenge, taken by all our clans at the instigation of Raik Na Seem. The corpse is not present because its owner will not know he is dead, perhaps for several months. We bury him now because we cannot reach him. He is not one of us, not of the desert. He is dead, however, but merely unaware of that fact. There is no mistake, though. We lack only the physical body."

"He is an enemy of your people, sister?"

"Aye, indeed. He is an enemy. He sent men to steal our greatest treasure. They failed, but they have done us profound harm in their failing. I know you, do I not? You are the one Raik Na Seem hoped would return. He sent for a dreamthief." And she looked back to the dais, where, beneath the light of a single torch, a huge figure stood, bowed as if in prayer. "You are our friend, Alnac Kreb, who aided us once before."

"I have been privileged to do your people a trifling service in the past, aye." Alnac Kreb acknowledged her recognition with his habitual grace.

"Raik Na Seem waits upon you," she said. "Go in peace, and peace be with your family and friends."

Puzzled, Alnac Kreb turned to Elric. "I know not why Raik Na Seem should have sent for me but I feel obliged to find out. Will you stay here or accompany me, Prince Elric?"

"I am growing curious about this whole affair," said Elric, "and would know more, if that's possible."

They made their way through the trees until they stood on the banks of the great oasis, waiting respectfully while the old man remained in the position he had assumed since the coffin had been carried off. Eventually he turned and it was clear that he had been weeping. When he saw them he straightened up and, as he recognised Alnac Kreb, he smiled, making a gesture of welcome. "My dear friend!"

"Peace be upon you, Raik Na Seem." Alnac stepped forward and embraced the old man, who was at least a head and shoulders taller than himself. "I bring with me a friend. His name is Elric of Melniboné, of that same people who were the great enemies of the Quarzhasaatim."

"The name has substance in my heart," said Raik Na Seem. "Peace be upon you, Elric of Melniboné. You are welcome here."

"Raik Na Seem is First Elder to the Bauradim Clan," Alnac said, "and a father to me."

"I am blessed by a good, brave son." Raik Na Seem gestured back towards the tents. "Come. Take refreshment in my tent."

"Willingly," said Alnac. "I would learn why you are burying an empty casket and who your enemy is that he should merit such elaborate ceremony."

"Oh, he is the worst of villains, make no mistake of that." A deep sigh escaped the old man as he led them through the throngs of tents until he reached a massive pavilion into which he led them, their feet treading on richly patterned carpets.

The pavilion was actually a series of compartments, one leading into another, each occupied by members of Raik Na Seem's
family, which seemed vast enough to be almost a tribe in itself.
The smell of delicious food came through to them as they were
seated on cushions and offered bowls of scented water with
which to wash themselves.

Eventually, as they ate, the old man told his story and, while
it unfolded, Elric came to realise that Fate had brought him to
the Silver Flower Oasis at an auspicious time, for he slowly
recognised the significance of what was being said. At the time
of the most recent Blood Moon, said Raik Na Seem, a group
of men had come to the Silver Flower Oasis asking after the
road to the Place of the Pearl. The Bauradim had recognised
the name, for it was in their literature, but they understood
the references to be poetic metaphor, something for scholars
and other poets to discuss and interpret. They had told the
newcomers this and hoped that they would leave, for they were
Quarzhasaatim, members of the Sparrow Sect of Sorcerer Adventurers and as such notorious for their murky wizardry and
cruelty. The Bauradim wanted no quarrel, however, with any
Quarzhasaatim, with whom they traded. The men of the Sparrow Sect did not leave, however, but continued to ask anyone
they could about the Place of the Pearl, which was how they
came to learn of Raik Na Seem's daughter.

"Varadia?" Alnac Kreb knew alarm. "They surely did not
think she knew anything of this jewel?"

"They heard that she was our Holy Girl, the one we believe
will grow to be our spiritual leader and bring wisdom and
honour to our clan. Because we say that our Holy Girl is the
receptacle of all our knowledge, they believed she must know
where this Pearl was to be found. They attempted to steal her."

Alnac Kreb growled with sudden anger. "What did they do,
Father?"

"They drugged her, then made to ride away with her. We
learned of their crime and followed them. We caught them
before they had completed half the length of the Red Road
back to Quarzhasaat and in their terror they threatened us with

the power of their master, the man who had commissioned them to seek out the Pearl and use any means to bring it back to him."

"Was his name Lord Gho Fhaazi?" asked Elric softly.

"Aye, Prince, it was." Raik Na Seem looked at him with new curiosity. "Do you know him?"

"I know him. And I know him for what he is. Is that the man you buried?"

"It is."

"When do you plan his death?"

"We do not plan it. We have been promised it. The Sorcerer Adventurers attempted to use their arts against us, but we have such people of our own and they were easily countered. It is not something we like to use, that power, but sometimes it is necessary. A certain creature was summoned from the netherworld. It devoured the men of the Sparrow Sect and before it left it granted us a prophecy, that their master would die within the year, before the next Blood Moon had faded."

"But Varadia?" said Alnac Kreb urgently. "What became of your daughter, your Holy Girl?"

"She had been drugged, as I said, but she lived. We brought her back."

"And she recovered?"

"She half-wakes, perhaps once a month," said Raik Na Seem, controlling his sadness. "But the sleep will not lift from her. Shortly after we found her she opened her eyes and told us to take her to the Bronze Tent. There she sleeps, as she has slept for almost a year, and we know that only a dreamthief may save her. That was why I have sent word by every traveller and caravan we have encountered, asking for a dreamthief. We are fortunate, Alnac Kreb, that a friend heard our prayer."

The dreamthief shook his handsome head. "It was not your message which brought me hither, Raik Na Seem."

"Still," said the old man philosophically, "you are here. You can help us."

Alnac Kreb seemed disturbed, but disguised his emotions

quickly. "I will do my best, that I swear. In the morning we shall visit the Bronze Tent."

"It is well-guarded now, for more Quarzhasaatim have come since those first evil ones, and we have been forced to defend our Holy Girl against them. That has been a simple enough matter. But you spoke of the enemy we have buried, Prince Elric. What do you know of him?"

Elric paused for only a few seconds before he spoke. He told Raik Na Seem everything which had happened: how he had been tricked by Lord Gho, what he had been told to find, the hold which Lord Gho had over him. He refused to lie to the old man, and the respect he showed Raik Na Seem was apparently reciprocated, for though the First Elder's face darkened with anger at the tale, he reached out with a firm hand when it was finished and gripped Elric's arm in a gesture of sympathy.

"The irony is, my friend, that the Place of the Pearl exists only in our poetry and we have never heard of the Fortress of the Pearl."

"You must know that I would do your Holy Girl no further harm," said Elric, "and that if I can help you and yours in any way, that is what I shall do. My quest is ended here and now."

"But Lord Gho's potion will kill you unless you can find the antidote. Then he'll kill your friend, too. No, no. Let us look more positively at these problems, Prince Elric. We have them in common, I think, for we are all victims of that soon-dead lord. We must consider how to defeat his schemes. It is possible that my daughter does indeed know something about this fabulous Pearl, for she is the vessel of all our wisdom and has already learned more than ever my poor head could hold . . ."

"Her knowledge and her intelligence are as breathtaking as her beauty and her amiability," said Alnac Kreb, still fuming at the story of what the Quarzhasaatim had done to Varadia. "If you had known her, Elric . . ." He broke off, his voice shaking.

"We are all in need of rest, I think," said the First Elder of the Bauradim. "You shall be our guests and in the morning I shall take you to the Bronze Tent, there to look upon my sleeping daughter and hope, perhaps with the sum of all our wisdom, to find a means of bringing her waking mind back to this realm."

That night, sleeping in the luxury only a wealthy nomad's tent could provide, Elric dreamed again of Cymoril, trapped in a drug slumber by his cousin Yyrkoon, and it seemed that he slept beside her, that they were one and the same, as he had always felt when they lay together. But now he saw the dignified figure of Raik Na Seem standing over him and he knew that this was his father, not the neurotic tyrant, the distant figure of his childhood, and he understood why he was obsessed with questions of morality and justice, for it was this Bauradi who was his true ancestor. He knew a kind of peace then, as well as some kind of new, disturbing emotion, and when he awoke in the morning he was reconciled to the fact that he was craving the elixir which at once brought him life and death, and he reached for his flask and took a small sip before rising, washing himself and joining Alnac and Raik Na Seem at the morning meal.

When this was done, the old man called for the fleet, sturdy mounts for which the Bauradim were famous, and the three of them rode away from the Silver Flower Oasis, which bustled with every kind of activity, where comedians, jugglers and snake-charmers were already performing their skills and story-tellers had gathered groups of children whose parents had sent them there while they went about their business, and they rode towards the Ragged Pillars, seen faintly on the morning horizon. These mountains had been eroded by the winds of the Sighing Desert until they did, indeed, resemble huge columns of ragged red stone, as if they should have supported the roof of the sky itself. Elric had thought at first he observed the ruins of some ancient city. But Alnac Kreb had told him the truth.

"There are, indeed, many ruins in these parts. Farms, small villages, whole towns, which the desert sometimes reveals, all engulfed by the sands summoned by the foolish wizards of

Quarzhasaat. Many built here, even after the sands came, in the belief that they would disperse after a while. Forlorn dreams, I fear, like so many of the things built by men.''

Raik Na Seem continued to lead them across the desert, though he used no map or compass. Apparently he knew the way by habit and instinct alone.

They stopped once at a spot where a tiny growth of cacti had been all but covered by the sand and here Raik Na Seem took his long knife and sliced the plants close to their roots, peeling them swiftly and handing the juicy parts to his friends. ''There was once a river here,'' he said, ''and a memory of it remains, far below the surface. The cactus remembers.''

The sun had reached zenith. Elric began to feel the heat sapping him and was forced again to drink a little of the elixir, merely in order to keep pace with the other two. And it was not until evening, when the Ragged Pillars were considerably closer, that Raik pointed to something which flashed and glittered in the last rays of the sun. ''There is the Bronze Tent, where the peoples of the desert go when they must meditate.''

''It is your temple?'' said Elric.

''It is the nearest thing we have to a temple. And there we debate with our inner selves. It is also the nearest thing we have to the religions of the West. And it is there we keep our Holy Girl, the symbol of all our ideals, the vessel of our race's wisdom.''

Alnac was surprised. ''You keep her there always?''

Raik Na Seem shook his head, almost amused. ''Only while she sleeps in this unnatural slumber, my friend. As you know, before this she was a normal little child, a joy to all who met her. Perhaps with your help she will be that child again.''

Alnac's brow clouded. ''You must not expect too much of me, Raik Na Seem. I am an inexpert dreamthief at best. There are those with whom I learned my craft who would tell you so.''

''But you are our dreamthief.'' Raik Na Seem smiled sadly and put his hand on Alnac Kreb's shoulder. ''And our good friend.''

The sun had set by the time they approached the great tent which resembled those Elric had seen at the Silver Flower Oasis but was several times the size, its walls of pure bronze.

Now the moon made its appearance in the sky almost directly overhead. It seemed that the sun's rays reached for it even as they began to sink beneath the horizon, touching it with their colour, for it glowed with a richness Elric had never seen in Melniboné or the lands of the Young Kingdoms. He gasped in surprise, realising the specific nature of the prophecy.

A Blood Moon had risen over the Bronze Tent. Here he would find the path to the Fortress of the Pearl.

Though it meant that his own life might now be saved, the Prince of Melniboné discovered that he was only disturbed by this revelation.

5

The Dreamthief's Pledge

"**H**ere is our treasure," said Raik Na Seem. "Here is what greedy Quarzhasaat would steal from us." And there was sorrow as well as anger in his voice.

At the very centre of the Bronze Tent's cool interior, in which tiny lamps burned over hundreds of heaped cushions and carpets occupied by men and women in attitudes of deep contemplation, was a raised level and on this a bed carved with intricate designs of exquisite delicacy, set with mother-of-pearl and pale turquoise, with milky jade and silver filigree and blond gold. Upon this, her little hands folded on her chest, which rose and fell with profound regularity, lay a young girl of about thirteen years. She had the strong beauty of her people, and her hair was the colour of honey against her tawny skin. She might have been sleeping as naturally as any child of her age save for the single startling fact that her eyes, blue as the wonderful Vilmirian Sea, stared upward towards the roof of the Bronze Tent and were unblinking.

"My people believed that Quarzhasaat destroyed herself forever," said Elric. "Would that they had, or that Melniboné had shown less arrogance and completed what their wizards began!'' He rarely betrayed such ferocious emotion towards those his race had defeated but now he knew only loathing for Lord Gho, whose men, he was sure, had done this terrible thing. He recognised the nature of the sorcery, for it was not unlike that he had learned himself, though his cousin Yyrkoon had shown more interest in those specific arts and cared to practise them where Elric did not.

"But who can save her now?" said Raik Na Seem softly, perhaps a little embarrassed by Elric's outburst in this place of meditation.

The albino recovered himself and made a gesture of apology. "Are there no potions which will rouse her from this slumber?" he asked.

Raik Na Seem shook his head. "We have consulted everyone and everything. The spell was cast by the leader of the Sparrow Sect and he was killed when we took our premature revenge."

In deference to those who sat within the Bronze Tent, Raik Na Seem now led them out into the desert again. Here guards stood, their lamps and torches casting great shadows across the sand, while the rays of the ruby moon drenched everything with crimson, so it was almost as if they drowned in a tide of blood. Elric was reminded how, as a youth, he had peered into the depths of his Actorios, imagining the gem as a gateway into other lands, each facet representing a different realm, for by then he already read much of the multiverse and how it was thought to be constituted.

"Steal the dream which entraps her," Raik Na Seem was saying, "and you know that all we have will be yours, Alnac Kreb."

The handsome black man shook his head. "To save her would be all the reward I wanted, Father. Yet I fear I have not the skills . . . Has no other tried?"

"We have been deceived more than once. Sorcerer Adventurers from Quarzhasaat, either believing themselves possessed of your knowledge or thinking they could accomplish what only a dreamthief can accomplish, have come to us, pretending to be members of your craft. We have seen them all go mad before our eyes. Several died. Some we let run back to Quarzhasaat in the hope they would be a warning to others not to waste their lives and our time."

"You sound very patient, Raik Na Seem," said Elric, remembering what he had already heard and clearer now as to why Lord Gho so desperately sought a dreamthief for this work. The news brought back to Quarzhasaat by the maddened Sorcerer Adventurers had been garbled. What little Lord Gho had made of it, he had passed on to Elric. But now the albino saw that it was the child herself who possessed the secret of the path to the Pearl at the Heart of the World. Doubtless, as the recipient of all her people's wisdom, she had learned of its location. Perhaps it was a secret she must keep to herself. Whatever the reason, it was obvious that the girl, Varadia, must wake from her sorcerous sleep before any further progress could be made. And Elric knew that even if she did wake it was not in his nature to question her, to beg for a secret which was not his to know. His only hope would be if she offered the knowledge freely to him but he knew that no matter what occurred he would never be able to ask.

Raik Na Seem seemed to understand a little of the albino's dilemma. "My son, you are a friend of my son," he said in the formal manner of his people. "We know that you are not our enemy and that you did not come here willingly to steal what was ours. We know, too, that you had no intention of taking from us any treasure to which we are guardian. Know this, Elric of Melniboné, that if Alnac Kreb can save our Holy Girl, we shall do all we can to put you on the path to the Fortress of the Pearl. The only reason for hindering you would be if Varadia, awakened, warned us against giving this aid. Then, at least, you will be told as much."

"There could be no fairer promise," said Elric gratefully. "Meanwhile, I pledge myself to you, Raik Na Seem, to help guard your daughter against all those who would harm her and to watch over her until Alnac should bring her back to you."

Alnac had moved a little away from the other two and was standing in deep thought on the edge of the torchlight, his white night-cloak drenched a dark pinkish hue by the rays of the Blood Moon. From his belt he had drawn his hooked staff and was holding it in his two hands, looking at it and murmuring to it, much as Elric might speak to his own runesword.

At length the dreamthief turned back to them, his face full of great seriousness. "I will do my best," he said. "I will call upon every resource within myself and upon everything I have been taught, but I should warn you that I have weaknesses of character I have not yet overcome. These are weaknesses which I can control if called upon to exorcise an old merchant's nightmares or a boy's love-trance. What I see here, however, might defeat the cleverest dreamthief, the most experienced of my calling. There can be no partial success. I succeed or I fail. I am willing, because of the circumstances, because of our old friendship, because I loathe everything that the Sorcerer Adventurers represent, to attempt the task."

"It is all I would hope," said Raik Na Seem somberly. He was impressed by Alnac's tone.

"If you succeed you bring the child's soul back to the world where it belongs," said Elric. "What do you lose if you fail, Master Dreamthief?"

Alnac shrugged. "Nothing of any great value, I suppose."

Elric, looking hard into his new friend's face, saw that he lied. But he saw, too, that he wished to be questioned no further in the matter.

"I must rest," said Alnac. "And eat." He wrapped himself in the folds of his night-cloak, his dark eyes staring back at Elric as if he wished for all the world to share some secret which he felt in his heart should never be shared. Then he turned away suddenly, laughing. "If Varadia should wake as a result of my efforts and if she knows the whereabouts of your terrible Pearl, why then, Prince Elric, I'll have done most of your work for you. I'll expect part of your reward, you know."

"My reward will be the slaying of Lord Gho," said Elric quietly.

"Aye," said Alnac, moving towards the Bronze Tent, which shifted and shimmered like some half-materialised artefact of Chaos, "that is exactly what I hope to share!"

The Bronze Tent consisted of the great central chamber and then a series of smaller chambers, where travellers could rest and revive themselves, and it was to one of these that the three men went to lay themselves down and, still wakeful, consider the work which must begin the next day. They did not talk, but it was several hours before all were eventually asleep.

In the morning, while Elric, Raik Na Seem and Alnac Kreb approached the place where the Holy Girl still lay, those who remained in the Bronze Tent drew back respectfully. Alnac Kreb held his dreamwand gently in his right hand, balancing it rather than gripping it, as he stared down into the face of the child he loved almost as his own daughter. A long sigh escaped him and Elric saw that his sleep had not apparently refreshed him. He looked drawn and unhappy. He turned, smiling, to the albino. "When I saw you partaking of the contents of that silver flask earlier, I had half a mind to ask you for a little . . ."

"The drug's poison and it's addictive," said Elric, shocked. "I thought I had explained as much."

"You had." Alnac Kreb again revealed by his expression that he possessed thoughts he felt unable to share. "I had merely thought that in the circumstances, there would be little point in fearing its power."

"That is because you do not know it," said Elric forcefully. "Believe me, Alnac, if there was any way in which I could help you in this task I would do so. But to offer you poison would not, I think, be an act of friendship . . ."

Alnac Kreb smiled a little. "Indeed. Indeed." He slid his dreamwand from hand to hand. "But you said that you would watch over me?"

"I promised that, aye. And as you asked, the moment you tell me to carry the dreamwand from the Bronze Tent, I shall do so."

"That is all you can do and I thank you for that," said the

dreamthief. "Now I'll begin. Farewell for the moment, Elric. I think we are fated to meet again, but perhaps not in this existence."

And with those mysterious words Alnac Kreb approached the sleeping girl, placing his dreamwand over her unblinking eyes, laying his ear against her heart, his own gaze growing distant and strange, as if he entered a trance himself. He straightened, swaying, then took the girl in his arms and lowered her gently to the carpets. Next he lay down beside her, putting her lifeless hand within his own, his dreamwand in the other. His breathing grew slower and deeper and Elric almost thought he heard a faint song coming from within the dreamthief's throat.

Raik Na Seem bent forward, peering into Alnac's face, but Alnac did not see him. With his other hand he brought up the dreamwand so that the hook passed over their clasped hands, as if to secure them, to bind them together.

To his surprise, Elric saw that the dreamwand was beginning to glow faintly and to pulse a little. Alnac's breathing grew deeper still, his lips opening, his eyes staring directly above him, just as Varadia's stared.

Elric thought he heard the child murmur and it was no illusion that a tremor passed between Alnac and the Holy Girl while the dreamwand pulsed in tempo with their mutual breathing and glowed brighter.

Then suddenly the dreamwand was curling and writhing, moving with astonishing speed between the two, as if it had entered their very veins and was following the blood itself. Elric had the impression of a tangle of arteries and nerves, all touched by the strange light from the dreamwand, then Alnac gave a single cry and his breathing was no longer the steady movement it had been. Instead it had become shallow, almost non-existent, while the child continued to breathe with the same slow, deep, steady rhythm.

The dreamwand had returned to Alnac. It seemed to burn from within his body, almost as if it had become fused with his spine and cortex. The hooked end appeared to glow from within his brain, flooding his flesh with indescribable luminance, displaying every bone, every organ, every vein.

The child herself seemed unchanged until Elric looked at her more closely, seeing almost with horror that her eyes had turned from vibrant blue to jet black. Reluctantly he looked from Varadia's face to Alnac's and saw what he had not wished to see: The dreamthief's own eyes now bright blue. It was as if the two of them had exchanged souls.

The albino, with all his experience of sorcery, had never witnessed anything like this and he found it disturbing. Gradually he was beginning to understand the strange nature of a dreamthief's calling, why it could be so dangerous, why there were so few who could practise the trade and why fewer still would wish to.

Now a further change began to take place. The crooked staff seemed to writhe again and begin to absorb the dreamthief's very substance, taking the blood and the vitality of flesh and bones and brain into itself.

Rail Na Seem groaned with terror. He stepped backward, unable to control himself. "Ah, my son! What have I asked of thee!"

Soon all that remained of Alnac Kreb's splendid body seemed little more than a husk, like the discarded skin of some transmuted dragonfly. But the dreamwand lay where Alnac had first placed it upon his own hand and Varadia's, though it seemed larger and glowed with an impossible brilliance, its colours constantly moving through a spectrum part natural, part supernatural.

"I think he is giving much in his attempt to save my daughter," said Raik Na Seem. "Perhaps more than anyone should give."

"He would give everything," Elric said. "I think that it is in his nature. That is why you call him your son and why you trust him."

"Aye," said Raik Na Seem. "But now I fear that I lose a son as well as a daughter." And he sighed and was troubled, perhaps wondering, if, after all, he had been wise in begging this service of Alnac Kreb.

For more than a day and a night Elric sat with Raik Na Seem and the men and women of the Bauradim within the shelter of the Bronze Tent, their eyes fixed upon the strangely wizened body of Alnac the Dreamthief which occasionally stirred and murmured yet still seemed as lifeless as the mummified goats which the sand-dunes sometimes revealed. Once Elric thought he heard the Holy Girl make a sound and once Raik Na Seem rose to put his hand on his daughter's brow, then returned shaking his head.

"This is not the time to despair, father of my friend," said Elric.

"Aye." The First Elder of the Bauradim drew himself up, then settled down again beside Elric. "We set high store by prophecies here in the desert. It seems that our longing for help might have coloured our reason."

They looked out of the tent into the morning. Smoke from the still burning brands drifted across the lilac-coloured sky, borne upward and to the north by the light breeze. Elric found the smell almost sickening now, but his concern for his new friend made him forgetful of his own health. Occasionally he drank sparingly of Lord Gho's elixir, unable to do more than control his craving, and when Raik Na Seem offered him water from his own flask Elric shook his head. Within him there were still many conflicts. He felt a strong comradeship with these people, a liking for Raik Na Seem which he valued. He had grown to care for Alnac Kreb, who had helped save his life in an action clearly as generous as the man's general character. Elric was grateful for the Bauradim's trust of him. Having heard his tale, they would have been within their rights to banish him at very least from the Silver Flower Oasis. Rather, they had taken him to the Bronze Tent when the Blood Moon burned, allowing him to follow Lord Gho's instructions, trusting him not to abuse their action. He was bound to them now by a loyalty he could never break. Perhaps they knew this. Perhaps they read his character as easily as they read Alnac's.

This sense of their trust heartened him, though it made his task all the more difficult, and he was determined in no way, however inadvertently, to betray it.

Raik Na Seem sniffed the wind and looked back towards the distant oasis. A column of black smoke marched into the sky, growing taller and taller, mingling with the smoke closer at hand: some released afrit joining its fellows. Elric would not have been surprised if it had taken shape before his eyes, so familiar had he become with strange events in past days.

"There has been another attack," said Raik Na Seem. He spoke unconcernedly. "Let us hope it is the last. They are burning the bodies."

"Who attacks you?"

"More men of the Sorcerer Adventurer societies. I suspect their decisions have something to do with the internal politics of the city. Dozens of them are battling for some favour or other—perhaps the seat on the Council you mentioned. From time to time their machinations involve us. This is familiar to us. But I suppose the Pearl at the Heart of the World has become the only price which will pay for the seat, eh? So as the story spreads, more and more of these warriors are sent here to find it!" Raik Na Seem spoke with fierce humour. "Let us hope they must soon run out of inhabitants and eventually only the scheming lords themselves will be left, squabbling for non-existent power over a non-existent people!"

Elric watched as a whole tribe of nomads rode past, keeping some distance away from the Bronze Tent in order to show their respect. These tanned, white-skinned people had burning blue eyes as bright as those which stared into nothing within the tent and, when their hoods were thrown back, startlingly blond hair, also like Varadia's. Their clothing distinguished them, however, from the Bauradim. It was predominantly of a rich lavender shade with gold and dark green trimming. They were heading towards the Silver Flower Oasis, driving herds of sheep and riding the odd humped bull-like beasts which, as Alnac had declared, were so well adapted to the desert.

"The Waued Nii," said Raik Na Seem. "They are amongst

the last at any gathering. They come from the very edge of the desert and they trade with Elwher, bringing that lapis lazuli and jade carving we all value so much. In the winter, when the storms grow too intense for them, they even raid across the plains and into the cities. Once, they boast, they looted Phum, but we believe it was some other, smaller place which they mistook for Phum." This was clearly a joke the desert peoples enjoyed at the expense of the Waued Nii.

"I had a friend who was once of Phum," said Elric. "His name was Rackhir and he sought Tanelorn."

"Rackhir I know. A good bowman. He travelled with us for a few weeks last year."

Elric was strangely pleased by this news. "He was well?"

"In excellent health." Raik Na Seem was glad of a subject to draw his mind away from the fate of his daughter and his adoptive son. "He was a welcome guest and hunted for us when we went close to the Ragged Pillars, for there's game there which we lack the skill to find. He spoke of his friend. A friend who had many thoughts and whose thoughts led him to many quandaries. That was you, no doubt. I remember now. He must have been joking. He said that you were a little on the pale side. He wondered what had become of you. He cared for you, I think."

"And I for him. We had something in common. As I feel a bond with your folk and with Alnac Kreb."

"You shared dangers together, I gather."

"We had many strange experiences. He, however, was tired of the quest for such things and hoped to retire, to find peace. Know you where he went from here?"

"Aye. As you say, he was searching for legendary Tanelorn. When he had learned all he could from us, he bade us farewell and rode on to the West. We counselled him not to waste himself in pursuit of a myth, but he believed he knew enough to continue. Did you not wish to journey with your friend?"

"I have other duties which call me, though I, too, have sought Tanelorn." He would have added more but thought better of it. Any further explanation would have led him into memories and problems he had no wish to contemplate at present. His main concern was for Alnac Kreb and the girl.

"Ah, yes. Now I recall. You are a king in your own country, of course. But a reluctant one, eh? The duties are hard for a young man. Much is expected of you and you bear upon your shoulders the weight of the past, the ideals and loyalties of an entire people. It is difficult to rule well, to make good judgements, to dispense justice fairly. We have no kings here amongst the Bauradim, merely a group of men and women elected to speak for the whole clan, and I think it is better to share those burdens. If all share the burden, if all are responsible for themselves, then no single individual has to carry a weight that is too much for them."

"The reason I travel is to learn more of such means of administering justice," said Elric. "But I will tell you this, Raik Na Seem, my people are as cruel as any in Quarzhasaat, and have more real power. We have a scanty notion of justice, and the obligations of rule involve little more than inventing new terrors by which we may cow and control others. Power, I think, is a habit as terrible as the potion I must now sip in order to sustain myself. It feeds upon itself. It is a hungry beast, devouring those who would possess it and those who hate it—devouring even those who own it."

"The hungry beast is not power itself," said the old man. "Power is neither good nor evil. It is the use one makes of it which is good or evil. I know that Melniboné once ruled the world, or that part of it she could find and the part she did not destroy."

"You seem to know more of my nation than my nation knows of you!" The albino smiled.

"It is said by our folk that we all came to the desert because we fled first Melniboné and then Quarzhasaat. Each was as cruel as the other, each as corrupting, and it did not matter to us which destroyed which. We had hoped they would extinguish each other, of course, but that was not to be. The second best thing occurred: Quarzhasaat almost destroyed herself and Melniboné forgot all about her—and us! I believe that soon after their war, Melniboné became bored with expansion and withdrew to rule only the Young Kingdoms. Now I hear she rules even less."

"Only the Dragon Isle now." Elric found that his thoughts were going back to Cymoril and he tried to stop himself from thinking of her. "But many a reaver's sought to sail against her and loot her wealth. They discover, however, that she remains too powerful for them. They must continue to trade with her instead."

"Trade was ever War's superior," said Raik Na Seem, and looked suddenly back over his shoulder at Alnac's withered body. The golden outline of the dreamwand was glowing again and throbbing, as it had done from time to time since Alnac had first lain down beside the girl.

" 'Tis a strange organ," said Raik Na Seem softly. "Almost a second spine."

He was about to say more when there was a faint movement in Alnac's features and a dreadful, desolate groan escaped the bloodless lips.

They turned and went to kneel beside him. Alnac's eyes still blazed blue and Varadia's were still black.

"He is dying," whispered the First Elder. "Is it so, Prince Elric?"

Elric knew no more than the Bauradi.

"What can we do for him?" asked Raik Na Seem.

Elric touched the cold, leathery carcass. He lifted an almost weightless wrist and could hear no pulse beating. It was at this moment, startlingly, that Alnac's eyes turned from blue to black and looked at Elric with all their old intelligence. "Ah, you have come to help me. I have learned where the Pearl lies. But it is too well protected."

The voice was a whisper from the dust-dry mouth.

Elric cradled the dreamthief in his arms. "I will help you, Alnac. Tell me how."

"You cannot. There are caverns . . . These dreams are defeating me. They are drowning me. They are drawing me in.

I am doomed to join those already doomed. Poor company for one such as me, Prince Elric. Poor company . . .''

The dreamwand pulsed and glowed white as bleached bones. The dreamthief's eyes turned to blue again, then back to black. The thin air stirred in the leathery remains of his throat. Suddenly there was horror in his face. "Ah, no! I must find the will!"

The dreamwand moved like a snake through his body, then slithered into Varadia, then returned. "Oh, Elric," said the tiny voice, "help me if you can. Oh, I am trapped. This is the worst I have ever known . . ."

His words seemed to Elric to call to him directly from the grave, as if his friend were already dead. "Elric, if there is some way . . ."

Then the body shuddered, filled as if with a single huge breath, while the dreamwand flickered and writhed again and then grew still, lying as it had first done with the crook upon the two clasped hands.

"Ah, my friend, I was a fool even to consider myself able to survive this . . ." The tiny voice faded. "Would that I had understood the nature of her mind. It is so strong! So strong!"

"Who does he speak of?" asked Raik Na Seem. "My child? That which holds her? My daughter is of the Sarangli women. Her grandmother could charm whole tribes to believe they died of disease. I told him as much. What does he not understand?"

"Oh, Elric, she has destroyed me!" There was a tremor in the frail hand as it reached towards the albino.

Then, suddenly, all the colour and life came flooding back into Alnac's body. It seemed to expand to its former size and vitality. The hooked staff became nothing more than the artefact Elric had originally seen at Alnac's belt.

The handsome dreamthief grinned. He was surprised. "I live! Elric, I live!"

He took a firmer grip on his staff and made to rise. Then he coughed and something disgusting oozed from his lips, like a gigantic, half-digested worm. It was as if he regurgitated his own rotten organs. He wiped the stuff away. For a moment he was bewildered, the terror returning to his eyes.

"No." Alnac seemed reconciled suddenly. "I was too proud. I die, of course." He collapsed backward onto the sheet as Elric again tried to hold him. With his old irony the dreamthief shook his head. "A little too late, I think. It's not my fate, after all, to be your companion, Sir Champion, in this plane."

Elric, to whom the words made no sense, believed Alnac to be raving and sought to quieten him.

Then the staff fell from the dreamthief's grasp and he rolled onto his side before a wavering, sickly scream came out of him, then a stink which threatened to drive Elric and Raik Na Seem from the Bronze Tent. It was as if his body putrefied before their eyes even as the dreamthief tried to speak again and failed.

And then Alnac Kreb was dead.

Elric, mourning a brave, good man, felt then that his own doom and that of Anigh had been determined. The dreamthief's death suggested forces at work of which the albino understood nothing, for all his sorcerous wisdom. He had come across no grimoire which even hinted of such a fate. He had seen worse befall those who meddled with sorcery, but here was a sorcery which he could not begin to interpret.

"He is gone, then," said Raik Na Seem.

"Aye." Elric's own breath shuddered in his throat. "Aye. His courage was greater than any of us suspected. Including, I think, himself."

The First Elder walked slowly to where his child still slept in her terrible trance. He looked down into her blue eyes as if he almost hoped to see the black eyes somewhere there within her.

"Varadia?"

She did not respond.

Solemnly Raik Na Seem took the Holy Girl and placed her back upon the raised block, settling her into the cushions as if she merely slept a natural sleep and he, her father, laid her down for her nightly rest.

Elric stared at the remains of the dreamthief. He had doubt-less understood the cost of failure and perhaps that was the secret he had refused to share.

"It is over," said Raik Na Seem gently. "Now I can think of nothing to do for her. He gave too much." He was fighting not to lose himself in either self-mortification or despair. "We must try to think what to do. Will you help me in this, friend of my son?"

"If I can."

As Elric rose, shaking, to his feet he heard a sound behind him. He thought at first it was some Bauradi woman come to mourn. He looked back at the light which streamed in through the tent and saw only her outline.

It was a young woman, but she was not of the Bauradim. She entered the tent slowly and there were tears in her eyes as she stared down at Alnac Kreb's ruined body.

"I am too late, then?"

Her musical voice was full of the most intense sorrow. She reached a hand to her face. "He should not have attempted such a task. They told me at the Silver Flower Oasis that you had come here. Why could you not have waited a little longer? Just a day more?"

It was with great effort that she controlled her grief and Elric felt a sudden, obscure kinship with her.

She took another step towards the body. She was an inch or so shorter than Elric, with a heart-shaped face framed by thick, brown hair. Slender and well-muscled, she wore a padded jer-kin slashed to show its red silk lining. She had soft velvet breeches, embroidered felt riding boots and over all this an almost transparent cotton dust-cloak pushed back from her shoulders. At her belt was a sword, and cradled above her left shoulder was a hooked staff of gold and ebony, a more elabo-rate version of the one which lay on the carpet beside Alnac's corpse.

"I taught him all he knew of his craft," she said. "But it was not enough for this. How could he ever have thought that it would be! He could never have achieved such a goal. He had not the character for it.'' She turned away, brushing at her face. When she looked back her tears had gone and she stared directly back into Elric's eyes.

"I am Oone," she said. She bowed briefly to Raik Na Seem. "I am the dreamthief you sent for."

PART TWO

Is there a daughter born in dreams
Whose flesh is snow, whose ruby eyes
Stare into realms whose substance seems
Strong as agony, soft as lies?
Is there a girlchild born of dreams
Who carries blood as old as Time,
Destined one day to blend with mine
And give new lands a newer queen?

The Chronicle of the Black Sword

PART TWO

1

How a Thief May Instruct an Emperor

Oone removed a date stone from her mouth and dropped it into the sand of the Silver Flower Oasis. She reached her hand towards one of the brilliant cactus flowers which gave the place its name. She stroked the petals with long, delicate fingers. She sang to herself and it seemed to Elric that her words were a lament.

Respectfully he remained silent, sitting with his back to a palm tree looking to the distant camp and its continuing activity. She had asked him to accompany her but had said little to him. He heard a calling from the kashbeh high above but when he peered in that direction he saw nothing. The breeze blew over the desert and red dust raced like water towards the Ragged Pillars on the horizon.

It was almost noon. They had returned to the Silver Flower Oasis that morning and the few remains of Alnac Kreb were to be burned with honour according to the customs of the Bauradim that night.

Oone's staff was no longer slung on her back. Now she held the dreamwand in both hands, turning it over and over, watching the light on its burnish and polish as if she had only now

seen it for the first time. The other wand, Alnac's, she had
tucked into her belt.

"It would have made my task a little easier," she said suddenly, "if Alnac had not acted so precipitously. He did not
realise I was coming and was doing his best to save the child,
I know. But a few more hours and I could have used his help,
perhaps successfully. Certainly I might have saved him."

"I do not understand what happened to him," said Elric.

"Even I do not know the exact cause of his fall," she said.
"But I will explain what I can. That is why I asked you to
come with me. I would not wish to be overheard. And I must
demand your word that you will be discreet."

"I am ever that, madam."

"Forever," she said.

"Forever?"

"You must promise never to tell another soul what I tell you
today, nor recount any event which results from the telling.
You must agree to be bound by a dreamthief's code even
though you are not of our kind."

Elric was baffled. "For what reason?"

"Would you save their Holy Girl? Avenge Alnac? Free
yourself from the drug's slavery? Adjust certain wrongs in
Quarzhasaat?"

"You know I would."

"Then we may reach an agreement, for it is certain that,
unless we help each other, you and the girl and perhaps myself, too, will all be dead before the Blood Moon fades."

"Certain?" Elric was grimly amused. "Are you an oracle,
too, then, madam?"

"All dreamthieves are that, to some degree." She was almost impatient, as if she spoke to a slow child. She caught
herself. "Forgive me. I forget that our craft is unknown in the
Young Kingdoms. Indeed, it's rarely that we travel to this
plane at all."

"I have met many supernaturals in my life, my lady, but
few who seem so human as yourself."

"Human? Of course I am human!" She seemed puzzled.

Then her brow cleared. "Ah. I forget that you are at once more sophisticated and less learned than those of my own persuasion." She smiled at him. "I am still not recovered from Alnac's unnecessary dissolution."

"He need not have died." Elric's tone was flat, unquestioning. He had known Alnac long enough to care for him as a friend. He understood something of Oone's loss. "And there is no way to revive him?"

"He lost all essence," said Oone. "Instead of stealing a dream, he was robbed of his own." She paused, then spoke quickly, as if she feared she would regret her words. "Will you help me, Prince Elric?"

"Yes." He spoke without hesitation. "If it is to avenge Alnac and save the child."

"Even if you risk Alnac's fate? The fate which you witnessed?"

"Even that. Can it be worse than dying in Lord Gho's power?"

"Yes," she said simply.

Elric laughed aloud at her frankness. "Ah, well. Just so, madam! Just so! What's your bargain?"

She moved her hand again towards the silver petals, balancing her wand between her fingers. She was frowning, still not wholly certain of the rightness of her decision. "I think that you are one of the few mortals on this earth who could understand the nature of my profession, who'll know what I mean when I speak of the nature of dreams and reality and how they intersect. I think, too, that you have habits of mind which would make you, if not a perfect ally, then an ally on whom I could to some extent depend. We dreamthieves have made something of a science of a trade which logically can tolerate no consistent laws. It has enabled us to pursue our craft with some success, largely, I suspect, because we are able, to a degree, to impose our wills upon the chaos we encounter. Does this make sense to you, Prince?"

"I think so. There are philosophers of my own people who claim that much of our magic is actually the imposition of powerful will upon the fundamental stuff of reality, an ability, if you like, to make dreams come true. Some claim our whole world was created thus.''

Oone seemed pleased. ''Good. I knew there were certain ideas I would not have to explain.''

''But what would you have me do, lady?''

''I want you to help me. Together we can find a way to what the Sorcerer Adventurers call the Fortress of the Pearl and by so doing one or both of us might steal the dream which binds the child to perpetual sleep and free her to wakefulness, return her to her people to be their seeress and their pride.''

''The two are linked, then?'' Elric began to rise to his feet, ignoring the call of his ever-present craving. ''The child and the Pearl?''

''I think so.''

''What is the link?''

''In discovering that, we shall doubtless discover how to free her.''

''Forgive me Lady Oone,'' said Elric gently, ''but you sound almost as ignorant as I!''

''In some ways it is true that I am. Before I go further, I must ask you to swear to abide by the Dreamthief's Code.''

''I swear,'' said Elric, and he held up the hand on which his Actorios glowed to show that he swore by one of his people's most revered artefacts. ''I swear by the Rings of Kings.''

''Then I will tell you what I know and what I desire of you,'' said Oone. She linked her free hand in his arm and led him further into the groves of palms and cypress. Sensing the shuddering hunger in him which yearned for Lord Gho's terrible drug, she seemed to show some sympathy.

''A dreamthief,'' she began, ''does exactly what the title implies. We steal dreams. Originally our guild were true thieves. We learned the trick of entering the worlds of other peoples' dreams and stealing those which were most magnificent or exotic. Gradually, however, people began to call upon us to steal unwanted dreams—or rather the dreams which entrapped or plagued friends or relatives. So we stole those. Frequently the dreams themselves were in no way harmful to another, only to the one who was in their power . . .''

Elric interrupted. ''Are you saying that a dream has some material reality? That it can be seized, like a volume of verse, say, or money purse, and slipped free of its owner?''

''Essentially, yes. Or, I should say, our guild learned the trick of making a dream sufficiently real for it to be handled thus!'' She now laughed openly at his confusion and some of the care went away from her for a moment. ''There is a certain talent needed and a great deal of training.''

''But what do you do with these stolen dreams?''

''Why, Prince Elric, we sell them at the Dream Market, twice a year. There's a fine trade in almost any sort of dream, no matter how bizarre or terrifying. There are merchants who purchase them and customers who would buy them. We distill them, of course, into a form which can be transported and later translated. And because we make the dreams take substance, we are threatened by them. That substance can destroy us. You see what happened to Alnac. It takes a certain character, a certain cast of mind, a certain attitude of spirit, all combining, to protect oneself in the Dream Realms. But because we have codified these realms we have also to a degree made them our own to manipulate.''

''You must explain more to me,'' said Elric, ''if I am to follow you at all, madam!''

''Very well.'' She paused at the edge of the grove, where the earth grew dustier and formed a territory between oasis and desert that was a little of both and was neither. She studied the cracked earth as if the cracks were the outlines of a singularly complicated map, a geometry which only she could understand.

''We have made rules,'' she said. Her voice was distant, almost as if she spoke to herself. ''And codified what we have discovered over the centuries. And yet we are still subject to the most unimaginable hazards . . .''

''Wait, madam. Are you suggesting that Alnac Kreb, by some wizardry known only to your guild, entered the world of

the Holy Girl's dreams and there suffered adventures such as
you or I might suffer in this material world?''

"Well put." She turned with a strange smile on her lips.
"Aye. And his substance went into that world and was absorbed by it, strengthening the substance of her dreams . . .''

"The dreams he hoped to steal."

"He hoped to steal only one. The one which imprisons her
in that perpetual slumber.''

"And then he would sell it, you say, at your Dream Market?''

"Perhaps." She was clearly unwilling to discuss this aspect
of the matter.

"Where is that market held?''

"In a realm beyond this one, in a place where only those of
our profession, or those who attend upon us, may travel.''

"You'd take me there?" Elric spoke from curiosity.

Her glance was a mixture of amusement and caution. "Possibly. But first we must be successful. We must steal a dream
so that we may trade it there. Know you, Elric, I have every
desire to inform you of all you wish to learn, but there are
many things hard to explain to one who has not studied with
our guild. They can only be demonstrated or experienced. I
am not a native of your world, nor are most dreamthieves from
this sphere. We are wanderers—nomads, you might say—
between many times and many places. We have learned that
a dream in one realm can be an undeniable reality in another,
while what is utterly prosaic in that realm can elsewhere be the
stuff of the most fantastic nightmare.''

"Is all creation so malleable?" Elric asked with a shudder.

"What we create must ever be, lest it die," she said, her
tone one of ironical finality.

"The struggle between Law and Chaos echoes that struggle
within ourselves between unbridled emotion and too much
caution, I suppose," Elric mused, aware that she did not wish
to pursue this particular conversation.

With her foot Oone traced the cracks in the red earth. "To
learn more you must become an apprentice dreamthief . . .''

"Willingly," said Elric. "I'm sufficiently curious now, madam. You spoke of your laws. What are they?"

"Some are instructive, some are descriptive. First I'll tell you that we have determined that every Dream Realm shall have seven aspects, which we have named. By naming and describing we hope to shape that which has no shape and control that which few can begin to control. By such impositions we have learned to survive in worlds where others would be destroyed within minutes. Yet even when we perform such impositions, even that which our own wills define can become transmuted beyond our control. If you would accompany me and aid me in this adventure, you must know that I have determined we shall pass through seven lands. The first land we call Sadanor, or the Land of Dreams-in-Common. The second land is Marador, which we call the Land of Old Desires, while the third is Paranor, the Land of Lost Beliefs. The fourth land is known to dreamthieves as Celador, which is the Land of Forgotten Love. The fifth is Imador, the Land of New Ambition, and the sixth is Falador, the Land of Madness . . ."

"Fanciful names indeed, madam. The Guild of Dreamthieves has a penchant for poetry, I think. And the seventh? What is that named?"

She paused before she replied. Her wonderful eyes peered into his, as if exploring the recesses of his own skull. "That has no name," she said quietly, "save any name the inhabitants shall give it. But there, if anywhere, you will find the Fortress of the Pearl."

Elric felt himself trapped by that gentle yet determined gaze. "And how may we enter these lands?" The albino forced himself to engage with these questions though by now his whole body was crying out for a draft of Lord Gho's elixir.

She sensed his tension, and her hand on his arm was meant to calm and reassure him. "Through the child," said Oone.

Elric remembered what he had witnessed in the Bronze Tent and he shuddered. "How is such a thing achieved?"

Oone frowned and the pressure of her hand increased. "She is our gateway and the dreamwands are our keys. There is no way in which I will harm her, Elric. Once we have reached the seventh aspect, the Nameless Land, there we might in turn find the key to her particular prison.''

"She is a medium, then? Is that what has happened to her? Did the Sorcerer Adventurers know something of her power and in attempting to use her put her into this trance?''

Again she hesitated, then she nodded. "Close enough, Prince Elric. It is written in our histories, of which we have many, though most are inaccessible to us in the libraries of Tanelorn, *'What lies within always has a form without and that which is without takes a shape within.'* Put another way, we sometimes say that what is visible must always have an invisible aspect, just as everything invisible must be represented by the visible.''

Elric found this too cryptic for him, though he was familiar enough with such mysterious utterances from his own grimoires. He did not dismiss them, but he knew they frequently required much pondering and certain experience before they made complete sense. "You speak of supernatural realms, madam. The worlds inhabited by the Lords of Chaos and of Law, by the elementals, by immortals and the like. I know something of such realms and have even journeyed in them some little way. But I have never heard of leaving part of one's physical substance behind and travelling into those realms by means of a sleeping child!''

She looked at him for a long moment as if she thought he was deliberately disingenuous, then she shrugged. "You will find the realms of the dreamthief very similar. And you would do well to memorise and obey our code.''

"You are a strict order, then, madam . . .''

"If we are to survive. Alnac had the instincts of a good dreamthief but he had not acquired the full discipline. That was one of the chief reasons for his dissolution. You on the other hand are familiar with the necessary disciplines, for they were how you came by your knowledge of sorcery. Without those disciplines you, too, would have perished.''

"I have rejected much of that, Lady Oone.''

"Aye. So I believe. But you have not lost the habit, I think.

Or so I hope. The first law the dreamthief obeys says, *Offers of guidance must always be accepted but never trusted.* The second says, *Beware the familiar,* and the third tells us, *What is strange should be cautiously welcomed.* There are many others, but it is those three which encompass the fundamentals by which a dreamthief survives.'' She smiled. Her smile was oddly sweet and vulnerable and Elric realised she was weary. Perhaps her grief had exhausted her.

The Melnibonéan spoke gently, looking back to the great red rocks of the Silver Flower's protection and sanctuary. The voices were stilled now. Thin lines of smoke ascended the rich blue of the sky. "How long does it take to instruct and train one of your calling?"

She recognised his irony now. "Five years or more," she said. "Alnac had been a full member of the guild for perhaps six years."

"And he failed to survive in the realm where the Holy Girl's spirit is held prisoner?"

"He was, for all his skills, only an ordinary mortal, Prince Elric."

"And you think I'm more than that?"

She laughed openly. "You are the last Emperor of Melniboné. You are the most powerful of your race, which is a race whose familiarity with sorcery is legendary. True, you have left your bride to be waiting for you while you place your cousin Yyrkoon on the Ruby Throne to reign as Regent until you return—a decision only an idealist would make—but nonetheless, my lord, you cannot pretend to me that you are in any way ordinary!"

In spite of his craving for the poisonous elixir, Elric found himself laughing back at her. "If I am such a man of qualities, madam, how is it that I find myself in this position, contemplating death from the tricks of a second-rate provincial politician?"

"I did not say you admired yourself, my lord. But it would be foolish to deny what you have been and what you could become."

"I prefer to consider the latter, my lady."

"Consider, if you will, the fate of Raik Na Seem's daughter. Consider the fate of his people deprived of their history and their oracle. Consider your own doom, to perish for no good reason in a distant land, your destiny unfulfilled."

Elric accepted this.

She continued. "It is probable, too, that you have no rival as a sorcerer in your world. While your specific skills might be of little use to you in the adventure I propose, your experience, knowledge and understanding might make the difference between success and failure."

Elric had become impatient as his body's demand for the drug grew unbearable. "Very well, Lady Oone. Whatever you decide, I shall agree to."

She took a step back from him and looked at him coolly. "You had best return to your tent and find your elixir," she said softly.

Familiar desperation filled the albino's mind. "I shall, madam. I shall." And turning he strode swiftly back towards the gathered tents of the Bauradim.

He scarcely spoke to any of those who greeted him as he passed. Raik Na Seem had moved nothing from the tent Elric had last shared with Alnac Kreb, and the albino hastily drew the flask from his saddle-bag, taking a deep draft and feeling, for a short while at least, the relief, the resurgence of energy, the illusion of health which the Quarzhasaati's drug gave him. He sighed and turned towards the entrance of the tent as Raik Na Seem came up, his brow furrowed, his eyes full of pain which he tried to disguise. "Have you agreed to help the dreamthief, Elric? Will you attempt to achieve what the prophecy predicted? Bring our Holy Girl back to us? There is now less time than there ever was. Soon the Blood Moon will be gone."

Elric dropped the flask onto the carpet which covered the ground. He bent and picked up the Black Sword, which he had unbuckled while he walked with Oone. The thing thrilled in his fingers and he felt vaguely nauseated. "I will do whatever is required of me," the albino said.

"Good." The older man gripped Elric by the shoulders. "Oone has told me that you are a great man with a great destiny and that this time is one of considerable moment in your life. We are honoured to be part of that destiny and grateful for your concern . . ."

Elric accepted Raik Na Seem's words with all his old grace. He bowed. "I believe that the health of your Holy Girl is more important than any fate of mine. I will do whatever is possible to bring her back to you."

Oone had entered behind the Bauradim's First Elder. She smiled at the albino. "You are ready now?"

Elric nodded and began to buckle on the Black Sword, but Oone stopped him with a gesture. "You'll find the weapons you need where we travel."

"But the sword is more than a weapon, Lady Oone!" The albino knew a kind of panic.

She held out Alnac's dreamwand to him. "This is all you need for our venture, my lord Emperor."

Stormbringer murmured violently as Elric let the sword fall back to the cushions of the tent. It seemed almost to threaten him.

"I am dependent . . ." he began.

She shook her head gently. "You are not. You believe that sword to be part of your identity but it is not. It is your nemesis. It is the part of you which represents your weakness, not your strength."

Elric sighed. "I do not understand you, my lady, but if you do not wish me to bring the sword, I'll leave it."

Another sound, a peculiar growl, from the blade, but Elric ignored it. He left both flask and sword in the tent and strode to where horses awaited them to carry them from the Silver Flower Oasis back to the Bronze Tent.

As they rode a little distance behind Raik Na Seem, Oone told Elric something more of what the Holy Girl meant to the Bauradim.

"As you perhaps have already realised, the child holds in trust the history and the aspirations of the Bauradim—their collected wisdom. Everything they know to be true and of value is contained within her. She is the living representation of her people's learning—what is the essence of their history—of a time before they became desert dwellers even. If they lose her, there is every chance, they believe, that they must begin their history all over again—relearn hard-won lessons, relive experience and make the mistakes and blunders which so painfully informed their people's understanding down the centuries. She is Time, if you like—their library, museum, religion and culture personified in a single human being. Can you imagine, Prince Elric, what her loss means to them? She is the very soul of the Bauradim. And that soul is imprisoned where only those of a certain skill can even find her, let alone free her."

Elric fingered the dreamwand which now replaced his runesword at his hip. "If she were only an ordinary child, bringing sorrow to her family through her condition, I would be inclined to help if I could," he said. "For I like this people and their leader."

"Her fate and yours are intertwined," said Oone. "Whatever your sentiments, my lord, you probably have little real choice in the matter."

He did not wish to hear this. "It seems to me, madam, that you dreamthieves are altogether too familiar with myself, my family, my people and my destiny. It makes me somewhat uncomfortable. Yet I cannot deny you know more than anyone, save my betrothed, about my inner conflicts. How come you by this power of divination and prophecy?"

She spoke almost casually. "There is a land all dreamthieves have visited. It is a place where all dreams intersect, where all that we have in common meets. And we call that land the Birthplace of the Bone, where mankind first assumed reality."

"This is legend! And primitive legend at that!"

"Legend to you. Truth to us. As one day you'll discover."

"If Alnac could foretell the future, why did he not wait for you to come to help him?"

"We rarely know our own destinies, only the general movements of the tides and of the figures who stand out in their
world's histories. All dreamthieves, it is true, know the future,
for half their lives are spent without Time. For us there is no
past or future, only a changing present. We are free of those
particular chains while bound as strongly by others."

"I have read of such ideas, but they mean very little to me."

"Because you lack experience to make sense of them."

"You have already spoken of the Land of Dreams-in-
Common. Is that the same as the Birthplace of the Bone?"

"Perhaps. Our people are undecided on the point."

Temporarily invigorated by the drug, Elric began to enjoy
the conversation, much of which he saw as mere pleasant abstraction. Free of his runesword he knew a kind of lightness of
spirit which he had not experienced since the first months of
his courtship of Cymoril in those relatively untroubled years
before Yyrkoon's growing ambition had begun to contaminate
life at the Melnibonéan Court.

He recalled something from one of his own people's histories. "I have seen it said that the world is no more than what
its denizens agree it is. I remember reading something to that
effect in *The Gabbling Sphere* which said, 'For who is to say which
is the inner world and which the outer? What we make reality
may be what will alone decides, and what we define as dreams
may be the greater truth.' Is that a philosophy close to your
own, Lady Oone?"

"Close enough," she said. "Though it seems a little airy."

They rode like this, almost like two children on a picnic,
until they reached the Bronze Tent when the sun was setting
and were led, once more, into the place where men and women
sat or lay around the great raised bed on which rested the little
girl who symbolised their entire existence.

It seemed to Elric that the illuminating braziers and lamps
were burning lower than when last he was here, and that the
child looked even paler than before, but he forced an expression of confidence when he turned to Raik Na Seem. "This
time we shall not fail her," he said.

Oone appeared to approve of Elric's words and watched carefully as, on her instructions, Varadia's frail body was lifted from the bed and placed this time upon a huge cushion which, in its turn, was set between two other cushions, also of great size. She signed to the albino to lay his body down on the far side of the child while she herself took up her position on the girl's left.

"Grasp her hand, my lord Emperor," said Oone ironically, "and place the crook of the dreamwand over both yours and hers, as you saw Alnac do."

Elric felt some trepidation as he obeyed her, but he knew no fear for himself, only for the child and her people, for Cymoril waiting for him in Melniboné, for the boy who prayed in Quarzhasaat that he would return with the jewel his jailer had demanded. His hand locked to the girl's by the dreamwand, he knew a sense of fusion that was not unpleasant, yet seemed to burn as hot as any flame. He watched as Oone did the same thing.

Immediately Elric felt a power possess him and for a moment it was as if his body grew lighter and lighter until it threatened to drift away on the slightest breeze. His vision faded, yet dimly he could still see Oone. She seemed to be concentrating.

He looked into the face of the Holy Girl and for a second thought he saw her skin turn still whiter, her eyes glow as crimson as his own, and a strange thought came and went in his mind: *If I had a daughter she would look thus . . .*

And then it was as if his bones were melting, his flesh dissolving, his whole mind and spirit dissipating. He gave himself up to this sensation as he had determined he must, since he now served Oone's purpose, and now the flesh became flowing water, the veins and blood were coloured strands of air, his skeleton flowed like molten silver, mingling with the Holy Girl's, becoming hers, then flowing on beyond her, into caverns and tunnels and dark places, into places where whole worlds existed in hollowed rock, where voices called to him and knew him and sought to comfort him or frighten him or tell him truths he did not wish to learn; and then the air grew bright again and he felt Oone beside him, guiding him, her hand on his, her body almost his body, her voice confident and even cheerful, like one who moves towards familiar danger; danger which she had overcome many times. Yet there was an edge to her voice which made him believe she had never faced a danger as great as this one and that there was every chance neither of them would return to the Bronze Tent or the Silver Flower Oasis.

And there was music which he understood was the very soul of this child turned into sound. Sweet, sad, lonely music. Music so beautiful he would have wept had he anything more than the airiest substance.

Then he saw blue sky before him, a red desert stretching away towards red mountains on the horizon, and he had the strangest of sensations, as if he were coming home to a land he had somehow lost in his childhood and then forgotten.

2

In the Marches
at the Heart's Edge

As Elric felt his bones re-form
and the flesh resume its familiar weight and contour he saw
that the land they had entered seemed scarcely any different
from that which they had left. Red desert stretched before them,
red mountains lay beyond. So familiar was the landscape that
Elric looked back, expecting to see the Bronze Tent, but immediately behind him now yawned a chasm so vast that no
further side could be seen. He knew sudden vertigo and
checked his balance, somewhat to Oone's amusement.

The dreamthief was dressed in her same functional velvets and
silks and seemed a little amused by his response. "Aye, Prince
Elric! Now we are indeed at the very edge of the world! We have
only certain choices here and they do not include retreat!"

"I had not considered it, madam." Looking more closely,
he realised that the mountains were considerably taller and
were all leaning in the same direction, as if bent by a tremendous wind.

"They are like the teeth of some ancient predator," said
Oone with a shudder of one who might actually have stared
into such a maw at some time in their career. "Doubtless the

first stage of our journey takes us there. This is the land we dreamthieves call Sadanor. The Land of Dreams-in-Common.''

''Yet you seem unfamiliar with the scenery.''

''The scenery varies. We know only the *nature* of the land. It may change in its details. But where we travel is frequently dangerous not because it is unfamiliar but because of its familiarity. That is the second rule of the dreamthief.''

''Beware the familiar.''

''You learn well.'' She seemed unduly pleased by his response, as if she had doubted her own description of his qualities and was glad to have them confirmed. Elric began to realise the degree of desperation involved in this adventure and was seized by that wild carelessness, that willingness to give himself up to the moment, to any experience, which so set him apart from the other lords of Melniboné, whose lives were ruled by tradition and a desire to maintain their power at any cost.

Smiling, his eyes alight with all their old vitality, he bowed ironically. ''Then lead on, madam! Let us begin our journey towards the mountains.''

Oone, a little startled by his mood, frowned. But she began to walk through sand so light it stirred like water around her feet. And the albino followed.

''I must admit,'' he said, after they had walked for perhaps an hour, without noting any shift in the position of the light, ''the more I am in this place, the more it begins to disturb me. I thought the sun obscured, but now I realise there is no sun in the sky at all.''

''Such normalities come and go in the Land of Dreams-in-Common,'' said Oone.

''I would feel more secure with my sword at my side.''

''Swords are easily come by here,'' she said.

''Drinkers of souls?''

''Perhaps. But do you feel the need for that peculiar form of sustenance? Do you crave Lord Gho's drug?''

Elric admitted to his own surprise that he had lost no energy. For perhaps the first time in his adult life he had the sense that he was physically as other people, able to sustain himself without calling on any form of artifice. "It occurs to me," he said, "that I might be well-advised to make my home here."

"Ah, now you begin to fall into another of this realm's traps," she said, lightly enough. "First there is suspicion and maybe fear. Then there is relaxation, a feeling that you have always belonged here, that this is your natural home, or your spiritual home. These are all illusions common to the traveller, as I am sure you know. Here those illusions must be resisted, for they are more than sentiment. They may be traps set to snare you and destroy you. Be grateful that you have more apparent energy than that which you normally know, but remember another rule of the dreamthief: *Every gain is paid for, either before or after the event.* Every apparent benefit could well have its contrary disadvantage."

Privately Elric still thought the price for such a sense of well-being might be worth the paying.

It was at that moment that he saw the leaf.

It drifted down from over his head, a broad, red-gold oak leaf, falling gently as any ordinary autumn shedding, and landed upon the sand at his feet. Without at first finding this extraordinary, he bent to pick the leaf up.

Oone had seen it, too, and made as if to caution him, then changed her mind.

Elric laid the leaf on the palm of his hand. There was nothing unusual about it, save that there was not a tree visible in any direction. He was about to ask Oone to explain this phenomenon when he noticed that she was staring beyond him, over his shoulder.

"Good afternoon to you," said a jaunty voice. "This is luck indeed, to find some fellow mortals in such a miserable wilderness. What trick of the Wheel brought us here, do you think?"

"Greetings," said Oone, her smile growing broad. "You're ill-dressed, sir, for this desert."

"I was told neither of my destination nor of the fact that I was leaving . . ."

Elric turned and to his surprise saw a small man whose sharp, merry features were shadowed by an enormous turban of yellow silk. This headdress, at least as wide as the man's shoulders, was decorated with a pin containing a great green gem and from it sprouted several peacock feathers. He seemed to be wearing many layers of clothing, all highly coloured, of silk and linen, including an embroidered waistcoat and a long jacket of beautifully stitched blue patchwork, each shade subtly different from the one next to it. On his legs were baggy trousers of red silk and his feet sported curling slippers of green and yellow leather. The man was unarmed, but in his hands he held a startled black and white cat upon whose back were folded a pair of silky black wings.

The man bowed when he saw Elric. "Greetings, sir. You would be the incarnation of the Champion on this plane, I take it. I am—" He frowned as if he had for a second forgotten his own name. "I am something beginning with 'J' and something beginning with 'C.' It will return to me in a moment. Or another name or event will occur, I'm sure. I am your— what?—amanuensis, eh?" He peered up into the sky. "Is this one of those sunless worlds? Are we to have no night at all?"

Elric looked to Oone, who did not seem wary of this apparition. "I did not ask for a secretary, sir," he said to the small man. "Nor did I expect to be assigned one. My companion and I are on a quest in this world . . ."

"A quest, naturally. It is your role, as it is mine to accompany you. That's in order, sir. My name is—" But again his own name eluded him. "Yours is?"

"I am Elric of Melniboné and this is Oone the Dreamthief."

"Then this is the Land the dreamthieves call Sadanor, I take it. Good, then I am called Jaspar Colinadous. And my cat's name is Whiskers, as always."

At this, the cat gave voice to a small, intelligent noise, to which its owner listened carefully and nodded.

"I recognise this land now," he said. "You'll be seeking the Marador Gate, eh? For the Land of Old Desires."

"You are a dreamthief yourself, Sir Jaspar?" Oone asked in some surprise.

"I have relatives who are."

"But how came you here?" Elric asked. "Through a medium? Did you use a mortal child, as we did?"

"Your words are mysterious to me, sir." Jaspar Colinadous adjusted his turban, the little cat tucked carefully under one voluminous silk sleeve. "I travel between the worlds, apparently at random, usually at the behest of some force I do not understand, frequently to find myself guiding or accompanying venturers such as yourselves. Not," he added feelingly, "always dressed appropriately for the realm or the moment of my arrival. I dreamed, I think, I was the sultan of some fabulous city, where I possessed the most astonishing variety of treasures. Where I was waited upon . . ." Here he coloured and looked away from Oone. "Forgive me. It was a dream. I have awakened from it now. Unfortunately the clothes followed me from the dream . . ."

Elric believed the man's words were close to nonsense, but Oone had no difficulty with them. "You know a road, then, to the Marador Gate?"

"Surely I must, if this is the Land of Dreams-in-Common." Carefully he placed the cat on his shoulder and then began to rummage in his sleeves, within his shirt, in the pockets of his several garments, producing all manner of scrolls and papers and little books, boxes, compacts, writing instruments, lengths of cord and reels of thread, until one of the rolled pieces of vellum caused him to cry out in relief. "Here it is, I think! Our map." He replaced all the other items in exactly the places he had drawn them from and unrolled the parchment. "Indeed, indeed! This shows us the road through yonder mountains."

"Offers of guidance . . ." began Elric.

"And beware the familiar," said Oone softly. Then she made a dismissive gesture. "Here we have conflict already, you see, for what is unfamiliar to you is highly familiar to me. That is part of the nature of this land." She turned to Jaspar Colinadous. "Sir? May I see your map?"

Without hesitation, the small man handed it to her. "A straight road. It's always a straightish road, eh? And only one. That's the joy of these Dream Realms. One can interpret and control them so simply. Unless, of course, they swallow one up completely. Which they are wont to do.''

''You have the advantage of me,'' said Elric, ''for I know nothing of this world. Neither was I aware that there are others like it.''

''Aha! Then you have so much wonder to anticipate, sir! So many marvels yet to witness. I would tell you of them, but my own memory is not what it should be. I frequently have only the vaguest of recollections. But there is an infinity of worlds and some are yet unborn, some so old they have grown senile, some born of dreams, some destroyed by nightmares.'' Jaspar Colinadous paused apologetically. ''I grow over-enthusiastic. I do not intend to confuse you, sir. Just know you that I am a little confused myself. I am ever that. Does my map make sense to you, Lady Dreamthief?''

''Aye.'' Oone was frowning over the parchment. ''There is only one pass through those mountains, which are called the Shark's Jaws. If we assume that the mountains are lying to our north, then we must bear to the north-east and there find the Shark's Gullet, as it's named here. We are much obliged to you, Master Jaspar Colinadous.'' She rolled up the map and returned it to him. It disappeared into one of his sleeves and the cat crept down to lie, purring, in the crook of his arm.

For a moment, Elric had the strongest instinct that this likable individual had been called up by Oone from her own imagination, though it was impossible to believe he did not exist in his own right, such a self-confident personality was he. Indeed, Elric had the passing fancy that perhaps he, himself, was the phantasy.

''You'll note there are dangers in that pass,'' said Jaspar Colinadous casually, as he fell in beside them. ''I'll let Whiskers scout for us, if you like, when we get closer.''

''We should be much obliged to you, sir,'' said Oone.

They continued their journey across the bleak landscape, with Jaspar Colinadous telling tales of previous adventures, most of which he could only half recall, of people he had known, whose names escaped him, and of great moments in the histories of a thousand worlds whose importance now eluded him. To hear him was like coming upon the old halls of Imrryr, on the Dragon Isle, where once huge series of windows had told in pictures the tales of the first Melnibonéans and how they had come to their present home. Now they were mere shards, small fragments of the story, brilliant details whose context was only barely imaginable and whose information was gone forever. Elric ceased trying to follow Jaspar Colinadous's conversation but, as he had learned to do with the fragments of glass, let himself enjoy them for their texture and their colour instead.

The consistency of the light had begun to disturb him and eventually he interrupted the little man in his flow and asked him if he, too, was not made uncomfortable by it.

Jaspar Colinadous took this opportunity to stop and remove his slippers, shaking sand from them as Oone waited ahead of them, her stance impatient. "No, sir. Supernatural worlds are frequently sunless, for they obey none of the laws we are familiar with in our own. They may be flat, half-spheres, oval, circular, even shaped like cubes. They exist only as satellites to those realms we call 'real,' and therefore are dependent not upon any sun or moon or planetary system for their ordering, but upon the demands—spiritual, imaginative, philosophical and so on—of worlds which do, in fact, require a sun to heat them and a moon to move their tides. There is even a theory that our worlds are the satellites and that these supernatural worlds are the birthplaces of all our realities." His shoes again free from sand, Jaspar Colinadous began to follow Oone, who was some distance on, having refused to wait upon them.

"Perhaps this is the land ruled by Arioch, my patron Duke of Hell," said Elric. "The land from which the Black Sword sprung."

"Oh, quite possibly, Prince Elric. For, see, there's a hellish sort of creature stooping on your friend at this very moment and us without a weapon between us!"

The three-headed bird must have flown at such a great height it had not been seen to approach, but now it was dropping at terrifying speed from above and Oone, alerted by Elric's cry of warning, began to run, perhaps hoping to divert it in its descent upon her. It was like a gigantic crow, with two of its heads tucked deep into its neck, while the other stretched out to help its downward flight, its wings spread behind it, its claws extended, ready to seize the woman.

Elric began to run forward, screaming at the thing. He, too, hoped that this activity would disturb the creature enough to make it lose its momentum.

With a terrible cawing which seemed to fill the entire heavens, the monster slowed its descent a trifle in order to make a more accurate strike on the woman.

It was then that Jaspar Colinadous cried from behind Elric: "Jack Three Beaks, thou naughty bird!"

The beast wavered in the air, turning all heads towards the turbanned figure who strode decisively towards it across the sand, his cat alert on his arm.

"What's this, Jack? I thought you were forbidden living meat!" Jaspar Colinadous's voice was contemptuous, familiar. Whiskers growled and gibbered at the thing, though it was many times larger than the little cat.

With a croak of defiance the bird flopped onto the sand and began to run at some considerable speed towards Oone, who had stopped to witness this bizarre event. Now she took to her heels again, the three-headed crow in pursuit.

"Jack! Jack! Remember the punishment."

The bird's cry was almost mocking. Elric began to stumble through the desert in its track, hoping to find means of saving the dreamthief.

It was then that he felt something cut through the air above his head, fanning him with unexpected coolness, and a dark shape sped in pursuit of the thing Jaspar Colinadous had called Jack Three Beaks.

It was the black and white cat. The beast flung his little body at the bird's central neck and sank all four sets of claws into the feathers. With a shrill scream the gigantic three-headed crow whirled round, its other heads trying to peck at the tenacious cat and just failing to reach it.

To Elric's astonishment the cat seemed to swell larger and larger as if feeding on the life-stuff of the crow, while the crow appeared to grow smaller.

"Bad Jack Three Beaks! Wicked Jack!" The almost ridiculous figure of Jaspar Colinadous strutted up to the thing now, wagging a finger, at which beaks snapped but dared not bite. "You were warned. And now you must perish. How came you here at all? You followed me, I suppose, when I left my palace." He scratched his head. "Not that I recall leaving the palace. Ah, well . . ."

Jack Three Beaks cawed again, glaring with mad, frightened eyes in the direction of his original prey. Oone was approaching again.

"This creature is your pet, Master Jaspar?"

"Certainly not, madam. It is my enemy. He knew he'd had his last warning. But I think he did not expect to find me here and believed he could attack living prey with impunity. Not so, Jack, eh?"

The answering croak was almost pathetic now. The little black and white cat resembled nothing so much as a feeding vampire bat as it sucked and sucked of the monster's life-stuff.

Oone watched in horror as gradually the crow shrank to a tiny, wizened thing and Whiskers at last sat back, huge and round, and began to clean himself, purring with considerable pleasure. Clearly pleased with his pet, Jaspar Colinadous reached up to pat his head. "Good lad, Whiskers. Now poor Jack's not even gravy for an old man's bread." He smiled proudly at his two new friends. "This cat has saved my life on many an occasion."

"How had you the name of that monster?" Oone wished to know. Her lovely features were flushed and she was out of breath. Elric was reminded suddenly of Cymoril, though he could not exactly identify the similarity.

"Why, it was Jack frightened the principality I visited before this." Jaspar Colinadous displayed his rich clothing. "And how I came to be so favoured by the folk of that place. Jack Three Beaks always knew the power of Whiskers and was afraid of him. He had been terrorising the people when I arrived. I tamed Jack—or strictly speaking, Whiskers did—but let him live, since he was a useful carrion eater and the province was given to terrible heat in the summer. When I fell through that particular rent in the fabric of the multiverse he must have come with me, without realising I was already here with Whiskers. There's little mystery to it, Lady Oone.''

She drew a deep breath. ''Well, I'm grateful for your aid, sir.''

He inclined his head. ''Now, had we better not move on toward the Marador Gate? There are more, if less unexpected, dangers ahead of us in the Shark's Gullet. The map marks 'em.''

''Would that I had a weapon at my side,'' said Elric feelingly. ''I would be more confident, whether it were an illusion or no!'' But he marched beside the others as they moved on towards the mountain.

The cat remained behind, licking his paws and cleaning himself, for all the world like an ordinary domestic creature which had killed a pantry-raiding mouse.

At last the ground began to rise as they reached the shallow foothills of the Shark's Jaws and saw ahead of them a great, dark fissure in the mountains, the Gullet which would lead them through to the next land of their journey. In the heat of the barren wilderness the pass looked cool and almost welcoming, though even from here Elric thought he could see shapes moving in it. White shadows flickered against the black.

''What manner of people live here?'' he asked Oone, who had not shown him the map.

''Chiefly those who have either lost their way or become too fearful to continue the journey inward. The other name for the pass is the Valley of Timid Souls.'' Oone shrugged. ''But I suspect it is not from them that we shall be in danger. At least, not greatly. They'll ally themselves with whatever power rules the pass.''

''And the map says nothing of its nature?''

''Only that we should be wary.''

There came a noise from behind them and Elric turned,

expecting a threat, but it was only Whiskers, looking a little plumper, a little sleeker, but back to his normal size, who had at last caught up with them.

Jaspar Colinadous laughed and bent to let the cat leap onto his shoulder. "We have no need of weapons, eh? Not with such a handsome beast to defend us!"

The cat licked his face.

Elric was peering into the dark pass, trying to determine what he might find there. For a moment he thought he saw a rider at the entrance, a man mounted on a silvery grey horse, wearing strange armour of different shades of white and grey and yellow. The warrior's horse reared as he turned it and rode back into the blackness and Elric knew a sensation of foreboding, though he had never seen the figure before.

Oone and Jaspar Colinadous were apparently unaware of the apparition and continued with untiring stride in the direction of the pass.

Elric said nothing of the rider but instead asked Oone how it was that they had all walked for hours and felt neither hungry nor weary.

"It is one of the advantages of this realm," she said. "The disadvantages are considerable, however, since a sense of time is easily lost and one can forget direction and goals. Moreover, it's wise to bear in mind that while one does not appear to lose physical energy or experience hunger, other forms of energy are being expended. Psychic and spiritual they may be, but they are just as valuable, as I'm sure you appreciate. Conserve those particular resources, Prince Elric, for you'll have urgent need of them soon enough!"

Elric wondered if she, too, had caught sight of the pale warrior but, for a reason he could not understand, was reluctant to ask her.

The hills were growing taller and taller around them as, subtly, they moved into the Shark's Gullet. The light was dimmer already, blocked by the mountains, and Elric felt a chill which was not altogether the result of the shade.

He became aware of a rushing sound and Jaspar Colinadous

ran towards a high bank of rocks to peer over them and look down. He turned, a little baffled. "A deep chasm. A river. We must find a bridge before we can go on." He murmured to his winged cat, which immediately took flight over the abyss and was soon lost in the gloom beyond.

Forced to pause, Elric knew sudden gloom. Unable to gauge his physical needs, uncertain of what events took place in the world he had left, perturbed by the knowledge that their time was running short and that Lord Gho would certainly keep his word to torture young Anigh to death, he began to believe that he could well be on a fool's errand, embarked on an adventure which could only end in disaster for all. He wondered why he had trusted Oone so completely. Perhaps because he had been so desperate, so shocked by the death of Alnac Kreb . . .

She touched him on the shoulder. "Remember what I told you. Your weariness is not physical here, but it manifests itself in your moods. One must seek spiritual sustenance as assiduously as you would normally seek food and water."

He looked into her eyes, seeing warmth and kindness there. Immediately his despair began to dissipate. "I must admit I was beginning to know strong doubt . . ."

"When that feeling overwhelms you, try to tell me," she said. "I am familiar with it and might be able to help you . . ."

"So I am entirely in your hands, madam." He spoke without irony.

"I thought you understood that when you agreed to accompany me," she said softly.

"Aye." He turned in time to see the little cat coming back and alighting on Jaspar Colinadous's shoulder. The turbanned man listened carefully and intelligently and Elric was certain that the cat was speaking.

At last Jaspar Colinadous nodded. "There's a good bridge not a quarter of a mile from here and it leads to a trail winding directly into the pass. Whiskers tells me that the bridge is guarded by a single mounted warrior. We can hope, I suppose, that he will let us cross."

They followed the course of the river as the sky overhead

grew darker and darker and Elric wished that, together with his lack of hunger and tiredness, he did not feel the rapid drop in temperature which made his body shake. Only Jaspar Colinadous was unaffected by the cold.

The rough wall of rocks at the chasm's edge gradually fell away, curving inward towards the pass, and very soon they saw the bridge ahead of them, a narrow spur of natural stone pushing outward over the foaming river below. And they heard the echo of the water as it plunged yet deeper down the gorge. Yet nowhere was there the guard which the little cat had reported.

Elric moved cautiously in the lead now, again wishing he had a weapon to give him reassurance. He reached the bridge and set a foot upon it. Far down at the foot of the chasm's granite walls grey foam leapt and danced and the river gave voice to its own peculiar song, half triumph, half despair, almost as if it were a living thing.

Elric shivered and took another step. Still he saw no figure in that deepening gloom. Another step and he was high above the water, refusing to look down lest the water call him to it. He knew the fascination of such torrents and how one could be drawn into them, hypnotised by their rush and noise.

"See you any guard, Prince Elric?" called Jaspar Colinadous.

"Nothing," the albino cried back. And he took two more steps.

Oone was behind him now, moving as cautiously as he. He peered to the bridge's further side. Great slabs of dank rock, covered in lichen and oddly coloured creepers, rose up and disappeared into the dark air above. The sound of the river made him think he heard voices, little skittering sounds, the scuffle of threatening limbs, but still he saw nothing.

Elric was half-way across the bridge before he detected the suggestion of a horse in the shadows of the gorge, the barest hint of a rider, perhaps wearing armour which was the colour of his own bone-white skin.

"Who's that?" The albino raised his voice. "We come in peace. We mean no harm to anyone here."

Again it might have been that the water made him believe he heard a faint, unpleasant chuckle.

Then it seemed the rush of water grew louder and he realised he heard the sound of hooves on rock. Formed as if by the spray, a figure suddenly appeared on the far side of the bridge, bearing down on him, its long, pale sword poised to strike.

There was nowhere to turn. The only way of avoiding the warrior was to jump from the bridge into the torrent below. Elric found his vision dimmed even as he prepared to spring forward, hoping to catch the horse's bridle and at least halt the rider in his tracks.

Then again there was a whirring of wings and something fixed itself on the attacker's helm, slashing at the face within. It was Whiskers, spitting and yowling like any ordinary alley cat engaged in a brawl over a piece of ripe fish.

The horse reared. The rider gave out a shriek of rage and pain and released the bridle in order to try to pull the little cat from him. Whiskers rushed upward into the air, out of reach. Elric glimpsed glaring, silvery eyes, a skin which glowed with the leper's mark, and then the horse, out of control, had slipped on the wet rock and fallen sideways. For a moment it tried to get back to its feet, the rider yelling and roaring as if demented, the long, white sword still in his hand. And then both had tumbled over the edge of the bridge and went falling, a chaotic mixture of arms and hooves, down into the echoing chasm to be swallowed by the distant, murky waters.

Elric was gasping for breath. Jaspar Colinadous came to grip his arm and steady him, helping him and Oone cross to the far side of the rocky slab and stand upon the bank, still scarcely aware of what had happened to them.

"I'm grateful again to Whiskers," said Elric with an unstable grin. "That's a valuable pet you have, Master Colinadous."

"More valuable than you know," said the little man feelingly. "He has played a crucial part in more than one world's history." He patted the cat as the beast returned to his arms, purring and pleased with himself. "I'm glad we were able to be of service to you."

"We're well rid of the bridge's guardian." Elric peered down into the foam. "Are we to encounter more such attacks, my lady?"

"Most certainly," she said. She was frowning as if lost in some conundrum only she perceived.

Jaspar Colinadous pursed his lips. "Here," he said. "Look how the gorge narrows. It becomes a tunnel."

It was true. They could now see how the rocks leaned in upon one another so that the pass was little more than a cave barely large enough to let Elric enter without bending his head. A set of crude steps led up to it and from time to time a little flicker of yellow fire appeared within, as if the place were lit by torches.

Jaspar Colinadous sighed. "I had hoped to journey with you further than this, but I must turn back now. I can go no further than the Marador Gate, which is what this seems to be. To do so would be to destroy me. I must find other companions now, in the Land of Dreams-in-Common." He seemed genuinely regretful. "Farewell, Prince Elric, Lady Oone. I wish you success in your adventure."

And suddenly the little man had turned and walked swiftly back over the bridge, not looking behind him. He left them almost as suddenly as he had arrived and was gone back into the darkness before either could speak, his cat with him.

Oone seemed to accept this and, at Elric's questioning glance, said: "Such people come and go here. Another rule the dreamthief learns is *Hold on to nothing but your own soul*. Do you understand?"

"I understand that it must be a lonely thing to be a dreamthief, madam."

And with that Elric began to climb the great rough-hewn steps which led into the Marador Gate.

3

Of Beauty Found in Deep Caverns

The tunnel began to descend almost as soon as they had entered it. Where it had first been cool, now the air became hot and humid so that sometimes it seemed to Elric he was wading through water. The little lights which gave faint illumination were not, as he had first thought, lamps or brands, but seemed naturally luminescent, delicate nodes of soft, glowing substance, almost fleshlike in appearance. He and Oone found that they were whispering, as if unwilling to disturb any denizens of this place. Yet Elric did not feel afraid here. The tunnel had the atmosphere of a sanctuary and he noticed that Oone, too, had lost some of her normal caution, though her experience had taught her to be wary of anything as a potentially dangerous illusion.

There was no obvious transition from Sadanor to Marador, save perhaps a slight change of mood before the tunnel opened up into a vast natural hall of richly glowing blues and greens and golden yellows and dark pinks, all flowing one to the other, like lava which had only recently cooled, more like exotic plants than the rock they were. Scents, like those of the loveliest, headiest flowers, made Elric feel as though he walked in a garden, not unlike the gardens he had known as a child, places of the greatest security and tranquility; yet there was no doubt that the place was a cavern and that they had travelled underground to reach it.

At first delighted by the sight, Elric began to feel a certain sadness, for until now he had not remembered those gardens of childhood, the innocent happiness which comes so rarely to a Melnibonéan, no matter what their age. He thought of his mother, dead in childbirth, of his infinitely mourning father, who had refused to acknowledge the son who, in his opinion, had killed his wife.

A movement from the depths of this natural hall and Elric again feared danger, but the people who began to emerge were unarmed and they had faces full of restrained melancholy.

"We have arrived in Marador," whispered Oone with certainty.

"You are here to join us?" A woman spoke. She wore flowing robes of myriad, glistening colour, mirroring the colours of the rock on walls and roof. She had long hair of faded gold and her eyes were the shade of old pewter. She reached to touch Elric—a greeting—and her hand was cold on his. He felt himself becoming infected with the same sad tranquility and it seemed to him that there could be worse fates than remaining here, recalling the desires and pleasures of his past, when life had been so much simpler and the world had seemed easily conquered, easily improved.

Behind him Oone said in a voice which sounded unduly harsh to his ear: "We are travellers in your land, my lady. We mean you no harm, but we cannot stay."

A man spoke. "Travellers? What do you seek?"

"We seek," said Elric, "the Fortress of the Pearl."

Oone was clearly displeased by his frankness. "We have no desire to tarry in Marador. We wish only to learn the location of the next gate, the Paranor Gate."

The man smiled wistfully. "It is lost, I fear. Lost to all of us. Yet there is no harm in loss. There is comfort in it, even, don't you feel?" He turned dreaming, distant eyes on them.

"Better not to seek that which can only disappoint. Here we prefer to remember what we most wanted and how it was to want it . . ."

"Better, surely, to continue looking for it?" Elric was surprised by his own blunt tone.

"Why so, sir, when the reality can only prove inadequate when compared against the hope?"

"Think you so, sir?" Elric was prepared to consider this notion, but Oone's grip on his arm tightened.

"Remember the name that dreamthieves give this land," she murmured.

Elric reflected that it was truly the Land of Old Desires. All of his own forgotten yearnings were returning to him, bringing a sense of simplicity and peace. Now he remembered how those sensations had been replaced by anger as he began to realise that there was little likelihood of his dreams ever coming true. He had raged at the injustice of the world. He had flung himself into his sorcerous studies. He had become determined to change the balance of things and introduce greater liberty, greater justice by means of the power he had in the world. Yet his fellow Melnibonéans had refused to accept his logic. The early dreams had begun to fade and with them the hope which had at first lifted his heart. Now here was the hope offered him again. Perhaps there were realms where all he desired was true? Perhaps Marador was such a world.

"If I went back and found Cymoril and brought her here, we could live in harmony with these people, I think," he said to Oone.

The dreamthief was almost contemptuous.

"This is called the Land of Old Desires—not the Land of Fulfilled Desire! There is a difference. The emotions you feel are easy and easily maintained—while the reality remains out of your reach, while you merely long for the unattainable. When you set out to discover fulfillment, Elric of Melniboné, then you achieved stature in the world. Turn your back on that determination—your own determination to help build a world where justice reigns—and you'll lose my respect. You'll lose respect for yourself. You'll prove yourself a liar and you'll prove me a fool for believing you could help me save the Holy Girl!''

Elric was shocked by her outburst, which seemed offensive in that particular atmosphere of serenity. ''But I think it is impossible to build such a world. Better to have the prospect, surely, than the knowledge of failure?''

''That is what all in this realm believe. Remain here, if you will, and believe what they believe forever. But I think one must always make an attempt at justice, no matter how poor the prospect of success!''

Elric felt tired and wished to settle down and rest. He yawned and stretched. ''These people seem to have a secret I would learn. I think I will talk to them for a while before continuing.''

''Do so and Anigh dies. The Holy Girl dies. And everything of yourself that you value, that dies also.'' Oone did not raise her voice. She spoke almost in a matter-of-fact tone. But her words had an urgency which broke Elric's mood. It was not for the first time that he had considered retreating into dreams. Had he done so, his people would now be ruled by him, and Yyrkoon would be dead or exiled.

Thought of his cousin and his cousin's ambition, of Cymoril waiting for him to return so that they might be married, helped remind Elric of his purpose here and he shook off the mood of reconciliation, of retreat. He bowed to the people of the cavern. ''I thank you for your generosity, but my own path lies forward, through the Paranor Gate.''

Oone drew a deep breath, perhaps in relief. ''Time's not measured in any familiar way here, Prince Elric, but be assured it's passing more rapidly than I would like . . .''

It was with a sense of deep regret that Elric left the melancholy people behind him and followed her further into the glowing caverns.

Oone added: ''These lands are well-called. Be wary of the familiar.''

''Perhaps we could have rested there? Restored our energies?'' said Elric.

"Aye. And died full of sweet melancholy."

He looked at her in surprise and saw that she had not been unaffected by the atmosphere. "Is that what befell Alnac Kreb?"

"Of course not!" She recovered herself. "He was fully able to resist so obvious a trap."

Elric now felt ashamed. "I almost failed the first real test of my determination and my discipline."

"We dreamthieves have the advantage of having been tested thus many times," she told him. "It gets easier to confront, though the lure remains as strong."

"For you, too."

"Why not? You think I have no forgotten desires, nothing I would not wish to dream of? No childhood which had its sweet moments?"

"Forgive me, madam."

She shrugged. "There's an attraction to that aspect of the past. To the past in general, I suppose. But we forget the other aspects—those things which forced us into fantasy in the first place."

"You're a believer in the future, then, madam?" Elric tried to joke. The rock beneath their feet became slippery and they were forced to make the gentle descent with more caution. Ahead Elric thought he heard again the sound of the river, perhaps where it now raced underground.

"The future holds as many traps as the past," she said with a smile. "I am a believer in the present, my lord. In the eternal present." And there was an edge to her voice, as if she had not always held this view.

"Speculation and regret offer many temptations, I suppose," said Elric; then he gasped at what he saw ahead.

Molten gold was cascading down two well-worn channels in the rock, forming a gigantic V-shaped edifice. The metal flowed unchecked and yet as they approached it became obvious that it was not hot. Some other agent had caused the effect, perhaps a chemical in the rock itself. As the gold reached the floor of the cavern it spread into a pool and the pool in turn fed a brook which bubbled, brilliant with the precious stuff, down towards another stream which seemed at first to contain ordinary water, but when Elric looked more carefully he saw that that stream was, in turn, comprised of silver and the two elements blended as they met. Following the course of this stream with his eyes, he saw that they met, some distance away, with a further river, this one of glistening scarlet, which might be liquid rubies. In all his travels, in the Young Kingdoms and the realms of the supernatural, Elric had seen nothing like it. He made to move towards it, to inspect it further, but she checked him.

"We have reached the next gate," she said. "Ignore that particular wonder, my lord. Look."

She pointed between twin streams of gold and he could just make out something shadowy beyond. "There is Paranor. Are you ready to enter that land?"

Remembering the dreamthieves' term for it, Elric allowed himself an ironic smile. "As ready as I shall ever be, madam."

Then, just as he stepped towards the portal, there came the sound of galloping hooves behind them. They rang sharply on the rock of the cavern. They echoed through the gloomy roof, through a thousand chambers, and Elric had no time to turn before something heavy struck his shoulder and he was flung to one side. He had the impression of a deathly white horse, of a rider wearing armour of ivory, mother-of-pearl and pale tortoiseshell, and then it was gone through the gate of molten gold and disappearing into the shadows beyond. But there was no doubt in Elric's mind that he had encountered one of the warriors who had already attacked him on the bridge. He had the impression of the same mocking chuckle as the hooves faded and the sound was absorbed by whatever lay beyond the gate.

"We have an enemy," said Oone. Her face was grim and she clenched her hands to her sides, clearly taking a grip on herself. "We have been identified already. The Fortress of the Pearl does not merely defend. She attacks."

"You know those riders? You have seen them before?"

She shook her head. "I know their kind, that's all."

"And we've no means of avoiding them?"

"Very few." She was frowning to herself again, considering some problem she was not prepared to discuss. Then she seemed to dismiss it and taking his arm led him under the twin cascades of cool gold into a further cavern, which this time suddenly filled with a gentle green glow, as if they walked beneath a canopy of leaves in autumn sunlight. And Elric was reminded of Old Melniboné, at the height of her power, when his people were proud enough to take the whole world for granted, when entire nations had been remoulded for their passing pleasure. As they emerged into a further cavern, so vast he did not at first realise they were still underground, he saw the spires and minarets of a city, glowing with the same warm green, which was as beautiful as his own beloved Imrryr, the Dreaming City, which he had explored throughout his boyhood.

"It is like Imrryr and yet it is not like Imrryr at all," he said in surprise.

"No," she said, "it is like London. It is like Tanelorn. It is like Ras-Paloom-Atai." And she did not speak sarcastically. She spoke as if she really did believe the city resembled those other cities, only one of which Elric recognised.

"But you have seen it before. What is it called?"

"It has no name," she said. "It has all names. It is called whatever you desire to call it." And she turned away, as if resting herself, before she led him onward down the road past the city.

"Should we not visit it? There may be people there who can help us find our way."

Oone gestured. "And there may be those who would hamper us. It is now clear, Prince Elric, that our mission is suspected and that certain forces could well have the intention of stopping us at any cost."

"You think the Sorcerer Adventurers have followed us?"

"Or preceded us. Leaving at least something of themselves here." She was peering cautiously towards the city.

"It seems such a peaceful place," said Elric. The more he

looked at the city the more he was impressed by the architecture, all of the same greenish stone but varying from yellow to blue. There were vast buttresses and curving bridges between one tower and another; there were spires as delicate as cobwebs yet so tall they almost disappeared into the roofs of the cavern. It seemed to reflect some part of him which he could not at once recall. He longed to go there. He grew resentful of Oone's guidance, though he had sworn to follow it, and began to believe that she herself was lost, that she was no better suited to discover their goal than was he.

"We must continue," she said. She was speaking more urgently now.

"I know I would find something within that city which would make Imrryr great again. And in her greatness I could lead her to dominate the world. But this time, instead of bringing cruelty and terror, we could bring beauty and good will."

"You are more prone to illusion than I thought, Prince Elric," said Oone.

He turned to her angrily. "What's wrong with such ambitions?"

"They are unrealistic. As unreal as that city."

"The city looks solid enough to me."

"Solid? Aye, in its way. Once you enter its gate it will embrace you as thoroughly as any long-lost lover! Come then, sir. Come!" She seemed seized by an equally poor temper and strode on up an obsidian road which twisted along the hill towards the city.

Startled by her sudden change, Elric followed. But now his own anger was dissipating. "I'll abide, madam, by your judgement. I am sorry . . ."

She was not listening to him. Moment by moment the city came closer until soon they were overshadowed by it, looking up at walls and domes and towers whose size was so tremendous it was almost impossible to guess at their true extent.

"There's a gate," she said. "There! Go through and I'll say farewell. I'll try to save the child myself and you can give yourself up to lost beliefs and so lose the beliefs you currently hold!''

And now Elric looked closer at the walls, which were like jade, and he saw dark shapes within the walls and he saw that the dark shapes were the figures of men, women and children. He gasped as he stepped forward to peer at them, observing living faces, eyes which were undying, lips frozen in expressions of terror, of anguish, of misery. They were like so many flies in amber.

''That's the unchanging past, Prince Elric,'' said Oone. ''That's the fate of those who seek to reclaim their lost beliefs without first experiencing the search for new ones. This city has another name. Dreamthieves call it the City of Inventive Cowardice. You would not understand the twists of logic which brought so many to this pass! Which made them force those they loved to share their fate. Would you stay with them, Prince Elric, and nurse your lost beliefs?''

The albino turned away with a shudder. ''But if they could see what had happened to earlier travellers, why did they continue into the city?''

''They blinded themselves to the obvious. That is the great triumph of mindless need over intelligence and the human spirit.''

Together the two returned to the path below the city and Elric was relieved when the beautiful towers were far behind and they had passed through several more great caverns, each with its own city, though none as magnificent as the first. These he had felt no desire to visit, though he had detected movement in some and Oone had said she suspected not all were as dangerous as the City of Inventive Cowardice.

''You called this world the Dream Realm,'' he said, ''and indeed it's well-named, madam, for it seems to contain a catalogue of dreams, and not a few nightmares. It's almost as if the place were born of a poet's brain, so strange are some of the sights.''

''I told you,'' she said, speaking more warmly now that he had acknowledged the danger, ''much of what you witness here is the semi-formed stuff of realities that other worlds, such as yours and mine, are yet to witness. To what extent they will come to exist elsewhere I do not know. These places have been fashioned over centuries by a succession of dreamthieves, imposing form on what is otherwise formless.''

Elric was now beginning to understand better what he had been told by Oone. ''Rather than making a map of what exists, you impose your own map upon it!''

''To a degree. We do not invent. We merely describe in a particular way. By that means we can make pathways through each of the myriad Dream Realms, for, in this alone, the realms comply one with the other.''

''In reality there could be a thousand different lands in each realm?''

''If you would see it so. Or an infinity of lands. Or one with an infinity of aspects. Roads are made so that the traveller without a compass may not wander too far from their destination.'' She laughed almost gaily. ''The fanciful names we give these places are not from any poetical impulse, nor from whim, but from a certain necessity. Our survival depends on accurate descriptions!''

''Your words have a profundity to them, madam. Though my survival has also tended to depend on a good, sharp blade!''

''While you depend upon your blade, Prince Elric, you condemn yourself to a singular fate.''

''You predict my death, eh, madam?''

Oone shook her head, her beautiful lips forming an expression of utmost sympathy and tenderness. ''Death is inevitable to almost all of us, in some shape or another. And I'll admit, if Chaos ever conquered Chaos, then you will be the instrument of that remarkable conquest. It would be sad, indeed, Prince Elric, if in taming Chaos you destroyed yourself and all you loved into the bargain!''

''I promise you, Lady Oone, to do my best to avoid such a fate.'' And Elric wondered at the look in the dreamthief's eyes and then chose not to speculate further.

They walked through a forest of stalagmites and stalactites

now, all of the same glowing colours, dark greens and dark blues and rich reds, and there was a musical sound as water splashed from roof to floor. Every so often a huge drop would fall on one or the other of them but such was the nature of the caverns that they were soon dry again. They had begun to relax and walked arm in arm, almost merry, and it was only then that they saw the figures flitting between the upward-thrusting fangs of rock.

"Swordsmen," murmured Elric. He added ironically, "This is when a weapon would be useful . . ." His mind was half with the situation, half feeling its way out through the worlds of the elementals, seeking some kind of spell, some supernatural aid, but he was baffled. It seemed that the mental paths he was used to following were blocked to him.

The warriors were veiled. They were dressed in heavy flowing cloaks and their heads were protected by helms of metal and leather. Elric had the impression of cold, hard eyes with tattooed lids and knew at once that these were members of the Sorcerer Assassin guild from Quarzhasaat, left behind when their fellows had retreated from the Dream Realms. Doubtless they were trapped here. It was clear, however, that they did not intend to parley with Elric and Oone, but were closing in, following a familiar pattern of attack.

Elric was struck by a strangeness about these men. They lacked a certain fluidity of movement and, the closer they came, the more he realised that it was almost possible to see past their eyes and into the hollows of their skulls. These were not ordinary mortals. He had seen men like them in Imrryr once, when he had gone with his father on one of those rare times when Sadric chose to take him upon some local expedition, out to an old arena whose high walls imprisoned certain Melnibonéans who had lost their souls in pursuit of sorcerous knowledge, but whose bodies still lived. They, too, had seemed to be possessed by a cold, raging hatred against any not like themselves.

Oone cried out and moved rapidly, dropping to one knee as a sword struck at her, then clattered against one of the great

pointed pillars. So close together were the stalagmites that it
was difficult for the swordsmen to swing or to stab and for a
while both the albino and the dreamthief ducked and dodged
the blades until one cut Elric's arm and he saw, almost in
surprise, that the man had drawn blood.

The Prince of Melniboné knew that it was just a matter of
time before they were both killed and, as he fell back against
one of the great rocky teeth, he felt the stalagmite move behind
him. Some trick of the cavern had weakened the rock and it
was loose. He flung all of his weight forward against it. It
began to topple. Quickly he got his body in front of it, supporting the thing on his shoulder, then with all his energy he
ran with the great rocky spear at his nearest assailant.

The point of the rock drove full into the veiled man's chest.
The Sorcerer Assassin uttered a bleak, agonised shout, and
strange, unnatural blood began to well up around the stone,
gushing down and soaking into the warrior's bones, almost
reabsorbed by him. Elric sprang forward and dragged the sabre and the poignard from his hands even as another of the
attackers came upon him from the rear. All his battle cunning,
all his war skills, returned to Elric. Long before he had come
by Stormbringer he had learned the arts of the sword and the
dagger, of the bow and the lance, and now he had no need of
an enchanted blade to make short work of the second Sorcerer
Assassin, then a third. Shouting to Oone to help herself to
weapons, he darted from rock to rock, taking the warriors one
at a time. They moved sluggishly, uncertainly now, yet none
ran from him.

Soon Oone had joined him, showing that she was as accomplished a fighter as he. He admired the delicacy of her tech-
nique, the sureness of her hands as she parried and thrust,
striking with the utmost efficiency and piling up her corpses
with all the economy of a cat in a nest of rats.

Elric took time to grin over his shoulder. "For one who so
recently extolled the virtues of words over the sword, you show
yourself well-accomplished with a blade, madam!"

"It is often as well to have the experience of both before one

makes the choice,'' she said. She despatched another of their
assailants. ''And there are times, Prince Elric, I'll admit, when
a decent piece of steel has a certain advantage over a neatly
turned phrase!''

They fought together like two old friends. Their techniques
were complementary but not dissimilar. Both fought as the best
soldiers fight, with neither cruelty nor pleasure in the killing,
but with the intention of winning as quickly as possible, while
causing as little pain to their opponents.

These opponents appeared to suffer no pain, as such, but
every time one died he offered up the same disturbing wail of
anguish, and the blood which poured from the wounds was
strange stuff indeed.

At last the man and woman were done and stood leaning on
their borrowed blades panting and seeking to control that nau-
sea which so often follows a battle.

Then, as Elric watched, the corpses around them swiftly
faded, leaving only a few swords behind. The blood, too, disappeared. There was virtually nothing to say that a fight had
taken place in the great cavern.

''Where have they gone?''

Oone picked up a sheath and fitted her new sabre into it.
For all her words, she clearly had no intention of proceeding
any further without arms. She placed two daggers in her belt.
''Gone? Ah.'' She hesitated. ''To whatever pool of half-living
ectoplasm they came from.'' She shook her head. ''They were
almost phantasms, Prince Elric, but not quite. They were, as
I told you, what the Sorcerer Adventurers left behind.''

''You mean part of them returned to our own world, as part
of Alnac returned?''

''Exactly.'' She drew a breath and made as if to continue.

''Then why shall we not find Alnac here? Still alive?''

''Because we do not seek him,'' she said. And she spoke
with all her old firmness; enough to make Elric proceed only a
degree further with the subject.

''And perhaps anyway we would not find him here, as we

found the Sorcerer Adventurers, in the Land of Lost Beliefs,"
said the albino quietly.

"True," she said.

Then Elric took her in his arms for a moment and they
remained, embracing, for a few seconds, until they were ready
to continue forward seeking the Celador Gate.

Later, as Elric helped his ally across another natural bridge,
below which flowed a river of dull brown stuff, Oone said to
him: "This is no ordinary adventure for me, Prince Elric. That
is why I needed you to come with me."

A little puzzled as to why she should, after all, say something
which they had both taken for granted, Elric did not reply.

When the snout-faced women attacked them, with nets and
spikes, it did not take them long to cut their way free and drive
the cowardly creatures off, and neither were they greatly in-
convenienced by the vulpine things which loped on their hind-
legs and had claws like birds. They even joked together as they
despatched packs of snapping beasts which resembled nothing
so much as horses the size of dogs and spoke a few words of a
human tongue, though without any sense of the meaning.

Now at least they were reaching the borders of Paranor and
saw looming ahead of them two enormous towers of carved
rock, with little balconies and windows and terraces and cren-
ellations, all covered in old ivy and climbing brambles bearing
light yellow fruit.

"It is the Celador Gate," said Oone. She seemed reluctant
to approach it. Her hand on the hilt of her sword, her other
arm linked with Elric's, she stopped and drew a deep, slow
breath. "It is the land of forests."

"You called it the Land of Forgotten Love," said Elric.

"Aye. That's the dreamthieves' name." She laughed a little
sardonically.

Elric, uncertain of her mood and not wishing to intrude upon
her, held back also, looking from her to the gate and back
again.

She reached a hand to his bone-white features. Her own skin
was golden, still full of enormous vitality. She stared into his

face. Then, with a sigh, she turned away and stepped towards the gate, taking his hand and pulling him after her.

They passed between the towers and here Elric's nostrils immediately were filled with the rich smells of leaf and turf. All around them were massive oak trees and elms and birches and every other kind of tree, yet all of them, though they formed a canopy, grew not beneath the light of the open sky but were nurtured by the oddly glowing rocks in the cavern ceilings. Elric had thought it impossible for trees to grow underground and he marvelled at the health, the very ordinariness, of everything.

It was therefore with some astonishment that he observed a creature emerge from the wood and plant itself firmly on the path along which they must move.

"Halt! I must know your business!" His face was covered in brown fur and his teeth were so prominent, his ears so large, his eyes so doelike, he resembled nothing so much as an overgrown rabbit, though he was armoured solidly in battered brass, with a brass cap upon his head, and his weapons, a sword and spear of workmanlike steel, were also bound in brass.

"We seek merely to pass through this land without doing harm or being harmed," said Oone.

The rabbit-warrior shook his head. "Too vague," he said, and suddenly he hefted his spear and plunged the point deep into the bole of an oak. The oak tree screamed. "That's what he told me. And many more of these."

"The trees were travellers?" said Elric.

"Your name, sir?"

"I am Elric of Melniboné and, like my lady Oone here, I mean you no disturbance. We travel on to Imador."

"I know no 'Elric' or 'Oone.' I am the Count of Magnes Doar and I hold this land as my own. By my conquest. By my ancient right. You must go back through the gate."

"We cannot," said Oone. "To retreat would mean our destruction."

"To proceed, madam, would mean the same thing. What? Shall you camp at the gates forever?"

"No, sir," she said. She put her hand to the hilt of her sword. "We will hack our way through your forest if need be. We are on urgent business and will accept no halt."

The rabbit-warrior pulled the spear from the oak, which ceased to scream, and flung it into another tree. This, in turn, set up a wailing and a moaning until even the Count of Magnes Doar shook his head in irritation and drew his weapon out of the trunk. "You must fight me, I think," he said.

It was then that they heard a yell from the other side of the right pillar and something white and rearing appeared there. It was another of the pale riders in armour of bone, tortoise-shell and mother-of-pearl, his horrible eyes slitted with hatred, his horse's hooves beating at a barrier which had not been there when Oone and Elric passed through.

Then it was down and the warrior was charging.

The albino and the dreamthief made to defend themselves, but it was the Count of Magnes Doar who moved ahead of them and jabbed his spear up at the warrior's body. Steel was deflected by an armour stronger than it looked and the sword rose and fell, almost contemptuously, slicing down through the brass helm into the brain of the rabbit-warrior. He staggered backward, his hands clutching at his head, his sword and spear abandoned. His round brown eyes seemed to grow still wider and he began to squeal. He turned slowly, round and round, then fell to his knees.

Elric and Oone had positioned themselves behind the bole of one of the oaks, ready to defend themselves when the rider attacked.

The horse reared again, snorting with the same mindless fury as its master, and Elric darted from his cover, seized the dropped spear and stabbed up to where the breastplate and gorget joined, sliding the spearhead expertly into the warrior's throat.

There came a choking sound which in turn grew to a familiar chuckling and the rider had turned his horse and was riding

ahead of them again, along the path through the forest, his
body swaying and jerking as if in its death agonies, yet still
borne on by the horse.

They watched it disappear.

Elric was trembling. "If I had not already seen him die on
the bridge from Sadanor I would swear that was the same man
who attacked me there. He has a puzzling familiarity."

"You did not see him die," said Oone. "You saw him
plunge into the river."

"Well, I think he is dead now, after that stroke. I almost
severed his head."

"I doubt if he is," she said. "It's my belief he is our most
powerful enemy and we shall not have to deal with him in any
serious way until we near the Fortress of the Pearl itself."

"He protects the Fortress?"

"Many do." She embraced him again, swiftly, then sank to
one knee to inspect the dead Count of Magnes Doar. In death
he more resembled a man, for already the hair on his face and
hands was fading to grey and even his flesh seemed on the
point of disappearance. The brass helm, too, had turned an
ugly shade of silver. Elric was reminded of Alnac's dying. He
averted his eyes.

Oone, too, stood up quickly and there were tears in her eyes.
The tears were not for the Count of Magnes Doar. Elric took
her in his arms. He was suddenly full of longing for someone
he barely remembered from old dreams, the dreams of his
youth; someone who, perhaps, had never existed.

He thought he felt a slight shudder run through Oone as he
embraced her. He reached out for a memory of a little boat,
of a fair-haired girl sleeping at the bottom of the vessel as it
drifted out to open sea, of himself sailing a skiff towards her,
full of pride that he might be her rescuer. Yet he had never
known such a girl, he was sure, though Oone reminded him
of that girl grown up.

With a gasp Oone moved away from him. "I thought you
were . . . It's as if I'd always known you . . ." She put her
hands to her face. "Oh, this damned land is well-called, Elric!"

Elric could only agree.

"Yet what danger is there to us?" he asked.

She shook her head. "Who knows? Much or little. None? The dreamthieves say that it is in the Land of Forgotten Love that the most important decisions are made. Decisions which can have the most monumental consequences."

"So one should do nothing here? Make no decisions?"

She passed her fingers through her hair. "At least we should be aware that the consequences might not manifest themselves for a long while yet."

Together they left the dead rabbit-warrior behind them and continued down the tunnel of trees. Now from time to time Elric thought he saw faces peering at him from the green shadows. Once he was sure he saw the figure of his dead father, Sadric, mourning for Elric's mother, the only creature he had ever truly loved. So strong was the image that Elric called out:

"Sadric! Father! Is this your Limbo?"

At this Oone cried urgently. "No! Do not address him. Do not bring him to you. Do not make him real! It is a trap, Elric. Another trap."

"My father?"

"Did you love him?"

"Aye. Though it was an unhappy kind of love."

"Remember that. Do not bring him here. It would be obscene to recall him to this gallery of illusions."

Elric understood her and used all his habits of self-discipline to rid himself of his father's shade. "I tried to tell him, Oone, how much I grieved for him in his loss and his sorrow." He was weeping. His body was shaking with an emotion from which he believed he had long since freed himself. "Ah, Oone. I would have died myself to let him have his wife returned to him. Is there no way . . . ?"

"Such sacrifices are meaningless," she said, gripping him in both her hands and holding her to him. "Especially here. Remember your quest. We have already crossed three of the seven lands which will bring us to the Fortress of the Pearl. We have crossed half this. That means we have already accomplished more than most. Hold on to yourself, Prince of Melniboné. Remember who and what depends upon your success!''

''But if I have the opportunity to make something right that was so wrong. . . ?''

''That is to do with your own feelings, not what is and what can be. Would you invent shadows and make them play out your dreams? Would that bring happiness to your tragic mother and father?''

Elric looked over his shoulder into the forest. There was no sign of his father now. ''He seemed so real. Of such solid flesh!''

''You must believe that you and I are the only solid flesh in this entire land. And even we are—'' She stopped herself. She reached up to his face and kissed it. ''We will rest for a little, if only to restore our psychic strength.''

And Oone drew Elric down into the soft leaves at the side of the path. And she kissed him and she moved her lovely hands over his body and slowly she became all that he had lost in his love of women and he knew that he, in turn, became everything she had ever refused to allow herself to desire in a man. And he knew, without guilt or regret, that their love-making had no past and that its only future lay somewhere beyond their own lives, beyond any realm they would ever visit, and that neither would ever witness the consequences.

And in spite of this knowledge they were careless and they were happy and they gave each other the strength they would need if they ever hoped to fulfill their quest and reach the Fortress of the Pearl.

4

The Intervention
of a Navigator

Surprised by his own lack of
confusion, filled with an apparent clarity, Elric stepped, side
by side with Oone, through the shimmering silver gateway into
Imador, called mysteriously by the dreamthieves the Land of
New Ambition, and found himself at the top of an heroic flight
of steps which curved downward towards a plain which
stretched towards a horizon turned a pale, misty blue and which
he could almost have mistaken for the sky. For a moment he
thought that he and Oone were alone on that vast stairway and
then he saw that it was crowded with people. Some were engaged in hectic conversation, some bartering, some embracing,
while others were gathered around holy men, speech-makers,
priestesses, story-tellers, either listening avidly or arguing.

The steps down to the plain were alive with every manner
of human intercourse. Elric saw snake-charmers, bear-baiters,
jugglers and acrobats. They were dressed in costumes typical
of the desert lands—enormous silk pantaloons of green, blue,
gold, vermilion and amber; coats of brocade or velvet; turbans,
burnooses and caps of the most intricate needlework; bur-
nished metal and silver, gold, precious jewels of every kind.

And there was an abundance of animals, stalls, baskets overflowing with produce, with fabrics, with goods of leather and
copper and brass.

"How handsome they are!" he remarked. It was true that
though they were of all shapes and sizes the people had a beauty
which was not easily defined. Their skins were all healthy, their
eyes bright, their movements dignified and easy. They bore
themselves with confidence and good humour and while it was
clear they noticed Oone and Elric walking down the steps, they
acknowledged them without making any great effort to greet
them or ask them their business. Dogs, cats and monkeys ran
about in the crowd and children played the cryptic games all
children play. The air was warm and balmy and full of the
scents of fruit, flowers and the other goods being sold. "Would
that all worlds were like this," Elric added, smiling at a young
woman who offered him embroidered cloth.

Oone bought oranges from a boy who ran up to her. She
handed one to Elric. "This is a sweet realm indeed. I had not
expected it to be so pleasant." But when she bit into the fruit
she spat it into her hand. "It has no taste!"

Elric tried his own orange and he, too, found it a dry, fla-
vourless thing.

The disappointment he felt at this was out of all proportion
to the occurrence. He threw the orange from him. It struck a
step below and bounced until it was out of sight.

The grey-green plain appeared unpopulated. There was a
road sweeping across it, wide and well-paved, but there was
not a single traveller visible, in spite of the great crowd. "I
wonder why the road is empty," he said to Oone. "Do all
these people sleep at nights on these steps? Or do they disappear into another realm when their business here is done?"

"Doubtless that question will be answered for us soon
enough, my lord."

She linked her arm in his own. Since their love-making in
the wood, a sense of considerable comradeship and mutual
liking had grown up between them. He knew no guilt; he knew
in his heart that he had betrayed no one and it was clear Oone

was equally untroubled. In some strange way they had restored each other, making their combined energy something more than the sum. This was the kind of friendship he had never really known before and he was grateful for it. He believed that he had learned much from Oone and that the dreamthief would teach him more that would be valuable to him when he returned to Melniboné to claim his throne back from Yyrkoon.

As they descended the steps it seemed to Elric that the costumes became more and more elaborate, the jewels and headdresses and weapons richer and more exotic, while the stature of the people increased and they grew still more handsome.

From curiosity he stopped to listen to a story-teller who held a crowd entranced, but the man spoke in an unfamiliar language—high and flat—which meant nothing to him. He and Oone paused again, beside a bead-seller, whom he asked politely if those gathered on the steps were all of the same nation.

The woman frowned at him and shook her head, replying in still another language. There seemed few words in it. She repeated much. Only when they were stopped by a sherbet-seller, a young boy, could they ask their question and be understood.

The lad frowned, as if translating their words in his head. "Aye, we are the people of the steps. Each of us has a place here, one below the other."

"You grow richer and more important as you descend, eh?" asked Oone.

He was puzzled by this. "Each of us has a place here," he said again, and, as if alarmed by their questions, he ran off up into the dense crowd above. Here, too, there were fewer people and Elric could see that their numbers thinned increasingly as the steps neared the plain. "Is this an illusion?" he murmured to Oone. "It has the air of a dream."

"It is our sense of what should be that intrudes here," she said, "and it colours our perception of the place, I think."

"It is not an illusion?"

"It is not what you would call an illusion." She made an effort to find words but eventually shook her head. "The more it seems an illusion to us, the more it becomes one. Does that make sense?''

''I think so.''

At last they were nearing the bottom of the stairway. They were on the last few steps when they looked up to see a horseman riding towards them across the plain, creating a huge pillar of dust as he came.

There was a cry from the people behind them. Elric looked back and saw them all rushing rapidly up the stairs and his impulse was to join them, but Oone stayed him. ''Remember we cannot go back,'' she said. ''We must meet this danger as best we can.''

Gradually the figure on the horse became distinguishable. It was either the same warrior in the armour of mother-of-pearl, ivory and tortoiseshell or one who was identical. He bore a white lance tipped with a point of sharpened bone and the thing was aimed directly at Elric's heart.

The albino jumped forward in a manoeuvre designed to confuse his attacker. He was almost under the horse's hooves when he struck upward with his swiftly drawn sword and cut at the lance. The force of the blow sent him reeling to one side while Oone, reacting with almost telepathic coordination, almost as if they were controlled by a single brain, leapt and thrust beneath the raised left arm, seeking their assailant's heart.

Her thrust was parried by a sudden movement of the rider's gauntleted right hand and he kicked out at her. Now, for the first time, Elric saw his face clearly. It was thin, bloodless, with eyes like the flesh of long-dead fish and a sneering gash of a mouth, opening now in a grimace of contempt. Yet with a shock he saw, too, something of Alnac Kreb! The lance swung to strike Oone's shoulder and send her, too, to the ground.

Elric was up again before the lance could return, his sword slashing at the horse's girth-strap in an old trick learned from the Vilmirian bandits, but he was blocked by an armoured leg and the lance returned to thrust at him while he darted clear, giving Oone her opportunity.

Though Elric and Oone fought as a single entity, their attacker was almost prescient, seeming to guess their every move.

Elric began to believe the rider to be wholly supernatural in origin and even as he feinted again he sent his mind out into the realms of the elementals, seeking any aid which might possibly be available to him. But there was none. It was as if every realm were deserted, as if, overnight, the entire world of elementals, demons and spirits, had been banished to Limbo. Arioch would not aid him. His sorcery was completely useless here.

Oone cried out sharply and Elric saw that she had been flung back against the lowest step. She tried to climb to her feet but something was paralysed. She could hardly move her limbs.

Again the pale rider chuckled and began to advance for the kill.

Elric roared out his old battle-shout and raced towards their opponent, trying to distract him. The albino was horrified at the possibility of harm coming to the woman for whom he felt both profound love and comradeship and was willing to die to save her.

"Arioch! Arioch! Blood and souls!"

But he had no runesword to aid him here. Nothing save his own wits and skills.

"Alnac Kreb. Is this what remains of you?"

The rider turned, almost impatiently, and flung the lance at the running man. His answer.

Elric had not anticipated this. He tried to throw his body aside but the haft of the lance struck his shoulder and he fell heavily into the dust, losing his grip on the unfamiliar sabre. He began to scrabble towards it even as he saw the rider draw his own long blade and continue towards the helpless Oone. He raised himself to one knee and threw his poignard with desperate accuracy. The blade went true, between the plates of the rider's back armour, and the lifted sword fell suddenly.

Elric reached his sabre, got to his feet and saw to his horror that the rider was rearing over Oone, the sword again raised, ignoring the wound in his shoulder.

"Alnac?"

Again Elric tried to appeal to whatever part of Alnac Kreb was there, but this time he was completely ignored. That same hideous, inhuman chuckling filled the air, the horse snorted, its hooves pawing at the woman as she struggled on the step.

Scarcely aware of his own movement, Elric reached the rider and leapt upward, dragging at his back, trying to haul him from the horse. The rider growled and managed to turn. His whistling sword was parried by Elric's and the albino unseated him. Together the pair fell to the sand, a few inches from where Oone lay. Elric's sword-hand was crushed under his attacker's armoured back, but he managed to tug the poignard free with his left hand and would have struck at those hideous dead eyes had not the man's fingers closed on his wrist.

"You'll kill me before you harm her!" Elric's normally melodic voice was a snarl of hatred. But the warrior merely laughed again, the ghost of Alnac fading from his eyes.

They fought thus for several moments, neither gaining any true advantage. Elric could hear his own breathing, the grunting of the armoured man, the whinnying of the horse and Oone's gasp as she tried to get to her feet.

"Pearl Warrior!"

It was another voice. Not Oone's, but a woman's; and it carried considerable authority.

"Pearl Warrior! You must do no further violence to these travellers!"

The warrior grunted but ignored the woman. His teeth snapped at Elric's throat. He tried to turn the poignard towards the albino's heart. There were drops of foaming saliva on his lips now—beads of white rimming his mouth.

"Pearl Warrior!"

Suddenly the warrior began to speak, whispering to Elric as if to a fellow conspirator. "Don't listen to her. I can aid thee. Why do you not come with us and learn to explore the Great Steppe, where all the hunting is rich? And there are melons, tasting like the most delicate cherries. I can give thee such wonderful clothing. Do not listen. Do not listen. Yes, I am Alnac, thy friend. Yes!''

Elric was repelled by the insane babble, more than he had been by the creature's horrible appearance and his violence.

''Think of all the power there is. They fear thee. They fear me. Elric. I know thee. Let us not be rivals. Together we can succeed. I am not free, but thou couldst journey for us both. I am not free, but thou wouldst never bear responsibilities. I am not free, but, Elric, I have so many slaves at my disposal. They are thine. I offer thee new wealth and new philosophies, new ways of fulfilling every desire. I fear thee and thou fearest me. So we will bind us together, one to the other. It is the only tie that ever means anything. They dream of thee, all of them. Even I, who do not dream. Thou are the only enemy . . .''

''Pearl Warrior!''

With a rattle of bone and ivory, of tortoiseshell and mother-of-pearl, the leprous-skinned warrior disentangled himself from Elric. ''Together we can defeat her,'' he mumbled urgently. ''There would be no force to resist us. I will give thee my ferocity!''

Nauseated by all this, Elric climbed slowly to his feet, turning to stare in the same direction as Oone, who now sat on the step, nursing limbs to which life seemed to be restored.

A woman, taller than either Elric or Oone, stood there. She was veiled and hooded. Her eyes moved steadily from them to the one she called Pearl Warrior and then she raised the great staff she held in her right hand and struck at the ground with it.

''Pearl Warrior! You must obey me!''

The Pearl Warrior was furious. ''I do not wish this!'' He snarled and, clattering, brushed at his breastplate. ''You anger me, Lady Sough.''

''These are my charges and under my protection. Go, Pearl Warrior. Kill elsewhere. Kill the true enemies of the Pearl.''

''I do not want you to order me!'' He was surly, sulking like a child. ''All are enemies of the Pearl. You, too, Lady Sough.''

"You are a silly creature! Begone!" And she lifted the staff to point beyond the stairway, where hazy rock could be seen, rising up forever.

He spoke again, warningly. "You make me angry, Lady Sough. I am the Pearl Warrior. I have the strength from the Fortress." He turned to Elric as if to a comrade. "Ally yourself with me and we'll kill her now. Then we shall rule—thou in thine freedom, me in my slavery. All of this and many other realms beside, unknown to dreamthieves. Safety is there forever. Be mine. We shall be married. Yes, yes, yes . . ."

Elric shuddered and turned his back on the Pearl Warrior. He went to help Oone to her feet.

Oone was able to move all her limbs but she was still dazed. She looked back at the steps which disappeared above them. Not a single one of the people who had occupied that vast staircase was visible.

Troubled, Elric glanced at the newcomer. Her robes were of different shades of blue, with silver threads running through them, hemmed with gold and dark green. She carried herself with extraordinary grace and dignity and stared back at Oone and Elric with an air of amusement. Meanwhile the Pearl Warrior climbed to his feet and stood defiantly to one side, alternately glaring at Lady Sough and offering Elric a hideous conspiratorial smile.

"Where are all the folk of the steps gone?" Elric asked her.

"They have merely returned to their home, my lord," said Lady Sough. Her voice, when she addressed him, was warm and full, yet retained all the authority with which she had ordered the Pearl Warrior to stop his attack. "I am Lady Sough and I bid you welcome to this land."

"We are grateful for your intervention, my lady." Oone spoke for the first time, though with a degree of suspicion. "Are you the ruler here?"

"I am merely a guide and a navigator."

"That mad thing there accepts your command." Oone rose, rubbing at her arms and legs, glaring at the Pearl Warrior, who sneered, becoming shifty as Lady Sough gave him her attention.

"He is incomplete." Lady Sough was dismissive. "He guards the Pearl. But he has such an insubstantial intelligence, he cannot understand the nature of his task, nor who is friend or who foe. He can make only the most limited choices, poor corrupt thing. The ones who put him to this work had, themselves, only the faintest understanding of what was required in such a warrior."

"Bad! I will not!" The Pearl Warrior began to utter his chuckle again. "Never! It is why! *It is why!*"

"Go!" cried Lady Sough, gesturing once more with her staff, her eyes glaring above her veil. "You have no business with these."

"Dying is unwise, madam," said the Pearl Warrior, lifting his shoulder in a gesture of defiant arrogance. "Beware thine own corruption. We may all dissolve if this achieves that resolution."

"Go, stupid brute!" She pointed at his horse. "And leave that spear behind you. Destructive, insensate grotesque that you are."

"Am I mistaken," said Elric, "or does he speak gibberish?"

"Possibly," murmured Oone. "But it could be he speaks more of the truth than those who would protect us."

"Anything will come and anything will have to be resisted!" said the Pearl Warrior darkly as he mounted. He began to ride to where his lance had fallen after he had thrown it at Elric. "This is why we are to be!"

"Begone! Begone!"

He leaned from his saddle, reaching towards the lance.

"No," she said firmly, as if to a silly child. "I told you that you should not have it. Look what you have done, Pearl Warrior! You are forbidden to attack these people again."

"No alliance, then. Not now! But soon this freedom will be exchanged and all shall come together!" Another appalling chuckle from the half-crazed rider and he was digging his spurs into his horse's flanks, going at a gallop in the direction he had come. "There shall be bonds! Oh, yes!"

"Do his words make sense to you, Lady Sough?" Elric asked politely, when the warrior had disappeared.

"Some of them," she said. It seemed that she was smiling behind her veil. "It is not his fault that his brain is malformed. There are few warriors in this world, you know. He is perhaps the best."

"Best?"

Oone's sardonic question went unanswered. Lady Sough reached out a hand on which delicately coloured jewels glowed and she beckoned to them. "I am a navigator here. I can bear you to sweet islands where two lovers could be happy forever. I have a place that is hidden and safe. Can I take you there?"

Elric glanced at Oone, wondering if perhaps she was attracted by Lady Sough's invitation. For a second he forgot their purpose here. It would be wonderful to spend a short idyll in Oone's company.

"This is Imador, is it not, Lady Sough?"

"It is the place the dreamthieves call Imador, aye. We do not call it by that name." She seemed disapproving.

"We are grateful for your help in this matter, my lady," said Elric, thinking Oone a little brusque and seeking to apologise for his friend's manner. "I am Elric of Melniboné and this is Lady Oone of the Dreamthieves' Guild. Do you know that we seek the Fortress of the Pearl?"

"Aye. And this road is a straight one for you. It can lead you forward to the Fortress. But it might not lead you by the best route. I will guide you by whatever route you wish." She sounded a little distant, almost as if she were half-asleep herself. Her tone had become dreamy and Elric guessed she was offended.

"We owe you much, Lady Sough, and your advice is of value to us. What would you suggest?"

"That you raise an army first, I think. For your own safety. There are such terrible defences at the Fortress of the Pearl. Why, and before that, too. You are brave, the both of you. There are several roads to success. Death lies at the end of many other paths. Of this, you are, I am sure, aware . . .''

''Where could we recruit such an army?'' Elric ignored Oone's warning look. He felt that she was being obstinate, overly suspicious of this dignified woman.

''There is an ocean not far from here. There is an island in it. The people of that island long to fight. They will follow anyone who promises them danger. Will you come there? It is very good. There is warmth and secure walls. Gardens and much to eat.''

''Your words have a strong degree of common-sense,'' said Elric. ''It would be worth, perhaps, pausing in our quest to recruit those soldiers. And I was offered alliance by the Pearl Warrior. Will he help us? Can he be trusted?''

''For what you wish to do? Yes, I think.'' Her forehead furrowed. ''Yes, I think.''

''No, Lady Sough.'' Oone spoke suddenly and with considerable force. ''We are grateful for your guidance. Will you take us to the Falador Gate? Do you know it?''

''I know what you call the Falador Gate, young woman. And whatever your questions or your desires, they are mine to answer and fulfill.''

''What is your own name for this land?''

''None.'' She seemed confused by Oone's question. ''There is not one. It is this place. It is here. But I can guide you through it.''

''I believe you, my lady.'' Oone's voice softened. She took Elric by the arm. ''Our other name for this land is the Land of New Ambition. But new ambitions can mislead. We invent them when the old ambition seems too hard to achieve, eh?''

Elric understood her. He felt foolish. ''You offer a diversion, Lady Sough?''

''Not so.'' The veiled woman shook her head. The movement had all her gracefulness in it and she seemed a little wounded by the directness of his question. ''A fresh goal is sometimes preferable when the road becomes impassable.''

"But the road is not impassable, Lady Sough," said Oone. "Not yet."

"That is true." Lady Sough bowed her head a fraction. "I offer you all truth in this matter. Every aspect of it."

"We shall retain the aspect of which we are most sure," Oone continued softly, "and thank you greatly for your help."

"It is yours to take, Lady Oone. Come." The woman whirled, her draperies lifting like clouds in a gale, and led them away from the steps to a place where the ground dipped and revealed, when they were closer, a shallow river. There a boat was moored. The boat had a curling prow of gilded wood, not unlike the crook of Oone's dreamwand, and its sides were covered with a thin layer of beaten gold, and bronze, and silver. Brass gleamed on rails, on the single mast, and a sail, blue with threads of silver, like Lady Sough's robes, was furled upon the yardarm. There was no visible crew. Lady Sough pointed with her staff. "Here is the boat with which we shall find the gate you seek. I have a vocation, Lady Oone, Prince Elric, to protect you. Do not fear me."

"My lady, we do not," said Oone with great sincerity. Still, her voice was gentle. Elric was mystified by her manner but accepted that she had a clear notion of their situation.

"What does this mean?" Elric murmured as Lady Sough descended towards her boat.

"I think it means we are close to the Fortress of the Pearl," said Oone. "She tries to help us but is not altogether sure how best to do it."

"You trust her?"

"If we trust ourselves, we can trust her, I think. We must know what are the right questions to ask her."

"I'll trust you, Oone, to trust her." Elric smiled.

At Lady Sough's insistent beckoning they clambered into the beautiful boat, which rocked only slightly on the dark waters of what seemed to Elric an entirely artificial canal, straight and deep, moving in a sweeping curve until it disappeared from sight a mile or two from them. He peered upward, still not sure if he looked upon a strange sky or the roof of the largest cavern of all. He could just see the stairs stretching away in the distance and wondered again what had happened to the inhabitants when they had fled at the Pearl Warrior's attack.

Lady Sough took the great tiller of the boat. With a single movement she guided the craft onto the centre of the water-way. Almost at once the ground levelled out so that it was possible to see the grey desert on all sides, while ahead was foliage, greenery, the suggestion of hills. There was a quality about the light which reminded Elric of a September evening. He could almost smell the early autumn roses, the turning trees, the orchards of Imrryr. Seated near the front of the boat with Oone beside him, leaning on his shoulder, he sighed with pleasure, enjoying the moment. "If the rest of our quest is to be conducted in such a way, I shall be glad to accompany you on many such adventures, Lady Oone."

She, too, was in good humour. "Aye. Then all the world would desire to be dreamthieves."

The boat rounded a bend of the canal and they were alerted by figures standing on both banks. These sad, silent people, dressed in white and yellow, regarded the sailing barge with tear-filled eyes, as if they witnessed a funeral. Elric was sure they did not weep for himself or Oone. He called out to them, but they did not seem to hear him. They were gone almost at once and they passed by gently rising terraces, cultivated for vines and figs and almonds. The air was sweet with ripening harvests and once a small, foxlike creature ran along beside them for a while before veering off into a clump of shrubs. A little later, naked, brown-skinned men prowled on all fours until they, too, grew bored and disappeared into the under-growth. The canal began to twist more and more and Lady Sough was forced to throw all her weight upon the tiller to keep the boat on course.

"Why would a canal be built so?" Elric asked her when they were once more upon a straight stretch of water.

"What was above us is now ahead and what was below is now behind," she replied. "That is the nature of this. I am the navigator and I know. But ahead, where it grows darker, the river is unbending. This is made to help understanding, I think.''

Her words were almost as confusing as the Pearl Warrior's, and Elric tried to make sense by asking her further questions. ''The river helps us understand what, Lady Sough?''

''Their nature—her nature—what you must encounter—ah, look!''

The river was widening rapidly into a lake. There were reeds growing on the banks now, silver herons flying against the soft sky.

''It is no great distance to the island I spoke of,'' said Lady Sough. ''I fear for you.''

''No,'' said Oone with determined kindness. ''Take the boat across the lake towards the Falador Gate. I thank you.''

''This thanks is . . .'' Lady Sough shook her head. ''I would not have you die.''

''We shall not. We are here to save her.''

''She is afraid.''

''We know.''

''Those others said they would save her. But they made her—they made it dark and she was trapped . . .''

''We know,'' said Oone, and laid a comforting hand on Lady Sough's arm as the veiled woman guided the boat out onto the open lake.

Elric said: ''Do you speak of the Holy Girl and the Sorcerer Adventurers? What imprisons her, Lady Sough? How can we release her? Bring her back to her father and her people?''

''Oh, it is a lie!'' Lady Sough almost shouted, pointing to where, swimming directly towards them, came a child. But the boy's skin was metallic, of glaring silver, and his silver eyes were begging them for help. Then the child grinned, reached to pull off its own head and submerged. ''We near the Falador Gate,'' said Oone grimly.

''Those who would possess her also guard her,'' said Lady Sough suddenly. ''But she is not theirs.''

''I know,'' said Oone. Her gaze was fixed on what lay ahead

of them. There was a mist on the lake. It was like the finest haze which forms on water in an autumn morning. There was an air of tranquility which, clearly, she mistrusted. Elric looked back at Lady Sough but the navigator's eyes were expressionless, offering no clue to what dangers they might soon be facing.

The boat turned a little and there was land just visible through the mist. Elric saw tall trees rising above a tumble of rocks. There were white pillars of limestone, shimmering faintly in that lovely light. He saw hummocks of grass and below them little coves. He wondered if Lady Sough had, after all, brought them to the island she had mentioned and was about to question her when he saw what appeared to be a massive door of carved stone and intricate mosaic bearing an air of considerable age.

"The Falador Gate," said Lady Sough, not without a hint of trepidation.

Then the gate had opened and a horrible wind rushed out of it, tearing at their hair and clothing, clawing at their skins, shrieking and wailing in their ears. The boat rocked and Elric feared it must capsize. He ran to the stern to help Lady Sough with the tiller. Her veil had been ripped from her face. She was not a young woman, but she bore an astonishing resemblance to the little girl they had left in the Bronze Tent, the Holy Girl of the Bauradim. And Elric, taking the tiller while Lady Sough replaced her veil, remembered that no mention had ever been made of Varadia's mother.

Oone was lowering the sail. The wind's initial strength had died and it was possible to tack gradually towards the dark, strangely smelling entrance which had been revealed as the mosaic door had blown down.

Three horses appeared there. Hooves flailed at the air. Tails lashed. Then they were galloping across the water in the direction of the boat. Then they had passed it and vanished into the mist. Not one of the beasts had possessed a head.

Now Elric knew terror. But it was a familiar terror and within seconds he had regained control of himself. He knew

Michael Moorcock

that, whatever its name, he was about to enter a land where Chaos ruled.

It was only as the boat sailed under the carved rocks and into the grotto beyond that he recalled he had none of his familiar spells and enchantments; not one of his allies, nor his patron Duke of Hell, was available to him here. He had only experience and courage and his ordinary sensibilities. And at that moment he doubted if they were enough.

5

The Sadness
of a Queen
Who Cannot Rule

The mighty barrier of obsidian rock suddenly started to flow. A mass of glassy green flooded down into the water which hissed and began to stink and mountains of steam rose ahead of them. As the steam gradually dissipated, another river was revealed. This one, flowing through the narrow walls of a deep canyon, appeared of natural origin and Elric, his mind now keyed to interpretation, wondered if it was not the same river they had crossed earlier, when he had fought the Pearl Warrior on the bridge.

Then the barge, which had seemed so sturdy, appeared all at once fragile as the waters tossed it, roaring steadily downward until Elric thought they must eventually reach the very core of the world.

Standing with Lady Sough in the prow of the boat, Oone and Elric helped her use the tiller to hold a course that was almost steady. And then, ahead, the river ended without warning and they had tipped over a waterfall and before they knew it were landing heavily in calmer water, the barge bobbing like a scrap of bread on a pond, and overhead they could see a sky like diseased pewter in which dark, leathery things flew and communicated with desolate cries above palms whose leaves resembled nothing so much as viridian skins stretched out to await a sun which never rose. There was a rich, rotten smell about the place and the constant splashing and distant roaring of the water filled a silence broken only by the flying creatures above the rocks and the foliage which surrounded them.

It was warm, yet Elric shivered. Oone drew up the collar of her doublet and even Lady Sough gathered her robes more tightly about herself.

"Are you familiar with this land, Lady Oone?" Elric asked. "You have visited this realm before, I know, but you seem as surprised as I."

"There are always new aspects. It is in the nature of the realm. Perhaps Lady Sough can tell us more." And Oone turned courteously to their navigator.

Lady Sough had secured her veils more firmly. She seemed unhappy that Elric had seen her face. "I am the Queen of this land," she said, exhibiting no pride or any other emotion.

"Then you have minions who can assist us?"

"It was a Queen for me, so that I had no power over it, only the land's protection. This is where you call Falador."

"And is it mad?"

"It has many defences."

"They keep out what might also wish to leave," said Oone, almost to herself. "Are you afraid of those who protect Falador, Lady Sough?"

"I am Queen Sough now." A drawing up of the graceful body, but whether in parody or in earnest Elric could not tell. "I am protected. You are not. Even I am not so able to guard you here."

The barge continued to float slowly along the water-course. The slime of the rocks appeared to shift and move as if alive and there were shapes in the water which disturbed Elric. He would have drawn his sword if it had not seemed ill-mannered.

"What must we fear here?" he asked the Queen.

Now they floated below a great spur of rock on which a horseman had positioned himself. It was the Pearl Warrior, glaring down with the same mixture of mockery and mindless-ness. He lifted a long stick to which he had tied some animal's sharp, twisted horn.

Queen Sough shook her hand at him. "Pearl Warrior shall not do this! Pearl Warrior cannot defy, even here!"

The warrior let out his hideous chuckle and turned his horse back from the rock. Then he was gone.

"Will he attack us?" Oone asked the Queen.

Queen Sough was concentrating on her tiller, steering the boat subtly along a smaller water-course, away from the main river. Perhaps she already aimed to avoid any conflict. "He is unpermitted," she said. "Ah!"

The water had turned a ruby red and there were now banks of glistening brown moss, gently rising towards the walls of rock. Elric was convinced he saw ancient faces staring at him both from the banks and from the cliffs, but he did not feel threatened. The red liquid looked like wine and there was a heady sweetness here. Did Queen Sough know all the secret, tranquil places of this world and was she guiding them through so as to avoid its dangers?

"Here my friend Edif has influence," she told them. "He is a ruler whose chief interest is poetry. Will it be now? I do not know."

They had quickly become used to her strange speech forms and were finding her more easily understood, though they had no idea who Edif might be and had passed through his land into a place where the desert appeared suddenly on both sides of them, beyond flanking lines of palms, as if they moved to-wards an oasis. Yet no oasis materialised.

Soon the sky was the colour of bad liver again and the rocky walls had risen around them and there was the sticky, oppres-sive odour which reminded Elric of some decadent court's ante-rooms. Perfume which had once been sweet but had now grown stale; food which had once made the mouth water but which was now too old; flowers which no longer enhanced but re-minded one only of death.

The walls on either side now had great jagged caves in them

where the water echoed and tumbled. Queen Sough seemed nervous of these and kept the barge carefully in the centre of the river. Elric saw shadows moving within the caves, both above and below the water. He saw red mouths opening and closing and saw pale, unblinking eyes staring. They had the air of Chaos-born creatures and he wished mightily then for his runesword, for his patron Duke of Hell, for his repertoire of spells and incantations.

The albino was not altogether surprised when at last a voice spoke from one of the caverns.

"I am Balis Jamon, Lord of the Blood, and I wish to have some kidneys."

"We sail on!" cried Queen Sough in response. "I am not your food nor shall I ever be."

"Their kidneys! Theirs!" the voice demanded implacably. "I have fed on no true grub for so long. Some kidneys! Some kidneys!"

Elric drew his sword and his dagger. Oone did the same.

"You'll not have mine, sir," said the albino.

"Nor mine," said Oone, seeking the source of the voice. They could not be sure which of the many caves sheltered the speaker.

"I am Balis Jamon, Lord of the Blood. You'll pay a toll here in my land. Two kidneys for me!"

"I'll take yours instead, sir, if you like!" said Elric defiantly.

"Will you, now?"

There was a great movement from the furthest cave and water foamed in and out. Then something stooped and came wading into midstream, its fleshy body festooned with half-decayed plants and ruined blooms, its horned snout lifted so that it could stare at them from two tiny black eyes. The fangs in the snout were broken, yellow and black, and a red tongue licked at them, flicking little pieces of rotten meat into the water. It held one great paw over its chest and when the paw was lowered it revealed a dark, gaping hole where the heart would have been.

"I am Balis Jamon, Lord of the Blood. Look what I must

fill for me to live! Have mercy, little creatures. A kidney or two and I'll let you pass. I have nothing here, while you are complete. You must make justice and share with me.''

"This is my only justice for you, Lord Balis," said Elric, gesturing with a sword, which seemed a feeble thing even to him.

"You will never be complete, Balis Jamon!" called out Queen Sough. "Not until you know more of mercy!"

"I am fair! One kidney will do!" The paw began to reach towards Elric, who cut at it but missed, then cut again and felt the sword strike the creature's hide, which scarcely showed a mark. The paw grabbed at the sword. Elric withdrew it. Balis Jamon growled with a mixture of frustration and self-pity and reached both paws towards the albino.

"Stop! Here's your kidney!" Oone held up something which dripped. "Here it is, Balis Jamon. Now let us pass. We are agreed.''

"Agreed." He turned, evidently mollified, delicately took what she handed up to him and popped it into the hole in his chest. "Good. Go!" And he waded passively back towards his cave, honour and hunger both satisfied.

Elric was baffled, though grateful that she had saved his life. "What did you do, Lady Oone?"

She smiled. "A large bean. Some of the provisions I still carried in my purse. It looked similar to a kidney, especially when dipped in water. And I doubt if he knows the difference. He seemed a simple creature."

Queen Sough's eyes were lifted upward even as she steered the barge past the caves and into a wider stretch of water where buffalo lifted their heads from where they drank and stared at them with wary curiosity.

Elric followed the navigator's gaze but saw only the same lead-coloured sky. He sheathed his sword. "These creatures of Chaos seem simple enough. Less intelligent in some ways than others I've encountered."

"Aye." Oone was unsurprised. "That's likely, I think. She would be—"

The boat was lifted suddenly and for a second Elric thought

Lord Balis had returned to take vengeance on them for tricking him. But they appeared to be on the crest of a huge wave. The water level rose rapidly between the slimy walls and now, on the cliffs' edges figures appeared. They were of every kind of distorted shape and unlikely size and Elric was reminded a little of the beggar populace of Nadsokor, for these, too, were dressed in rags and bore the evidence of self-mutilation, as well as disease, wounding and ordinary neglect. They were filthy. They moaned. They looked greedily at the boat and they licked their lips.

Now, more than ever before, Elric wished he had Stormbringer with him. The runesword and a little elemental aid would have driven this rabble away in terror. But he had only the blades captured from the Sorcerer Adventurers. He must rely upon those, his alliance with Oone and their naturally complementary fighting skills. There came a juddering from the bottom of the barge and the wave receded as suddenly as it had risen, but now they were stranded on the very top of the cliff, with the misshapen horde all around them, panting and grunting and sniffing at their prey.

Elric wasted no time with parleying but jumped at once from the boat's prow and cut at the first two who grabbed for him. The blade, still sharp enough, severed their heads and he stood over their bodies grinning at them like the wolf he was sometimes called. "I want you all," he said. He used the battle bravado he had learned from the pirates of the Vilmirian Straits. He moved forward again and thrust, catching still another Chaos-creature in the chest. "I must kill every one of you before I am satisfied!"

They had not expected this. They shuffled. They looked at each other. They turned their weapons in their hands, they adjusted their rags and tugged at their limbs.

Now Oone was beside Elric. "I want my fair share of these," she cried. "Save them for me, Elric." Then she, too, darted forward and cut down an ape-faced thing which carried a jewelled axe of beautiful workmanship, clearly stolen from an earlier victim.

Queen Sough called from behind them. "They have not attacked you. They only threaten. Is this the true thing you must do?''

"It's our only choice, Queen Sough!'' cried Elric over his shoulder, and feinted at two more of the half-human things.

"No! No! It is not heroic. What can the guardian do, who is no longer a hero?''

Even Oone could not follow this and when Elric met her eye in a question she shook her head.

The rabble was gaining some confidence now, closing in. Snouts sniffed at them. Tongues licked saliva from slack lips. Hot, dirty eyes full of blood and pus squinted their hatred.

Then they had begun to close and Elric felt his blade meet resistance, for he had already blunted it on the first two creatures. Yet still the neck split and the head fell to one side, glaring the while, hands clutching. Oone had her back to his and together they moved so that they were protected from one side by the boat, which the rabble did not seem to wish to touch. Queen Sough, in obvious distress, wept as she watched but clearly had no authority over the Chaos-creatures. "No! No! This does not help her to sleep! No! No! She is in need of them, I know!''

It was at that point that Elric heard the sound of hooves and saw, over the heads of the closing crowd, the white armour of the Pearl Warrior.

"They are his creatures!'' he said in sudden understanding. "This is his own army and he is to be revenged on us!''

"No!'' Queen Sough's voice was distant now, as if very far away. "This cannot be useful! It is your army. They'll be loyal. Yes.''

Hearing her, Elric knew unexpected clarity. Was it that she was not really human? Were all of these creatures merely shape-changers of some kind, disguising themselves as humans? It would explain their strange cast of mind, the peculiar logic, the strange phrasing.

But there was no time for speculation, for now the creatures were hard about him and Oone, so that it was hardly possible to swing their blades to keep them back. Blood flowed, sticky and foetid, splashing on blades and arms and making them gag. Elric

felt he might be overwhelmed by the stench before he was defeated by their weapons.

It was clear they could not resist the mob and Elric was bitter,
feeling that they had come very close to the object of their quest
only to be cut down by the most wretched of the denizens of
Chaos.

Then more bodies fell at his feet and he realised that he had
not killed them. Oone, too, was astonished by this turn of events.

They looked up. They could not understand what was happening.

The Pearl Warrior was riding through the ranks of the rabble cutting this way and that, jabbing with his makeshift spear,
slicing with his sword, cackling and crowing at every fresh life
he took. His horrible eyes were alight with some sort of amusement and even his horse was slashing at the rabble with its
hooves, nipping at them with its teeth.

"This is the proper thing!" Queen Sough clapped her hands.
"This is true. This is to ensure honour for you!"

Gradually driven back by the Pearl Warrior, by Elric and Oone
as they resumed their attack, the rabble began to break up.

Soon the whole awful mob was running for the cliff edge,
leaping into the abyss rather than die by the Pearl Warrior's
bone spear and his silver sword.

His laughter continued as he herded the remainder to their
doom. He screamed his mockery at them. He raved at them
for cowards and fools. "Ugly things. Ugly! Ugly! Go! Perish!
Go! Go! Go! Banished now, they are. Banished to that! Yes!"

Elric and Oone leaned against the barge trying to catch their
breaths.

"I am grateful to you, Pearl Warrior," said the albino as
the armoured rider approached. "You have saved our lives."

"Yes." The Pearl Warrior nodded gravely, his eyes unusu-
ally thoughtful. "That is so. Now we shall be equal. Then we
shall know the truth. I am not free, as you. You believe this?"
His last question was addressed to Oone.

She nodded. "I believe that, Pearl Warrior. I, too, am glad
you helped us."

"I am the one who protects. This must be done. You go on? I was your friend."

Oone looked back to where Queen Sough was nodding, her arms outstretched in some kind of offering.

"Here I am not your enemy," said the Pearl Warrior, as if instructing the simple-minded. "If I were complete, we three would be a trinity of greatness! Aye! Thou knowest it! I have not the personal. These words are hers, you see. I think."

And with that particularly mystifying pronouncement he wheeled his horse and rode away over the grassy limestone.

"Too many defenders, not enough protectors, perhaps." Oone sounded as odd as the others. Before Elric could quiz her on this she had given her attention back to Queen Sough. "My lady? Did you summon the Pearl Warrior to our aid?"

"She called him to you, I think." Queen Sough seemed almost in a trance. It was odd to hear her speaking of herself in the third person. Elric wondered if this was the normal mode here and again it occurred to him that all the people of this realm were not human but had assumed human shape.

They were now stranded high above the river. Going to the edge of the abyss, Elric stared down. He saw only some bodies which had been caught on the rocks, others drifting downstream. He was glad then that their boat was not having to negotiate waters clogged with so many corpses.

"How can we continue?" he asked Oone. He had a vision of himself and her in the Bronze Tent, of the child between them. All were dying. He knew a pang of need, as if the drug were calling to him, reminding him of his addiction. He remembered Anigh in Quarzhasaat and Cymoril, his betrothed, waiting in Imrryr. Had he been right to let Yyrkoon rule in his place? Every one of his decisions seemed now to be foolish. His self-esteem, never high, was lower than he could remember. His lack of forethought, his failures, his follies, all reminded him that not only was he physically deficient, he was also lacking in ordinary common-sense.

"It is in the nature of the hero," said Queen Sough in relation to nothing. Then she looked at them and her eyes were maternal, kindly. "You are safe!"

"I think there is some urgency," said Oone. "I sense it. Do you?"

"Aye. Is there danger in the realm we left?"

"Perhaps. Queen Sough, are we far from the Nameless Gate? How can we continue?"

"By means of the moth-steeds," she said. "The waters always rise here and I have my moths. We have only to wait for them. They are on their way." Her tone was matter-of-fact. "It was that rabble which could have been yours. No more. But I cannot anticipate, you see. Every new trap is mysterious to me, as it is to you. I can navigate, as you navigate. This is together, you know."

Against the horizon there were rainbow lights winking and shimmering, like an aurora. Queen Sough sighed when she saw them. She was content.

"Good. Good. That is not late! Just the other."

The colours filled the sky now. As they came closer Elric realised that they belonged to huge, filmy wings supporting slender bodies, more butterfly than moth, of enormous size. Without hesitation the beasts began to descend until the three of them as well as the barge were engulfed by soft wings.

"Into the boat!" cried Queen Sough. "Quickly. We fly."

They hurried to obey her and at once the barge was rising into the air, apparently carried on the backs of the great moths who flew beside the canyon for a while before plunging down into the abyss.

"I watched but there was nothing," said Queen Sough by way of explanation to Elric and Oone. "Now we shall resume."

With astonishing gentleness the creatures had deposited the barge on the river and were flying back up between the walls of the canyon again, filling the whole gloomy place with brilliant multi-coloured light before they vanished. Elric rubbed at his brow. "This is truly the Land of Madness," he said. "I believe it is I who am mad, Lady Oone."

"You are losing confidence in yourself, Prince Elric." She

spoke firmly. "That is the particular trap of this land. You come to believe that it is yourself, not what surrounds you, that has little logic. Already we have imposed our sanity on Falador. Do not despair. It cannot be much longer before we reach the final gate."

"And what is there?" He was sardonic. "Sublime reason?" He felt the same strange sense of exhaustion. Physically he was still capable of continuing, but his mind and his spirit were depleted.

"I cannot begin to anticipate what we shall find in the Nameless Land," she said. "Dreamthieves have little power over what occurs beyond the seventh gate."

"I've noticed your considerable influence here!" But he did not mean to hurt her. He smiled to show that he joked.

From ahead they heard a howling, so painful that even Queen Sough covered her ears. It was like the baying of some monstrous hound, echoing up and down the abyss and threatening to shake the very boulders loose from the walls. As the river bore them round the bend they saw the beast standing there, a great shaggy wolflike beast, its head lifted as it howled again. The water rushed around its huge legs, foamed against its body. As it turned its gaze upon them the beast vanished completely. They heard only the echo of its howling. The speed of the water increased. Queen Sough had removed her hands from the tiller to block her ears. The boat swung in the water and bounced as it struck a rock. She made no attempt to steer it. Elric seized the long arm but in spite of using all his strength he could do nothing with the boat. Eventually he, too, gave up.

Down and down the river ran. Down into a gorge growing so deep that soon there was scarcely any light at all. They saw faces grinning at them. They felt hands reach out to touch them. Elric became convinced that every mortal creature who had ever died had come here to haunt him. In the dark rock he saw his own face many times, and that of Cymoril and Yyrkoon. Old battles were fought as he watched. And old, agonising emotions came back to him. He felt the loss of all he had ever loved, the despair of death and desertion, and soon his own voice joined the general babble and he howled as loudly as the hound had howled until Oone shook him and yelled at him and brought him back from the madness which had threatened to engulf him.

"Elric! The last gate! We are almost there! Hold on, Prince of Melniboné. You have been courageous and resourceful until now. This will require still more of you, and you must be ready!"

And Elric began to laugh. He laughed at his own fate, at the fate of the Holy Girl, at Anigh's fate and at Oone's. He laughed when he thought of Cymoril waiting for him on the Dragon Isle, not knowing even now if he lived or died, if he was free or a slave.

When Oone shouted at him again, he laughed in her face.

"Elric! You betray us all!"

He paused in his laughter long enough to say softly, almost in triumph, "Aye, madam, that is so. I betray you all. Have you not heard? It is my destiny to betray!"

"You shall not betray me, sir!" She slapped at his face. She punched him. She kicked his legs. "You shall not betray me and you shall not betray the Holy Girl!"

He knew intense pain, not from her blows but from his own mind. He cried out and then he began to sob. "Oh, Oone. What is happening to me?"

"This is Falador," she said simply. "Are you recovered, Prince Elric?"

The faces still gibbered at him from the rock. The air was still alive with all he feared, all he most misliked in himself.

He was trembling. He could not meet her gaze. He realised he was weeping. "I am Elric, last of Melniboné's royal line," he said. "I have looked upon horror and I have courted the Dukes of Hell. Why should I know fear now?"

She did not answer and he expected no answer from her.

The boat surged, swung again, lifted and dipped.

Suddenly he was calm. He took hold of Oone's hand in a gesture of simple affection.

"I am myself again, I think," he said.

"There is the gateway," said Queen Sough from behind

them. She had her grip on the tiller again and with her other hand was pointing ahead.

"There is the land you call the Nameless Land," she said. She spoke plainly now, not in the cryptic phrasing she had used since they had met her. "There you will find the Fortress of the Pearl. She cannot welcome you."

"Who?" said Elric. The waters were calm again. They ran slowly towards a great archway of alabaster, its edges trimmed by soft leaves and shrubs. "The Holy Girl?"

"She can be saved," said Queen Sough. "Only by you two, I think. I have helped her remain here, awaiting rescue. But it is all I can do. I am afraid, you see."

"We are all that, madam," said Elric feelingly.

The boat was caught by new currents and travelled still more slowly, as if reluctant to enter the last gate of the Dream Realm.

"But I am of no help," said Queen Sough. "I might even have conspired. It was those men. They came. Then more came. There was only retreat thereafter. I wish I could know such words. You would understand them if I had them. Ah, it is hard here!"

Elric, looking into her agonised eyes, realised that she was probably more of a prisoner in this world than he and Oone. It seemed to him that she longed to escape and was only kept here by her love of the Holy Girl, her protective emotions. Yet surely she had been here long before Varadia had come?

The boat had begun to pass under the alabaster arch now. There was a salty, pleasant taste to the air, as if they approached the ocean.

Elric decided he must ask the question which was on his mind.

"Queen Sough," he said. "Are you Varadia's mother?"

The pain in the eyes grew even more intense as the veiled woman turned away from him. Her voice was a sob of anguish and he was shocked by it.

"Oh, who knows?" she cried. *"Who knows?"*

PART THREE

Is there a brave lord birthed by Fate
To wield old weapons, win new estates
And tear down walls Time sanctifies,
Raze ancient temples as hallowed lies,
His pride to break, his love to lose,
Destroying his race, his history, his muse,
And, relinquishing peace for a life of strife,
Leave only a corpse that the flies refuse?

The Chronicle of the Black Sword

1

At the Court
of the Pearl

Again Elric experienced that
strange frisson of recognition at the landscape before him,
though he could not remember ever seeing anything like it.
Pale blue mist rose around cypresses, date palms, orange trees
and poplars whose shades of green were equally pale; flowing
meadows occasionally revealed the rounded white of boulders
and in the far distance were snow-peaked mountains. It was as
if an artist had painted the scenery with the most delicate of
washes, the finest of brushstrokes. It was a vision of Paradise
and completely unexpected after the insanity of Falador.

Queen Sough had remained silent since she had answered
Elric's question and a peculiar atmosphere had developed
among the three of them. Yet all the uneasiness failed to affect
Elric's delight at the world they had entered. The skies (if skies
they were) were full of pearly cloud, tinged by pink and the
faintest yellow, and a little white smoke rose up from a flat-
roofed house some distance away. The barge had come to rest
in a pool of still, sparkling water and Queen Sough gestured
for them to disembark.

"You will come with us to the Fortress?" asked Oone.

"She does not know. I do not know if it is permitted," said the Queen, her eyes hooded above her veil.

"Then I shall say farewell now," and Elric bowed and kissed the woman's soft hand. "I thank you for your assistance, madam, and trust you will forgive me for the crudeness of my manners."

"Forgiven, yes." Elric, looking up, thought Queen Sough smiled.

"I thank you also, my lady." Oone spoke almost intimately, as to one with whom she might share a secret. "Know you how we shall find the Fortress of the Pearl?"

"That one will know." The Queen pointed towards the distant cottage. "Farewell, as you say. You can save her. Only you."

"I am grateful for your confidence also," said Elric. He stepped almost jauntily onto the turf and followed Oone as they made their way across the fields to the little house. "This is a great relief, my lady. A contrast, indeed, to the Land of Madness!"

"Aye." She responded a trifle cautiously, and her hand went to the hilt of her sword. "But remember, Prince Elric, that madness takes many forms in all worlds."

He did not allow her wariness to let him lose his enjoyment. He was determined to restore himself to the peak of his energies, in preparation for whatever might lie ahead.

Oone was first to reach the door of the white house. Outside were two chickens scratching in the gravel, an old dog, tethered to a barrel, who looked up at them over a grey muzzle and grinned, a pair of short-coated cats cleaning their silvery fur on the roof over the lintel. Oone knocked and the door was opened almost immediately. A tall, handsome young man stood there, his head covered by an old burnoose, his body clad in a light brown robe with long sleeves. He seemed pleased to see visitors.

"Greetings to you," he said. "I am Chamog Borm, currently in exile. Have you come with good news from the Court?"

"We have no news at all, I fear," said Oone. "We are travellers and we seek the Fortress of the Pearl. Is it close by here?"

"At the heart and the centre of those mountains." He waved with his hand towards the peaks. "Will you join me for some refreshment?"

The name the young man had given, together with his extraordinary looks, caused Elric again to rack his brains, trying to recall why all this was so familiar to him. He knew that he had only recently heard the name.

Within the cool house, Chamog Borm brewed them a herbal drink. He seemed proud of his domestic skills and it was clear he was no simple farmer. In one corner of the room was heaped a pile of rich armour, steel chased with silver and gold, a helm decorated with a tall spike, that spike decorated with ornamental snakes and falcons locked in conflict. There were spears, a long, curved sword, daggers—weapons and accoutrements of every description.

"You are a warrior by trade?" said Elric as he sipped the hot liquid. "Your armour is very handsome."

"I was once a hero," said Chamog Borm sadly, "until I was dismissed from the Court of the Pearl."

"Dismissed?" Oone was thoughtful. "On what charge?"

Chamog Borm lowered his eyes. "I was charged with cowardice. Yet I believe that I was not guilty, that I was subject to an enchantment."

And now Elrich recalled where he had heard the name. When he had arrived in Quarzhasaat he had in his fever wandered in the market places and listened to the story-tellers. At least three of the stories he had heard had concerned Chamog Borm, hero of legend, the last brave knight of the Empire. His name was venerated everywhere, even in the camps of the nomads. Yet Elric was sure Chamog Borm had existed—if he had ever existed—at least a thousand years earlier!

"What was the action of which you were accused?" he asked.

"I failed to save the Pearl, which now lies under an enchantment, imprisoning us all in perpetual suffering."

"What was that enchantment?" Oone asked quickly.

"It became impossible for our monarch and many of the retainers to leave the Fortress. It was for me to free them. Instead I brought a worse enchantment upon us. And my punishment is contrary to theirs. They may not leave, and I may not return." As he spoke he became increasingly melancholy.

Elric, still astonished at this conversation with a hero who should have been dead centuries before, could say little, but Oone seemed to understand completely. She made a sympathetic gesture.

"Can the Pearl be found there?" Elric asked, conscious of the bargain he had made with Lord Gho, of Anigh's impending torture and death, of Oone's predictions.

"Of course." Chamog Borm was surprised. "Some believe it rules the whole Court, perhaps the world."

"Was this always so?" Oone asked softly.

"I have told you that it was not." He looked at them both as if they were simpletons. Then he lowered his eyes, lost in his own dishonour and humiliation.

"We hope to free her," said Oone. "Would you come with us, to help us?"

"I cannot help. She no longer trusts me. I am banished," he said. "But I can let you have my armour and my weapons so that part of me, at least, can fight for her."

"Thank you," said Oone. "You are generous."

Chamog Borm grew more animated as he helped them choose from his store. Elric found that the breastplate and greaves fitted him perfectly, as did the helmet. Similar equipment was found for Oone and the straps tightened to adjust to her slightly smaller body. They looked almost identical in their new armour and something in Elric was again struck, some deep sense of satisfaction that he could hardly understand but which he welcomed. The armour gave him not only a greater sense of security but a sense of deep recognition of his own inner strength, a strength which he knew he must call upon to the utmost in the encounter to come. Oone had warned him of subtler dangers at the Fortress of the Pearl.

Chamog Borm's gifts continued, in the shape of two grey horses which he led from their stable at the back of the house. "These are Taron and Tadia. Brother and sister, they were twin foals. They have never been separated. Once I rode them into battle. Once I took up arms against the Bright Empire. Now the last Emperor of Melniboné will ride in my place to fulfill my destiny and end the siege of the Fortress of the Pearl."

"You know me?" Elric looked hard at the handsome youth, seeking deception or even irony, but there was none in those steady eyes.

"A hero knows another, Prince Elric." And Chamog Borm reached out to grip Elric's forearm in the gesture of friendship of the desert peoples. "May you gain all you wish to gain and may you do so with honour. You, too, Lady Oone. Your courage is the greatest of all. Farewell."

The exile watched them from the roof of his little house until they were out of sight. Now the great mountains were close, almost embracing them, and they could see a wide, white road stretching through them. The light was like that of a late summer afternoon, though Elric could still not be sure if it was sky above them or the distant roof of a vast cavern, for the sun was still not in evidence. Was the Dream Realm a limitless series of such caverns or had the dreamthief mapped the entire world? Could they cross the mountains, or the Nameless Land beyond and begin again to travel through the seven gates, ultimately arriving back at the Land of Dreams-in-Common? And would they find Jaspar Colinadous waiting for them where they had left him?

The road, when they reached it, proved to be of pure marble, but the horses' hooves were so well shod they did not slip once. The noise of their galloping began to echo through the wide pass and herds of gazelles and wild sheep looked up from their grazing to watch them pass, two silver riders on silver horses on their way to do battle with the forces who had seized power at the Fortress of the Pearl.

"You have understood these people better than I," he said to Oone, as the road began to twist upward towards the centre of the range and the light had grown colder, the sky a bright, hard grey. "Do you know what we might expect to find at the Fortress of the Pearl?"

She shook her head in regret. "It is like understanding a code without knowing what the words actually relate to," she told him. "The force is powerful enough to banish a hero as potent as Chamog Borm."

"I know only the legend, and that from a little I heard in the Slave Market at Quarzhasaat."

"He was summoned by the Holy Girl as soon as she realised that she was under further attack. That is what I believe, at any rate. She did not expect him to fail her. Somehow, indeed, he made matters worse. She felt betrayed by him and banished him to the edge of the Nameless Land, there perhaps to greet and assist others who might come to help her. That is no doubt why we are given all the appurtenances of the hero, so that we may be as much like heroes as he."

"Yet we know this world less well. How may we succeed where he failed?"

"Perhaps because of our ignorance," she said. "Perhaps not. I cannot answer you, Elric." She rode close to him, leaning from her saddle to kiss that part of his cheek exposed by the helmet. "Only know this. I will betray neither her nor, if I can help it, you. Yet if I must betray one of you, I suppose it will be you."

Elric looked at her in bafflement. "Is that likely to be an issue?"

She shrugged and then she sighed. "I do not know, Elric. Look. I think we have come to the Fortress of the Pearl!"

It was like a palace carved from the most delicate ivory. White against the silver sky, it rose above the snows of the mountain, a great multitude of slender spires and turretted towers, of cupolas, of mysterious structures which seemed almost as if they had been arrested in mid-flight. There were bridges and stairways, curving walls and galleries, balconies and roof-gardens whose colours were a spectrum of pastel shades, a myriad of different plants, flowers, shrubs and trees. In all his travels Elric had only seen one place that was the equal to the Fortress of the Pearl and that was his own city, Imrryr. Yet the Dreaming City was exotic, rich, even vulgar— a romantic fancy compared to the complicated austerity of this palace.

As they approached on the marble road, Elric realised that the Fortress was not pure white, but contained shades of blue, silver, grey and pink, sometimes a little yellow or green, and he had the notion that the entire thing had been carved from a single gigantic pearl. Soon they had reached the Fortress's only gate, a great circular opening protected by spiked grilles which came from above and below and both sides to meet at the centre. The Fortress was vast but even its gate dwarfed them.

Elric could think of nothing to do but cry out. "Open in the name of the Holy Girl! We come to do battle with those who imprison her spirit here!"

His words echoed through the towers of the Fortress and through the jagged peaks of the mountains beyond and seemed to lose themselves in the heights of a cavern's roof. In the shadows beyond the gateway he saw something scarlet move and then vanish again. There came the smell of delicious perfume, mixed with the same strange ocean scent they had noticed when they first reached the Nameless Land.

Then the gates had parted, so swiftly that they seemed to melt into the air, and a rider confronted them, his humourless chuckling by now all too familiar.

"This is what should be, I think," said the Pearl Warrior.

"League yourself with us again, Pearl Warrior," said Oone, with all her considerable authority. "It is what she desires!"

"No. It is so that she shall not be betrayed. You must dissolve. Now! Now! Now!" His head was flung back as he screamed these last words, for all the world like a dog gone rabid.

Elric drew a sword from its scabbard. It shone with the same silver light that poured from the Pearl Warrior's blade. Oone followed his example, though more reluctantly.

"We shall pass now, Pearl Warrior."

"Nothing will here! I want your freedom."

"She shall have it!" said Oone. "It is not yours, not unless she bestows it upon you herself."

"She says it is mine. I will be that. I will be *that*!"

Elric could not follow this strange conversation and he chose not to waste time with it. He urged his silver horse forward, the blade glaring in his hand. So balanced was this sword, so familiar to his grip, that he felt for a moment that it was somehow the natural contrast to his runesword. Was this a sword forged by Law to serve its purposes, just as Stormbringer had, by all accounts, been forged by Chaos?

The Pearl Warrior guffawed and widened his awful eyes. Death was in them. The death of the world. He lowered the same misshapen lance he had brandished at them before and Elric saw it was encrusted with old blood. The warrior held his ground and the lance was suddenly threatening Elric's eyes so that the albino had to throw himself to one side to avoid its points, striking upward as he did so and feeling a greater resistance to his blow than anything he had felt before. The Pearl Warrior seemed to have gained strength since their last encounter.

"Ordinary soul!" The lips twisted in this insult, clearly as disgusting as any the Pearl Warrior could conceive. And he began to chuckle again, this time because Oone was riding at him, her sword stretched out full before her, a spear held in her other hand, her reins between her teeth. The sword drove forward, the spear swung back as she poised to throw. Then sword and spear struck the Pearl Warrior at the exact same moment so that his breastplate cracked like the shell of some great crustacean and was pierced by the sword.

Elric marvelled at this strategy which he had never witnessed before. Oone's strength and coordination were almost beyond credibility. It was a feat of arms warriors would speak of for a thousand years to come, which many would try to emulate and would die in the trying.

The spear had done its work in breaking open the Pearl Warrior's armour and the sword had completed the action. But the Pearl Warrior had not been killed.

He groaned. He cackled. He floundered. His sword came up as if to protect his chest from the blow already struck. His great horse reared and its nostrils flared with fury. Oone turned her own mount away. Her sword had left its tip in the Pearl Warrior's body. She was reaching for a second spear, for her dagger.

Elric drove forward again, his own spear aimed at the cracked armour, hoping to follow her example, but the blade struck the ivory and was turned. Elric lost balance long enough for the Pearl Warrior to take the advantage. The sword struck the steel of Elric's armour with a noise that made a cacophony within his helmet and brought bright sparks flashing like a fire. He fell onto his horse's neck, barely able to block the next thrust. Then the Pearl Warrior shrieked, the eyes growing still wider, the mouth gaping red and the foul breath steaming from it, while blood poured from under the gorget between his helmet and his breastplate. He fell towards Elric and the albino realised that the haft of a spear was sticking from his chest in exactly the same place where Oone had broken the creature's armour.

"This will not remain so!" cried the Pearl Warrior. It was a threat. "I cannot do that thing!"

Then he tumbled in a heap from his horse and clattered like old bones onto the flagstones of the courtyard. From behind him an ornamental fountain, representing a fig tree in full fruit, began to spurt water, filling the surrounding trough and overflowing until it touched the body of the Pearl Warrior. The riderless horse began to scream, turning round and round, rearing, foaming, then it galloped out through the gate and back down the marble road.

Elric turned the heavy corpse over to make sure that no life was left in the Pearl Warrior and to inspect the shattered armour. He remained admiring of Oone's manoeuvre. "I have never seen that done before," he said, "and I have fought beside and against famous warriors."

"A dreamthief must know many things," she said, by way of acknowledgement of his praise. "I learned such tactics from my mother, who was a greater battle-woman than I shall ever be."

"Your mother was a dreamthief?"

"No," said Oone absently as she inspected her ruined sword and then picked up the Pearl Warrior's, "she was a queen." She tested the weight of the dead creature's blade and discarded her own, trying it in her scabbard and finding that it was a little too wide. Carelessly she stuck it in her belt and unhooked the scabbard, throwing it upon the ground. The water from the fountain was around their ankles now and was disturbing their horses.

Leading the steeds, they passed under a heart-shaped arch and into another courtyard. Here, too, fountains played, but these were not flooding. They seemed carved out of ivory, like so much of the Fortress, and represented stylised herons, their beaks meeting at a point above their heads. Elric was reminded vaguely of the architecture of Quarzhasaat, though this had none of the decadence of that place, none of the look of senile old age which characterised the city at its worst. Had the Fortress been built by the ancestors of the present lords of Quarzhasaat, the Council of Six and One Other? Had some great king fled the city millennia before and journeyed here to the Dream Realm? Was that how the legend of the Pearl had come to Quarzhasaat?

Courtyard after courtyard, each in its own way of extraordinary beauty, followed until Elric began to wonder if this path was merely leading them through the Fortress to the other side.

"For such a large building it's somewhat underpopulated," he said to Oone.

"We shall find the inhabitants soon enough, I think," Oone murmured. Now they ascended a spiral causeway which led around a huge central dome. Although the palace had such a mood and look of austerity, Elric did not find its architecture cold and there was something almost organic about it, as if it had been formed from flesh, then petrified.

Their horses still with them, the sound now muffled by luxurious carpet, they moved through halls and corridors whose walls were hung with tapestries and decorated with mosaics, though they saw no pictures of living things, only geometrical designs.

"We near the heart of the Fortress, I think," Oone told him in a whisper. It was as if she feared to be overheard, yet they had seen no one. She looked beyond tall columns, through a series of rooms seemingly lit by sunshine from without. Following her gaze, Elric had the impression of blue fabric wafting through a door and vanishing. "Who was that?"

"All the same," said Oone to herself. "All the same." Her sword was drawn again, however, and she signed to Elric to imitate her. They entered another courtyard. This one seemed to be open to the sky—the same grey sky they had first seen in the mountains. Gallery after gallery rose up all around them, many storeys to the top. Elric thought he saw faces peering back at him, then something liquid struck his face and he almost inhaled the sickly red stuff which covered his body. More of it was pouring down on them from every part of the gallery and already the courtyard was knee-deep in what seemed to Elric to be human blood. He heard a muttering overhead, soft laughter, a cry.

"Stop this!" he shouted, wading to the side of the chamber. "We are here to parley. All we want is the Holy Girl! Give her spirit back to us and we shall leave!"

He was answered by a further shower of blood and he hauled his horse towards the next door. There was a gate across it. He tried to lift it. He tried to bounce it free of its mountings. He looked to Oone, who, wiping the red liquid from herself, joined him. She reached out her long fingers and found some kind of button. The gate opened slowly, almost reluctantly, but it opened. She grinned at him. "Like most men, you become a brute when you panic, my lord."

He was hurt by her joke. "I had no idea I should find such a means of opening the gate, my lady."

"Think of such things in future and you will stand a better chance of survival in this Fortress," she said.

"Why will they not parley with us?"

"They probably do not believe that we are ready to bargain," she said. Then she added: "In reality, I can only guess at their logic. Each adventure of a dreamthief is different from the others, Prince Elric. Come." She led them on past a series of pools full of warm water from which a little steam rose. There were no bathers in the pools. Then Elric thought he saw creatures, perhaps fish, swimming in the depths. He leaned forward to look, but Oone pulled him back. "I warned you. Your curiosity could bring your destruction and mine."

Something threshed and bubbled in the pool and then was gone. All at once the rooms began to shake and the water foamed. Cracks appeared in the marble floors. Their horses snorted with fear and threatened to lose their footing. Elric himself almost toppled down into one of the fissures which had opened. It was as if an earthquake had suddenly struck the mountains. Yet as they dashed hastily for the next gallery, which opened onto a peaceful lawn, all signs of the earthquake had vanished.

A man approached them. In bearing, he resembled Queen Sough, but he was shorter and older. His white beard hung upon a surcoat of gold cloth and in his hand he held a salver on which were placed two leather bags. "Will you accept the authority of the Fortress of the Pearl?" he said. "I am the seneschal of this place."

"Who do you serve?" Elric asked brusquely. His sword was still in his hand and he made no effort to disguise his readiness to use it.

The seneschal looked bewildered. "I serve the Pearl, of course. This is the Fortress of the Pearl!"

"Who rules here, old man?" Oone asked him pointedly.

"The Pearl. I have said so."

"Does no one rule the Pearl?" Elric was mystified.

"No longer, sir. Now, will you take this gold and go? We have no wish to expend more of our energies upon you. They flag, but they are not exhausted. I think you will be dissolved soon."

"We have defeated all your defenders," said Oone. "Why should we want gold?"

"Do you not desire the Pearl?"

Before Elric could answer, Oone silenced him with a warning gesture.

"We come only to secure the release of the Holy Girl."

The seneschal smiled. "They have all made that claim, but what they want is the Pearl. I cannot believe you, lady."

"How can we prove our words?"

"You cannot. We already know the truth."

"We have no interest in bargaining with you, Sir Seneschal. If you serve the Pearl, who does the Pearl serve?"

"The child, I think." His brow furrowed. Her question had confused him, yet to Elric it had seemed so simple. His admiration for the dreamsthief's skill increased.

"You see, we can help you in this," said Oone. "The child's spirit is imprisoned. And while it is imprisoned, so are you held captive."

The old man offered the bags of gold again. "Take this and leave us."

"I do not think we shall," said Oone firmly, and she led her horse forward, past the old man. "Come, Elric."

The albino hesitated. "We should question him more, Oone, surely?"

"He could not answer more."

The seneschal ran at her, swinging the heavy bags, the salver falling to the floor with a clang. "She is not! It will hurt! This is not to be. Pain will come! Pain!"

Elric felt sympathy for the old man. "Oone. We should listen to him."

She would not pause. "Come. You must."

He had learned to trust her judgement. He, too, pushed past the old man, who beat at his body with the bags of gold and wailed, the tears pouring down his cheeks and into his beard. It took a different courage to perform that particular action.

There was another great curving doorway ahead of them, all elaborate lattice-work and mosaic, bordered by bands of jade, blue enamel and silver. Two large doors of dark wood, hinges and studs of brass, blocked their way.

Oone did not knock. She reached gently towards the doors and placed her fingertips against them. Gradually, just as with the other gate, the doors began to part. They heard a faint noise from within, almost a whimper. The doors opened wider and wider until they were completely back on their hinges.

For a moment Elric was overwhelmed by what he saw.

A grey-gold glow filled the great chamber which had been revealed to them. The glow came from a column about the height of a tall man which was topped by a globe. At the centre of the globe shone a pearl of enormous size, almost as big as Elric's fist. Short flights of steps led up to the column from all sides, and around these steps were what at first appeared to be ranks of statues. Then Elric realised that they were men, women and children, dressed in all manner of costumes, though most of them in the styles favoured in Quarzhasaat and by the desert clans.

The old man came stumbling behind them. "Do not hurt this!"

"We defend ourselves, Sir Seneschal," Oone told him without turning to look at him. "That is all you need to know from us."

Slowly, still leading the silver horses, still with their silver swords in their hands, the light from the pearl touching their silver armour and their helmets and making these, too, glow with soft radiance, they made their way into the chamber.

"This is not to destroy. This is not to defeat. This is not to despoil."

Elric shivered when he heard the voice. He looked over towards the distant walls of the room and there was the Pearl Warrior, his armour all cracked and slimed with blood, his face a terrible bruise, the eyes seeming alternately to fade and take fire. And sometimes they were Alnac's eyes.

The warrior's next words were almost pathetic. "I cannot fight you. No more."

"We are not here to hurt," said Oone again. "We are here to free you."

There was a movement amongst the still figures. A blue-gowned veiled woman appeared. Queen Sough's own eyes had a suggestion of tears. "With these you come?" She indicated the swords, the horses, the armour. "But our enemies are not here."

"They will be here soon," said Oone. "Soon, I think, my lady."

Still baffled, Elric looked behind him, as if he would see their enemies. He made a movement towards the Pearl at the Heart of the World, merely to admire a marvel. At once all the figures came to life, blocking his path.

"You will steal!" The old man sounded even more wretched than before, even more impotent.

"No," said Oone. "It is not our purpose. You must understand that." She spoke urgently. "Raik Na Seem sent us to find her."

"She is safe. Tell him she is safe."

"She is not safe. Soon she will dissolve." Oone turned her gaze on the whispering throng. "She is separated, as we are separated. The Pearl is the cause."

"This is a trick," said Queen Sough.

"A trick," echoed the wounded Pearl Warrior, and there was a faint chuckle from his spoiled throat.

"A trick," said the seneschal, and held out the bags of gold.

"We come to steal nothing. We come to defend. Look!" Oone made a circular movement with her sword to show them what they had evidently not yet seen.

Emerging through the walls of the chamber, their hands filled with every imaginable weapon, came the hooded, tattooed soldiers of Quarzhasaat. The Sourcerer Adventurers.

"We cannot fight them," said Elric quietly to his friend. "There are too many of them." And he prepared himself for death.

2

The Destruction in the Fortress

Then Oone had mounted her silver horse and raised her silver sword. She called out: "Elric, do as I do!" and urged the stallion into a canter so that its hooves rattled like thunder in the chamber.

Prepared to die with courage, even at the moment of apparent triumph, Elric climbed into his saddle, took a spear in the hand that held the reins and with his sword already swinging charged against the invaders.

Only as they crowded around him, axes, maces, spears and swords lifted to attack, did Elric understand that Oone's action had not been one of mere desperation. These half-shades moved sluggishly, their eyes were misted, they stumbled and their blows were feeble.

The slaughter now became sickening to him. Following her example, he hacked and stabbed from side to side, almost mechanically. Heads came away from bodies like rotten fruit; limbs were sliced as easily as leaves from a stick; torsos collapsed under the thrust of a spear or sword. Their viscous blood, already the blood of the dead, clung to weapons and armour and their cries of pain were pathetic to Elric's ears. If

he had not sworn to follow Oone, he would have ridden back
and let her continue the work alone. There was little danger
to them as the veiled men continued to pour through the walls
and be met by sharp steel and cunning intelligence.

Behind them, around the column of the Pearl, the courtiers
watched. These clearly did not know what a mediocre threat
the two silver-armoured warriors confronted.

At last it was done. Decapitated, limbless bodies were piled
all around the hall. Elric and Oone rode out of that slaughter
and they were grim, unhappy, nauseated by their own actions.

"It is done," said Oone. "The Sorcerer Adventurers are
slain."

"You truly are heroes!" Queen Sough came down the steps
towards them, her eyes bright with admiration, her arms outstretched.

"We are who we are," said Oone. "We are mortal fighters
and we have destroyed the threat to the Fortress of the Pearl."
Her words had taken on a ritualistic tone and Elric, trusting
her, was content to listen.

"You are the children of Chamog Borm, Brother and Sister
of the Bone Moon, Children of Water and Cool Breezes, Parents of the Trees . . ." The seneschal had dropped his bags of
gold and was shaken by his weeping. He wept with relief and
with joy and Elric saw how much he resembled Raik Na Seem.

Oone, down from her horse again, was embraced by Queen
Sough. Meanwhile, a shuffling and cackling announced the
approach of the Pearl Warrior.

"This is no more for me," he said. Alnac's dead eyes had
nothing but resignation in them. "This is for dissolution . . ."
And he fell forward onto the marble floor, his armour all broken, his limbs sprawling, and there was no longer any flesh on
him, only bone, so that what was left of the Pearl Warrior
resembled little more than the inedible remains of a crab, the
supper of some sea-giant.

Queen Sough came towards Elric, her arms outstretched,
and she seemed much smaller than when he had first encountered her. Her head hardly reached to his lowered chin. Her

embrace was warm and he knew she, too, was weeping. Then her veil fell away from her face and he saw that she had lost years, that she was little more than a girl.

Behind Queen Sough the Lady Oone was smiling at him as astonished understanding filled him. Gently he touched the girl's face, the familiar folds of her hair, and he drew in a sudden breath.

She was Varadia. She was the Holy Girl of the Bauradim. She was the child whose spirit they had promised to free.

Oone joined him, placing a protective hand upon Varadia's shoulder. "You know now that we are truly your friends."

Varadia nodded, looking about her at the courtiers, who had assumed their earlier frozen stances. "The Pearl Warrior was the best there was," she said. "I could summon none better. Chamog Borm failed me. The Sorcerer Adventurers were too strong for him. Now I can release him from his exile."

"We combined his strength with our own," said Oone. "Your strength and our strength. That is how we succeeded."

"We three are not shadows," said Varadia, smiling, as if at a revelation. "*That* is how we succeeded."

Oone nodded agreement. "That is how we succeeded, Holy Girl. Now we must consider how to bring you back to the Bronze Tent, to your people. You carry all their pride and history with you."

"I knew that. I had to protect it. I thought I had failed."

"You have not failed," said Oone.

"The Sorcerer Adventurers will not attack again?"

"Never," said Oone. "Not here, nor anywhere. Elric and I will make sure of it."

And then Elric realised in admiration that it had been Oone, in the end, who had summoned the Sorcerer Adventurers, summoned those shades for the last time; summoned them so that she might demonstrate their defeat.

Oone looked at him and warned him with her eyes not to say too much. But now he realised that all that they had fought, save perhaps a little of the Pearl Warrior and the Sorcerer Adventurers, had been a child's dreams. The hero of legend,

Chamog Borm, could not save her because she knew he was not real. Similarly, the Pearl Warrior, chiefly her own invention, could not save her. But he and Oone were real. As real as the child herself! In her deep dream, in which she had disguised herself as a queen, seeking power but failing to find it, just as she had described, she had known the truth. Unable to escape from the dream, she had yet recognised the difference between her own invention and that which she had not invented—herself, Oone and Elric. But Oone had had to show that she could defeat what remained of the original threat, and in demonstrating the defeat, she freed the child.

And yet they were still within the dream, all three of them. The great Pearl pulsed as powerfully as before, the Fortress with all its mazes and intertwined passages and chambers was still their prison.

"You understood," Elric said to Oone. "You knew what they spoke of. The language was a child's language—a language seeking power and failing. A child's understanding of power."

But again Oone, with a glance, cautioned him to silence. "Varadia knows now that power is never discovered in retreat. All one can hope to do by retreating is to let one power destroy another or hide as one hides from a storm one cannot control, until the force has passed. One cannot gain anything, save one's own self. And ultimately one must always confront the evil that would destroy one." It was almost as if she herself were in a trance and Elric guessed that she repeated lessons learned in pursuit of her craft.

"You did not come to steal the Pearl but to save me from its prison," said Varadia as Oone took her young hands and held them tightly. "My father sent you to help me?"

"He asked our help and we gave it willingly," said Elric. At last he sheathed the silver sword. He felt slightly foolish in the armour of a fairy-tale hero.

Oone recognised his discomfort. "We shall give all this back to Chamog Borm, my lord. Is he permitted to return to the Fortress, Lady Varadia?"

The child grinned. "Of course!" She clapped her hands and

through the doorway to the Court of the Pearl, walking proudly, still in the clothes of his banishment, came Chamog Borm, to kneel at the feet of his mistress.

"My Queen," he said. There was strong emotion in his wonderful voice.

"I return to you your armour and your weapons, your twin horses, Tadia and Taron, and all your honour, Chamog Borm." Varadia spoke with warm pride.

Soon Elric and Oone had discarded the armour and again wore only their ordinary clothes. Chamog Borm was in his silver-and-gold-chased breastplate and greaves, his helmet of gleaming silver, his swords and his spears in their sheaths at hip and on horse. His other armour he bound to the back of Tadia. At last he was ready. Again he kneeled before his Queen. "My lady. What task wouldst thou have me accomplish for thee?"

Varadia said deliberately: "You are free to travel where you will, great Chamog Borm. But know only this—you must continue to fight evil wherever you find it and you must never again allow the Sorcerer Adventurers to attack the Fortress of the Pearl."

"I swear."

With a bow to Oone and Elric, the legendary hero rode slowly from the Court, his head high with pride and noble purpose.

Varadia was content. "I have made him again what he was before I called him. I now know that legends in themselves have no power. The power comes from the uses that the living make of the legend. The legends merely represent an ideal."

"You are a wise child," said Oone admiringly.

"Should I not be, madam? I am the Holy Girl of the Bauradim." Varadia spoke with considerable irony and good humour. "Am I not the Oracle of the Bronze Tent?" She lowered her eyes, perhaps in sudden melancholy. "I shall be a child only a little longer. I think I shall miss my palace and all its kingdoms . . ."

"Something is always lost here." Oone placed a comforting hand on the child's shoulder. "But much is gained also."

Varadia looked back at the Pearl. Following her gaze, Elric

saw that the entire Court had now vanished, just as the crowds
had vanished on the great staircase when they had been attacked by the Pearl Warrior just before they first met Lady
Sough. He now realised that in that guise she herself had guided
them to her own rescue, as best she could. She had reached
out to them. She had shown them the way in which they could,
with their wits and courage, accomplish her salvation.

Varadia was ascending the steps, her hands outstretched towards the Pearl. "This is the cause of all our misfortune," she
said. "What can we do with it?"

"Destroy it, perhaps," said Elric.

But Oone shook her head. "While it remains an undiscov-
ered treasure thieves will constantly seek it. This is the cause
of Varadia's imprisonment in the Dream Realm. This is what
brought the Sorcerer Adventurers to her. It is why they
drugged and attempted to abduct her. All the evil comes not
from the Pearl itself but what evil men have made of it."

"What shall you do?" asked Elric. "Trade it in the Dream
Market when you next go?"

"Perhaps that is what I should do. But it would not be the
means of ensuring Varadia's safety in the future. Do you understand?"

"While the Pearl is a legend, there will always be those who
will pursue the legend?"

"Exactly, Prince Elric. So we shall not destroy it, I think.
Not here."

Elric did not care. So absorbed had he become in the dream
itself, the revealing of the levels of reality existing in the Dream
Realm, that he had forgotten his original quest, the threat to
his life and that of Anigh in Quarzhasaat.

It was for Oone to remind him. "Remember, there are those
in Quarzhasaat who are not only your enemies, Elric of Melniboné. They are the enemies of this girl. The enemies of the
Bauradim. You have still a further task to accomplish, even
when we return to the Bronze Tent."

"Then you must advise me, Lady Oone," said Elric simply,
"for I am a novice here."

"I cannot advise you with any great clarity." She turned her eyes away from him, almost in modesty, perhaps in pain. "But I can make a decision here. We must claim the Pearl."

"As I understand it, the Pearl did not exist before the lords of Quarzhasaat conceived of it, before someone discovered the legend, before the Sorcerer Adventurers came."

"But it exists now," said Oone. "Lady Varadia, would you give the Pearl to me?"

"Willingly," said the Holy Girl, and she ran up the remaining steps and took the globe from the plinth and threw it to the ground so that shards of milky glass shattered everywhere, mingling with the bones and the armour of the Pearl Warrior, and she took the Pearl in one hand, as an ordinary child might grasp a lost ball. And she tossed it from palm to palm in delight, fearing it no longer. "It is very beautiful. No wonder they sought it."

"They made it, then they used it to trap you." Oone reached up and caught it as Varadia threw it to her. "What a shame those who could conceive of such beauty would go to such evil lengths to own it . . ." She frowned, looking about her in sudden concern.

The light was fading in the Court of the Pearl.

From all around them came an appalling noise, an anguished groaning; a great creaking and keening, a tortured screaming, as if all the tormented souls in all the multiverse had suddenly given voice.

It pierced their brains. They covered their ears. They stared in terror, watching as the floor of the Court erupted and undulated, as the ivory walls with all their wonderful mosaics and carvings began to rot before their eyes, crumbling and falling, like the fabric in a tomb suddenly exposed to daylight.

And then, over all the other noises, they heard the laughter.

It was sweet laughter. It was the unaffected laughter of a child.

It was the laughter of a freed spirit. It was Varadia's.

"It is dissolving at last. It is all dissolving! Oh, my friends, I am a slave no longer!"

Through all the falling filthy stuff, through all the decay and

dissolution which tumbled upon them, through the destroyed carcass of the Fortress of the Pearl, Oone came towards them. She
was hasty but she was careful. She held one of Varadia's hands.

"Not yet! Too soon! We could all dissolve in this!"

She made Elric take the child's other hand and they led her
through the crashing, shrieking darkness, out of the chamber,
down through the swaying corridors, out past the courtyards
where fountains now gushed detritus and where the very walls
were constructed of putrefying flesh which began to rot to nothing even as they went by. Then Oone made them run, until
the final gateway lay ahead of them.

They reached the causeway and the marble road. There was
a bridge ahead of them. Oone almost dragged the other two
towards it, running as fast as she could possibly run, with the
Fortress of the Pearl tumbling into nothing, roaring like a dying beast as it did so.

The bridge seemed infinite. Elric could not see to the further
side. But at length Oone stopped running and allowed them to
walk, for they had reached a gateway.

The gateway was carved of red sandstone. It was decorated
with geometrical tiles and pictures of gazelles, leopards and
wild camels. It had an almost prosaic appearance after so many
monumental doorways, yet Elric felt some trepidation in passing through it.

"I am afraid, Oone," he said.

"You fear mortality, I think." She pressed on. "You have
great courage, Prince Elric. Make use of it now, I beg you."

He quelled his terrors. His grip on the child's hand was firm
and reassuring.

"We go home, do we not?" said the Holy Girl. "What is
it you do not want to find there, Prince Elric?"

He smiled down at her, grateful for her question. "Nothing
much, Lady Varadia. Perhaps nothing more than myself."

They stepped together into the gateway.

3

Celebrations at the Silver Flower Oasis

Waking beside the still sleeping child, Elric was surprised to feel so refreshed. The dreamwand, which had helped them attain substance in the Dream Realm, was still hooked over their clasped hands and, looking across the child, he saw Oone beginning to stir.

"You have failed, then?"

It was Raik Na Seem's voice, full of resigned sadness.

"What?" Oone glanced at Varadia. Even as they watched, her skin began to shine with ordinary health and her eyes opened to see her anxious father staring down at her. She smiled. It was the easy, unaffected smile with which Oone and Elric were already familiar.

The First Elder of the Bauradim Clan began to weep. He wept as the seneschal of the Court of the Pearl had wept; he wept in relief and he wept in joy. He took up his daughter in his arms and he could not speak for the gladness in his heart. All he could do was reach one hand out towards his friends, the man and woman who had entered the Dream Realm to free his child's spirit, where it had fled to escape the evil of Lord Gho's hirelings.

They touched his hand and they left the Bronze Tent. They walked together into the desert and then they stood face to face, staring into one another's eyes.

"We have a dream in common now," said Elric. His voice was gentle, full of affection. "I think the memory will be a good one, Lady Oone."

She reached to hold his face in her hands. "You are wise, Prince Elric, and you are courageous, but there is a certain kind of ordinary experience you lack. I hope that you are successful in finding it."

"That is why I wander this world, my lady, and leave my cousin Yyrkoon as Regent on the Ruby Throne. I am aware of more than one deficiency."

"I am glad we dreamed together," she said.

"You lost your true love, I think," Elric told her. "I am glad if I helped you ease the pain of that parting."

She was baffled for a moment, then her brow cleared. "You speak of Alnac Kreb? I was fond of him, my lord, but he was more a brother to me than a lover."

Elric became embarrassed. "Forgive my presumption, Lady Oone."

She looked up into the sky. The Blood Moon had not yet waned. It cast its red rays onto the sand, onto the gleaming bronze of the tent where Raik Na Seem welcomed his daughter back to him. "I do not love easily in the way you mean." Her voice was significant. She sighed. "Do you still plan to return to Melniboné and your betrothed?"

"I must," he said. "I love her. And my duty lies in Imrryr."

"Sweet duty!" Her tone was sarcastic and she took a step or two away from him, her head bowed, her hand on her belt. She kicked at the dust the colour of old blood.

Elric had disciplined himself against his heart's pain for too long. He could only stand and wait until she walked back to him. And now she was smiling. "Well, Prince Elric, would you join the dreamthieves and make this your living for a while?"

Elric shook his head. "It is a calling which requires too much of me, my lady. Yet I am grateful for what this adventure has taught me, both about myself and about the world of dreams. I still understand only a little of it. I am still not wholly sure where we travelled or what we encountered. I do not know how much in the Dream Realm was the Lady Varadia's creation and how much was yours. It was as if I witnessed a battle of inventors! And did I contribute? I do not know."

"Oh, without you, believe me, Prince Elric, I think I would have failed. You have seen so much of other worlds! And you have read more. It does not do to analyse too closely the creatures and places one encounters in the Dream Realm, but be assured that you made your contribution. More, perhaps, than you'll ever know."

"Can reality ever be made from the fabric of those dreams?" he wondered.

"There was an adventurer of the Young Kingdoms called Earl Aubec," she said. "He knew how potent a creator of reality the human mind can be. Some say he and his kind helped make the world of the Young Kingdoms."

Elric nodded. "I've heard that legend. But I think it is as substantial as the story of Chamog Borm, my lady."

"You must think what you wish." She turned away from him to look at the Bronze Tent. The old man and his daughter were emerging. From somewhere within, the tent drums began to beat. There came a wonderful chanting, a dozen melodies linked together, interwoven. Slowly all the people who had remained at the Bronze Tent keeping vigil over the body of the Holy Girl began to gather around Raik Na Seem and Varadia. Their songs were songs of intense joy. Their voices filled the desert with the most gorgeous life and made even the distant mountains echo.

Oone linked her arm in Elric's, a gesture of comradeship, of reconciliation. "Come," she said, "let us join the celebrations."

They had only walked a few more paces before they were lifted on the shoulders of the crowd and soon they were borne, laughing and infected by the general joyousness, over the desert towards the Silver Flower Oasis.

The celebrations began at once, as if the Bauradim and all the other desert clans had been preparing for this moment. Every kind of delicious food was prepared until the air was rich with an enormous variety of mouth-watering smells and it seemed all the great spice warehouses of the world had been made to release their contents. Cooking fires blazed everywhere, as did great brands and lamps and candles, and from out of the Kashbeh Moulor Ka Riiz, overlooking the great oasis, rode the Aloum'rit guardians in all the glory of their ancient armour, their red-gold helmets and breastplates, their weapons of bronze and brass and steel. They had huge forked beards and massive turbans wound around the spikes of their helms. They wore surcoats of elaborate brocade and cloth-of-silver and their high boots were embroidered with designs almost as intricate as those on their shirts. They were proud, good-humoured men who rode at the sides of their wives, who were also armoured and carried bows and slender spears. All had soon mingled with the enormous crowd who had erected a large platform and placed a carved chair upon it and sat the smiling Varadia in the chair so that all could see the Holy Girl of the Bauradim restored to her clan, bringing back their history, their pride and their future.

Raik Na Seem still wept. Whenever he saw Oone and Elric he grasped them and pulled them to him, thanking them, telling them, as best he could, what it meant to him to have such friends, such saviours, such heroes.

"Your names will be remembered by the Bauradim for all time. And whatever favour you shall ask of us, so long as it be honourable, as we know it shall, then we shall grant it to you. If you are in danger ten thousand miles away you will send a message to the Bauradim and they will come to your aid. Meanwhile you must know that you have freed the spirit of a good-hearted child from dark captivity."

"And that is our reward," said Oone, smiling.

"Our wealth is yours," said the old man.

"We have no need of wealth," Oone told him. "We have discovered better resources, I think."

Elric agreed with her. "Besides, there is a man in Quarzhasaat who has promised me half an empire if I but do him a small service."

Oone understood Elric's reference and laughed.

Raik Na Seem was a little disturbed. "You go to Quarzhasaat? You still have business there?"

"Aye," said Elric. "There is a boy who is anxiously awaiting my return."

"But you have time to celebrate with us, to talk with us, to feast with myself and Varadia? You have scarcely exchanged a word with the child!"

"I think we know her pretty well," said Elric. "Enough to think highly of her. She is indeed the greatest treasure of the Bauradim, my lord."

"You were able to hold conversations in that gloomy realm where she was held prisoner?"

Elric thought to enlighten the First Elder, but Oone was quick to interrupt, so familiar was she with such questions.

"Some, my lord. We were impressed by her intelligence and her courage."

Raik Na Seem's brow furrowed as another thought occurred to him. "My son," he said to Elric, "were you able to sustain yourself in that realm without pain?"

"Without pain, aye," said Elric. Then he realised what had been said. For the first time he understood what good had come about from his adventure. "Aye, sir. There are benefits to assisting a dreamthief. Great benefits which I had not until now appreciated!"

With relish now Elric joined in the feasting, treasuring these hours with Oone, the Bauradim and all the other nomad clans. Again he felt as if he had come home, so welcoming were the people, and he wished that he could spend his life here, learning their ways, their philosophies and enjoying their pastimes.

Later, as he lay beneath a great date palm, rolling one of the silver flowers between his fingers, he looked up at Oone, who sat beside him, and said: "Of all the temptations I faced in the Dream Realm, this temptation is perhaps the greatest, Oone. This is simple reality and I am reluctant to leave it. And you."

"We have no further destiny together, I think." She sighed. "Not in this life, at any rate, or this world, perhaps. You shall be first a legend, then there will be none left to remember you."

"My friends will all die? I shall be alone?"

"I believe so. While you serve Chaos."

"I serve myself and my people."

"If you would believe that, Elric, you must do more to achieve it. You have created a little reality and perhaps will create a little more. But Chaos cannot be a friend without it betraying you. In the end, we have only ourselves to look to. No cause, no force, no challenge, will ever replace that truth . . ."

"It is to be myself that I travel as I do, Lady Oone," he reminded her. He looked out over the desert, over the tranquil waters of the oasis. He breathed in the cool, scented desert air.

"And you will leave here soon?" she asked.

"Tomorrow," he said. "I must. But I am curious to know what reality I have created."

"Oh, I think a dream or two has come true," she said cryptically, kissing him on the cheek. "And another will come true soon enough."

He did not pursue the question, for she had taken the great Pearl from the pouch at her belt and held it out to him.

"It exists! It was not the chimera we believed it to be! You still have it!"

"It is for you," she said. "Use it how you will. But that is what brought you here to the Silver Flower Oasis. It is what brought you to me. I think I will not trade it at the Dream Market. I would like you to have it. I think it might be yours by right, Elric. Be that as it may, the Holy Girl gave it to me and now I give it to you. It is what Alnac Kreb died because of, what all those assassins died to possess . . ."

"I thought you said that the Pearl did not exist before the Sorcerer Assassins sought to find it."

"That is true. But it exists now. Here it is. The Pearl at the Heart of the World. The great Pearl of legend. Have you no use for it?"

"You must explain to me . . ." he began, but she cut him short.

"Ask me not how dreams take substance, Prince Elric. That is a question that concerns philosophers in all ages and all places. I ask you again—have you no use for it?"

He hesitated, then reached out to take the lovely thing. He held it in his two palms, rolling it back and forth. He wondered at its richness, its pale beauty. "Aye," he said. "I think I have a use for it."

When he had placed the jewel in his own pouch, Oone said very softly: "I think it is an evil thing, that Pearl."

He agreed with her. "I think so, too. But sometimes evil can be used to counter evil."

"I cannot accept that argument." She seemed troubled.

"I know," he said, "you have already said as much." And then it was his turn to reach towards her and kiss her tenderly upon the lips. "Fate is cruel, Oone. It would be better if it provided us with one unaltering path. Instead it forces us to make choices and then never to know if those choices were for the best."

"We are mortals," she said with a shrug. "That is our particular doom."

She stroked his forehead. "You have a troubled mind, my lord. I think I will steal a few of the smaller dreams which make you uneasy."

"Can you steal pain, Oone, and turn it into something to sell in your market?"

"Oh, frequently," she said.

She took his head in her lap and began to massage his temples. Her look was tender.

He said sleepily: "I cannot betray Cymoril. I cannot . . ."

"I ask no more of you but that you sleep," she said. "One

day you will have much to regret and you will know real remorse. Until then, I can take away a little of what is unimportant."

"Unimportant?" His voice was slurred as she gradually stroked him into slumber.

"To you, I think, my lord. Though not to me . . ."

And the dreamthief began to sing. She sang a lullaby. She sang of a sickly child and a grieving father. She sang of happiness found in simple things.

And Elric slept. And as he slept the dreamthief performed her easy magic and took away just a few of the half-forgotten memories which had spoiled his nights in the past and might spoil those yet to come.

And when Elric awoke that next morning, it was with a light heart and an easy conscience, only the faintest memories of his adventures in the Dream Realm, a continuing affection for Oone and a determination to reach Quarzhasaat as soon as possible and take to Lord Gho what Lord Gho most desired in all the world.

His farewells to the people of the Bauradim were sincere and his sadness in parting was reciprocated. They begged him to return, to join them on their travels, to hunt with them as Rackhir, his friend, had once hunted.

"I will try to return to you one day," he said. "But first I have more than one oath to fulfill."

A nervous boy brought him his great black battle-blade. As he buckled on Stormbringer the sword seemed to moan with considerable satisfaction at being reunited with him.

It was Varadia, clasping his hands and kissing them, who gave him the blessing of her clan. It was Raik Na Seem who told him that he was now Varadia's brother, his own son, and then Oone the Dreamthief stepped forward. She had decided to remain a while as a guest of the Bauradim.

"Farewell, Elric. I hope that we may meet again. In better circumstances."

He was amused. "Better circumstances?"

"For me, at any rate." She grinned, contemptuously tapping the pommel of his runesword. "And I wish you well with your attempts to become that thing's master."

"I am its master now, I think," he said.

She shrugged. "I'll ride with you a little way up the Red Road."

"I would welcome your company, my lady."

Side by side, as they had done in the Dream Realm, Elric and Oone rode together. And, although he did not remember how he had felt before, Elric knew a certain resonance of recognition, as if he had found his soul's satisfaction, so that it was with sadness that eventually he parted from her to go on alone towards Quarzhasaat.

"Farewell, good friend. I'll remember how you defeated the Pearl Warrior in the Fortress of the Pearl. That is one memory I do not think will ever fade."

"I am flattered." There was a touch of melancholy irony in her voice. "Farewell, Prince Elric. I trust you will find all that you need and that you will know peace when you return to Melniboné."

"It is my firm intention, madam." A wave to her, not wishing to prolong the sadness, and he spurred his horse forward.

With eyes which refused to weep she watched him ride away up the long Red Road to Quarzhasaat.

4

Certain Matters Resolved in Quarzhasaat

When Elric of Melniboné rode into Quarzhasaat he was limp in his saddle, hardly controlling his horse at all, and the people who gathered around him asked him if he was ill, while some feared that he brought plague to their beautiful city and would have driven him out at once.

The albino lifted his strange head long enough to gasp out the name of his patron, Lord Gho Fhaazi, and to say that all he lacked was a certain elixir which that nobleman possessed. "I must have that elixir," he told them, "or I will be dead before I have accomplished my task . . ."

The old towers and minarets of Quarzhasaat were lovely in the fading rays of a huge red sun and there was a certain peace about the city which comes when the day's business is done and before it begins to take its pleasures.

A rich water-merchant, anxious to find favour with one who might soon be elected to the Council, personally led Elric's horse through the elegant alleys and impressive avenues until they came to the great palace, all golds and faded greens, of Lord Gho Fhaazi.

The merchant was rewarded by a steward's promise to mention his name to the nobleman, and Elric, now mumbling and whimpering to himself, sometimes groaning a little and licking anxious lips, passed through into the lovely gardens surrounding the main palace.

Lord Gho himself came to meet the albino. He was laughing heartily at the sight of Elric in such poor condition.

"Greetings, greetings, Elric of Nadsokor! Greetings, white-faced clown-thief. Oh, you are not so proud today! You were profligate with the elixir I gave you and now you return to beg for more—in worse condition than when you first arrived here!"

"The boy . . ." whispered Elric, as servants helped him from the horse. His arms hung limply as they carried him on their shoulders. "Does he live?"

"In better health than yourself, sir!" Lord Gho Fhaazi's pale green eyes were full of exquisite malice. "And in perfect safety. You were most adamant about that before you set off. And I am a man of my word." The politician stroked the ringlets of his oily beard and chuckled to himself. "And you, Sir Thief, do you also keep your word?"

"To the letter," muttered the albino. His red eyes rolled back in his head and it appeared for a second that he died. Then he turned a painful gaze in Lord Gho's direction. "Will you give me the antidote and all that you've promised? The water? The wealth? The boy?"

"No doubt, no doubt. But you have a poor bargaining position at present, thief. What of the Pearl? Did you find it? Or are you here to report failure?"

"I found it. And I have it hidden," said Elric. "The elixir has . . ."

"Yes, yes. I know what the elixir does. You must have a fundamentally strong constitution even to be able to speak by now." The Quarzhasaati supervised the men and women who carried Elric into the cool interior of the palace and placed him on great tasselled cushions of scarlet and blue velvet and gave him water to drink and food to eat.

"The craving grows worse, does it not?" Lord Gho took considerable pleasure at Elric's discomfort. "The elixir must feed off you, just as you appear to feed off it. You are cunning, eh, Sir Thief? You have hidden the Pearl, you say? Do you not trust me? I am a nobleman of the greatest city in the world!"

Elric, all dusty from his long ride, sprawled on the cushions and wiped his hands slowly on a cloth. "The antidote, my lord . . ."

"You know I shall not let you have the antidote until the Pearl is in my hands . . ." Lord Gho was expansively condescending as he looked down on his victim. "To tell you the truth, thief, I had not expected you to be as coherent as you are! Would you care for another draft of my elixir?"

"Bring it if you will."

Elric appeared to be careless, but Lord Gho understood how desperate he must actually be. He turned to give instructions to his slaves.

Then Elric said: "But bring the boy. Bring the boy so that I may see he has come to no harm and hear from his own lips what has taken place while I have been gone . . ."

"It's a small request. Very well." Lord Gho Fhaazi signed to a slave. "Bring the boy Anigh."

The nobleman crossed to a great chair, placed on a small dais between brocaded awnings, and slumped himself down in it while they waited. "I had scarcely expected you to survive the journey, Sir Thief, let alone succeed in finding the Pearl. Our Sorcerer Adventurers are the bravest, most skillful of warriors, trained in all the arts of sorcery and incantation. Yet those I sent, and all their brothers, failed! Oh, this is a happy day for me. I will revive you, I promise, so that you can tell me all that happened. What of the Bauradim? Did you kill many? You will recount everything so that when I present the Pearl to obtain my position I can give the story that goes with it. This will add to its value, you see. When I am elected, I shall be asked to retail such a story many times, I am sure. The Council will be so envious . . ." He licked his painted red lips. "Did you have to kill that child? What was the first thing you witnessed, for instance, when you reached the Silver Flower Oasis?"

"A funeral, as I recall . . ." Elric showed a little more animation. "Aye, that was it."

Two guards brought in a wriggling boy who did not seem greatly overjoyed when he saw Elric stretched upon the cushions. "Oh, master! You are more wretched than before." He stopped his struggling and tried to hide his disappointment. There were no marks of torture on him. He seemed not to have been harmed.

"Are you well, Anigh?"

"Aye. My chief problem has been in passing the time. Occasionally his lordship there has come to tell me what he will do if you fail to bring back the Pearl, but I have read such things on the walls of the lunatic stockades and they are nothing new to me."

Lord Gho scowled. "Be careful, boy . . ."

"You must have returned with the Pearl," said Anigh, glancing around him. "That is so, eh, my lord? Or you would not be here?" He was a little more relieved. "Are we to go now?"

"Not yet!" growled Lord Gho.

"The antidote," said Elric. "Do you have it here?"

"You are too impatient, Sir Thief. And your cunning is matched by mine." Lord Gho giggled and raised an admonishing finger. "I must have some proof that you possess the Pearl. Would you give me your sword as surety, perhaps? You are, after all, too weak to wield it. It is of no further use to you." He reached a greedy hand towards the albino's hip and Elric made a feeble movement away from him.

"Come, come, Sir Thief. Be not afraid of me. We are partners in this. Where is the Pearl? The Council congregates this evening at the Great Meeting House. If I can bring them the Pearl then . . . Oh, I shall be powerful by tonight!"

"The worm is so proud to be king of the dunghill," said Elric.

"Do not anger him, master!" cried Anigh in alarm. "You have still to learn where he hides the antidote!"

"I must have the Pearl!" Lord Gho grew petulant in his impatience. "Where have you hidden it, thief? In the desert? Somewhere in the city?"

Slowly Elric raised his body on the cushions. "The Pearl was a dream," he said. "It took your killers to make it real."

Lord Gho Fhaazi frowned, scratching at his whitened forehead and showing further nervousness. He looked suspiciously at Elric. "If you would have more elixir, you had best not insult me, thief. Nor play any game. The boy could die in an instant, and you with him, and I would be in no worse a position."

"But you would better yourself, my lord, I think. With the price of a place on the Council, I think." Elric seemed to gather strength and now he was upright on the luxurious velvet, signing for the boy to come towards him. The guards looked questioningly at their master, but he shrugged. Anigh walked, his brow furrowed with curiosity, towards the albino. "You are greedy, my lord, I think. You would own the whole of your world. This pathetic monument to your race's ruined pride!"

Lord Gho glared at him. "Thief, if you would recover yourself, if you would take the antidote to make you free of the drug I gave you, you will be more polite to me . . ."

"Ah, yes," said Elric thoughtfully, reaching into his jerkin. He pulled out a leather pouch. "The elixir which was to make me your slave!" He smiled. He opened the pouch.

Onto his extended palm now rolled the jewel for which Gho Fhaazi had offered half his fortune, for which he had sent a hundred men to their deaths, for which he had been prepared to abduct and kill one child and imprison another.

The Quarzhasaati began to tremble. His painted eyes rounded. He gasped and bent forward, almost fainting.

"It is true," he said. "You have found the Pearl at the Heart of the World . . ."

"Merely a gift from a friend," said Elric. The Pearl still

displayed on his hand, he rose to his feet and put a protective arm around the boy. "In obtaining it I found that my body lost its demand for the elixir and therefore has no need for your antidote, Lord Gho."

Lord Gho hardly heard him. His eyes were fixed on the great Pearl. "It is monstrous big . . . Even larger than I had heard . . . It is real. I can see it is real. The colour . . . Ah . . ." And he stretched towards it.

Elric drew his hand back. Lord Gho frowned and looked up at the albino with eyes that were hot with greed. "Did she die? Was it, as some said, in her body?"

Anigh shivered at Elric's side.

Full of loathing, Elric's voice was still soft. "No one died at my hand who was not already dead. As you are already dead, my lord. It was your funeral I witnessed at the Silver Flower Oasis. I am now the agent of the Bauradim prophecy. I am to avenge all the grief you brought to them and their Holy Girl."

"What? The others all sent their soldiers, too! The entire Council and half the candidates had sects of Sourcerer Adventurers seeking the Pearl. Every one. Most of those warriors failed or were killed. Or were executed for their failure. You killed no one, you said. Well, so there's no blood on your hands, eh. All's for the best. I'll give you what I promised, Sir Thief . . ."

Trembling with lust, Lord Gho extended his plump hand to take the Pearl.

Elric smiled and to Anigh's astonishment let the nobleman lift the Pearl from his palm.

Breathing heavily, Lord Gho caressed his prize. "Oh, it is lovely. Oh, it is so good . . ."

Elric spoke again, just as levelly as before. "And our reward, Lord Gho?"

"What?" He looked up absently. "Why yes, of course. Your lives. You no longer need the antidote, you say. Excellent. So you may go."

"I believe you also offered me a large fortune. All manner of wealth. Great stature amongst the lords of Quarzhasaat?"

Lord Gho dismissed this. "Nonsense. The antidote would
have sufficed. You are not the type of person to enjoy such
things. Breeding is required if they are to be used wisely and
with appropriate discretion. No, no. I will let you and the boy
go . . ."

"You will not keep your original bargain, my lord?"

"There was talk—but no bargain. The only bargain involved the boy's freedom and the antidote to the elixir. You
were mistaken."

"You remember nothing of your promises . . . ?"

"Promises? Certainly not." The ringletted beard and hair
quivered.

". . . and mine?"

"No, no. You are irritating me." His eyes were still upon
the Pearl. He fondled it as another might fondle a beloved
child. "Go, sir. While I am still pleased with you."

"I have many oaths to fulfill," said Elric, "and I do not
break my word."

Lord Gho looked up, his expression hardening. "Very well.
I am tired of this. By this evening I shall be a member of the
Six and One Other. By threatening me, you threaten the
Council. You are therefore enemies of Quarzhasaat. You are
traitors to the Empire and must be disposed of accordingly!
Guards!"

"Oh, you are a foolish fellow," said Elric. Then Anigh cried
out, for unlike Lord Gho, he had not forgotten the power of
the Black Sword.

"Do as he demands, Lord Gho!" shouted Anigh, fearing as
much for himself as for the nobleman. "I beg you, great lord!
Do what he says!"

"This is not how a member of the Council is addressed."
Lord Gho's tone was that of a baffled, reasonable individual.
"Guards—take them from my hall at once. Have them stran-
gled or cut their throats—I care not . . ."

The guards knew nothing of the runesword. They saw only
a slender man who might have been a leper and they saw a
young, defenceless boy. They grinned, as if at a joke of their

master's, and then drew their blades, advancing almost casually.

Elric pressed Anigh behind him. His hand went to Stormbringer's hilt. ''You are unwise to do this,'' he told the guards. ''I have no particular wish to kill you.''

Behind the soldiers one of the servants opened the door and slipped out into the corridor. Elric watched her go. ''Best copy her,'' he said. ''She has some idea, I think, of what will happen if you threaten us further . . .''

The guards laughed openly now. ''This is a madman,'' said one. ''Lord Gho is well rid of him!''

They came at Elric in a rush and then the runesword was howling in the cool air of that luxurious chamber—howling like a hungry wolf freed from a cage and longing only to kill and to feed.

Elric felt the power surge through him as the blade took the first guard, splitting him from crown to breastbone. The other tried to change direction from attack to flight, stumbled forward and was impaled on the blade's tip, his eyes horrified as he felt his soul being drawn from him into the runesword.

Lord Gho cringed in his great chair, too frightened to move. In one hand he clutched the great Pearl. His other hand was held palm outward as if he hoped to ward off Elric's blow.

But the albino, strengthened by his borrowed energy, sheathed the black blade and took five quick strides across the hall to mount the dais and stare down into Lord Gho's face, which twisted in terror.

''Take the Pearl back. For my life . . .'' whispered the Quarzhasaati. ''For my life, thief . . .''

Elric accepted the offered jewel, but he did not move. He reached into the pouch at his belt and drew forth a flask of the elixir Lord Gho had given him. ''Would you care for something to help you wash it down?''

Lord Gho trembled. Beneath the chalky substance on his skin his face had gone still paler. ''I do not understand you, thief.''

''I want you to eat the Pearl, my lord. If you can swallow

it and live, well, it will be clear that the prophecy of your death was premature.''

"Swallow it? It is too large. I could hardly get it into my mouth!'' Lord Gho sniggered, hoping that the albino joked.

"No, my lord. I think you can. And I think you can swallow it. After all, how else would it have got into the body of a child?''

"It was—they said it was a—a dream . . .''

"Aye. Perhaps you can swallow a dream. Perhaps you can enter the Dream Realm and so escape your fate. You must try, my lord, or else my runesword drinks your soul. Which would you prefer?''

"Oh, Elric. Spare me. This is not fair. We made a bargain.''

"Open your mouth, Lord Gho. Who knows? The Pearl might shrink or your throat expand like a snake's. A snake could easily swallow the Pearl, my lord. And you, surely, are superior to a snake?''

Anigh whispered from the window where he had been staring with studied gaze, unwilling to look upon a vengeance he regarded as just but distasteful. "The servant, Lord Elric. She has alarmed the city.''

For a second a desperate hope came into Lord Gho's green eyes and then faded as Elric placed the flask on the arm of the great chair and drew the runesword part-way from its scabbard. "Your soul will help me fight those new soldiers, Lord Gho.''

Slowly, weeping and whimpering, the great Lord of Quarzhasaat began to open his mouth.

"Here is the Pearl again, my lord. Put it in. Do your best, my lord. You have some chance of life this way.''

Lord Gho's hand shook. But eventually he began to force the lovely jewel between his reddened lips. Elric took the stopper from the elixir and poured some of the liquid into the nobleman's distorted cheeks. "Now swallow, Lord Gho. Swallow the Pearl you would have slain a child to own. And then I will tell you who I am . . .''

A few moments later the doors crashed inward and Elric recognised the tattooed face of Manag Iss, leader of the Yellow Sect and kinsman to the Lady Iss. Manag Iss looked from Elric to the distorted features of Lord Gho. The nobleman had failed completely to swallow the Pearl.

Manag Iss shuddered. "Elric. I heard that you had returned. They said you were close to death. Clearly this was a trick to deceive Lord Gho."

"Aye," said Elric. "I had this boy to free."

Manag Iss gestured with his own drawn sword. "You found the Pearl?"

"I found it."

"My Lady Iss sent me to offer you anything you desired for it."

Elric smiled. "Tell her I shall be at the Council Meeting House in half an hour. I shall bring the Pearl with me."

"But the others will be there. She wishes to trade privately."

"Would it not be wise to auction so valuable a thing?" said Elric.

Manag Iss sheathed his sword and smiled a little. "You're a cunning one. I do not think they know how cunning you are. Nor who you are. I have yet to tell them that particular speculation."

"Oh, you may tell them what I have just told Lord Gho. That I am the hereditary Emperor of Melniboné," said Elric casually. "For that is the truth of the matter. My Empire has survived rather more successfully than yours, I think."

"That could incense them. I am willing to be your friend, Melnibonéan."

"Thanks, Manag Iss, but I need no more friends from Quarzhasaat. Please do as I say."

Manag Iss looked at the slaughtered guards, at the dead Lord Gho, who had turned a strange colour, at the nervous boy, and he saluted Elric.

"The Meeting House in half an hour, Emperor of Melniboné." He turned on his heel and left the chamber.

After issuing certain specific instructions to Anigh concerning travel and the products of Kwan, Elric went out into the courtyard. The sun had set and there were brands burning all over Quarzhasaat as if the city were expecting an attack.

Lord Gho's house was deserted of servants. Elric went to the stables and found his horse and his saddle. He dressed the Baraudi stallion, carefully placing a heavy bundle over the pommel, then he had mounted and was riding through the streets, seeking the Meeting House where Anigh had told him it would be.

The city was unnaturally silent. Clearly some order had been given to uphold a curfew, for there was not even a city guard on the streets.

Elric rode at an easy canter along the wide Avenue of Military Success, along the Boulevard of Ancient Accomplishment and half a dozen other grandiosely named thoroughfares until he saw the long low building ahead of him which, in its simplicity, could only be the seat of Quarzhasaati power.

The albino paused. At his side the black runesword crooned a little, almost demanding a further letting of blood.

"You must be patient," said Elric. "Could be there will be no need for battle."

He thought he saw shadows moving in the trees and shrubberies around the Meeting House but he paid them no attention. He did not care what they plotted or who spied on him. He had a mission to fulfill.

At last he had reached the doors of the building and was not surprised to find them standing open. He dismounted, threw the bundle over his shoulder and walked heavily into a large, plain room, without decoration or ostentation, in which were placed seven tall-backed chairs and a lime-washed oak table. Standing in a semi-circle at one end of the table were six robed figures wearing veils not unlike certain sects of the Sorcerer Adventurers. The seventh figure wore a tall, conical hat which completely covered the face. It was this figure who spoke. Elric was not unsurprised to hear a woman's tones.

"I am the Other," she said. "I believe you have brought us a treasure to add to the glory of Quarzhasaat."

"If you believe this treasure to add to your glory, then my journey has not been fruitless," said Elric. He dropped the bundle to the ground. "Did Manag Iss tell you all I asked him to tell you?"

One of the Councillors stirred and said, almost as an oath: "That you are the progeny of sunken Melniboné, aye!"

"Melniboné is not sunken. Nor does she cut herself off from the world's realities quite as much as do you." Elric was contemptuous. "You challenged our power long ago, and defeated yourselves by your own folly. Now through your greed you have brought me back to Quarzhasaat when I would as readily have passed through your city unnoticed."

"Do you accuse us!" A veiled woman was outraged. "You who have caused us so much trouble? You, who are of the blood of that degenerate unhuman race which couples with beasts for its pleasures and produces"—she pointed at Elric—"the like of you!"

Elric was unmoved. "Did Manag Iss tell you to be wary of me?" he asked quietly.

"He said you had the Pearl and that you had a sorcerous sword. But he also said you were alone." The Other cleared her throat. "He said you brought the Pearl at the Heart of the World."

"I have brought it and that which contains it," said Elric. He bent down and tugged the velvet free of his bundle to reveal the corpse of Lord Gho Fhaazi, his face still contorted, the great lump in his throat making it seem as if he had an enormously enlarged Adam's apple. "Here is the one who first commissioned me to find the Pearl."

"We heard you had murdered him," said the Other with disapproval. "But that would be a normal enough action for a Melnibonéan."

Elric did not rise to this. "The Pearl is in Lord Gho Fhaazi's gullet. Would you have me cut it out for you, my nobles?"

He saw at least one of them shudder and he smiled. "You commission assassins to kill, to torture, to kidnap and to perform all other forms of evil in your name, but you would not see a little spilled blood? I gave Lord Gho a choice. He took this one. He talked so much and ate and drank so copiously I thought he might well have succeeded in getting the Pearl into his stomach. But he gagged a little and I fear that was the end of him.''

"You are a cruel rogue!'' One of the men came forward to look at his would-be colleague. "Aye, that's Gho. His colour has improved, I'd say.''

This jest did not meet with the leader's approval.

"We are to bid for a corpse, then?''

"Unless you wish to cut the Pearl free, aye.''

"Manag Iss,'' said one of the veiled women, lifting her head. "Step out, will you, sir?''

The Sorcerer Adventurer emerged from a door at the back of the hall. He looked at Elric almost apologetically. His hand went to his knife.

"We would not have a Melnibonéan spill more Quarzha-saati blood,'' said the Other. "Manag Iss will cut the Pearl free.''

The leader of the Yellow Sect drew a deep breath and then approached the corpse. Swiftly he did what he had been ordered to do. Blood poured down his arm as he held up the Pearl at the Heart of the World.

The Council was impressed. Several of the members gasped and they murmured amongst themselves. Elric believed they had suspected him of lying to them, since lies and intrigues were second nature to them.

"Hold it high, Manag Iss,'' said the albino. "It is this that you all desired so greedily that you were prepared to pay for it with what was left of your honour.''

"Be careful, sir!'' cried the Other. "We are patient with you now. Name your price and then begone.''

Elric laughed. It was not pleasant laughter. It was Melnibonéan laughter. At that moment he was a pure denizen of the Dragon Isle. "Very well,'' he said, "I desire this city. Not its citizens, not any of its treasure, nor its animals, not even its water. I would let you leave with everything you can carry. I desire only the city itself. It is, you see, mine by hereditary right.''

"What? This is nonsense. How could we agree?''

"You must agree," said Elric, "or you must fight me.''

"Fight you? There is only one of you.''

"There is no question of it," said another Councillor. "He is mad. He must be put down like a crazed dog. Manag Iss, call in your brothers and their men.''

"I do not believe it is advisable, cousin," said Manag Iss, clearly addressing Lady Iss. "I think it would be wise to parley.''

"What? Have you turned coward? Has this rogue an army with him?''

Manag Iss rubbed at his nose. "My lady . . .''

"Call in your brothers, Manag Iss!''

The captain of the Yellow Sect rubbed at one silk-clad arm and he frowned. "Prince Elric, I understand that you force us to a challenge. But we have not threatened you. The Council honestly came here to bid for the Pearl . . .''

"Manag Iss, you repeat their lies," said Elric, "and that is not an honourable thing to do. If they meant me no harm, why were you and all your brothers standing by? I saw almost two hundred warriors in the grounds.''

"That was a precaution only," said the Other. She turned to her fellow Councillors. "I told you I thought it was stupid to summon so many so soon.''

Elric said evenly: "Everything you have done, my nobles, has been stupid. You have been cruel, greedy, careless of others' lives and wills. You have been blind, thoughtless, provincial and unimaginative. It seems to me that a government so careless of anything but its own gratification should be at very least replaced. When you have all left the city I will consider electing a governor who will know better how to serve Quarzhasaat. Then, later perhaps, I will let you back into the city . . .''

"Oh, slay him!" cried the Other. "Waste no more time on

this. When that's done we can decide amongst ourselves who owns the Pearl.''

Elric sighed almost regretfully and said: "Best parley with me now, madam, before I myself lose patience. I shall not, once I have drawn my blade, be a rational and merciful being . . .''

"Slay him!" she insisted. "And have done with it!"

Manag Iss had the face of a man condemned to more than death. "Madam . . .''

She strode forward, her conical hat swaying, and tugged the sword from the scabbard. She raised the blade to behead the albino.

He reached out swiftly. His arm was a striking snake. He gripped her wrist. "No, madam! I am, I swear, giving you fair warning . . .''

Stormbringer murmured at his side and stirred.

She dropped the sword and turned away, nursing her bruised wrist.

Now Manag Iss reached for his fallen blade, making as if to sheath it, and then, with a subtle movement, tried to bring the weapon up and take Elric in the groin, an expression of resignation crossing his terrified features as the albino, anticipating him, sidestepped and in the same action drew the Black Sword, which began to sing its strange demonic song and glow with a terrible black radiance.

Manag Iss gasped as his heart was pierced. The hand that still held the Pearl seemed to stretch out, offering it back to Elric. Then the jewel had rolled from his fingers and rattled on the floor. Three Councillors rushed forward, saw Manag Iss's dying eyes and stepped backward.

"Now! Now! Now!" cried the Other, and, as Elric had expected, from every cranny of the Meeting House, members of the various sects of Sorcerer Adventurers came, their weapons at the ready.

And the albino began to grin his horrible battle-grin, and his red eyes blazed and his face was the skull of Death and his sword was the vengeance of his own people, the vengeance of the Bauradim and all those who had suffered under the injustice of Quarzhasaat over the millennia.

And he offered up the souls he took to his patron Duke of Hell, the powerful Duke Arioch who had grown sleek on many lives dedicated to him by Elric and his black blade.

"Arioch! Arioch! Blood and souls for my lord Arioch!"

Then the true slaughter began.

It was a slaughter to make all other such events pale into insignificance. It was a slaughter that would never be forgotten in all the annals of the desert peoples, who would learn of it from those who fled Quarzhasaat that night—flinging themselves into the waterless desert rather than face the white laughing demon on a Bauradi horse who galloped up and down their lovely streets and taught them what the price of complacency and unthinking cruelty could be.

"Arioch! Arioch! Blood and souls!"

They would speak of a white-faced creature from Hell whose sword poured with unnatural radiance, whose crimson eyes blazed with hideous rage, who seemed possessed, himself, of some supernatural force, who was no more master of it than were his victims. He killed without mercy, without distinction, without cruelty. He killed as a mad wolf kills. And as he killed, he laughed.

That laughter would never leave Quarzhasaat. It would remain on the wind which came in from the Sighing Desert, in the music of the fountains, the clang of the metal-workers' and jewellers' hammers as they fashioned their wares. And so would the smell of blood remain, together with the memory of slaughter, that terrible loss of life which left the city without a Council and an army.

But never again would Quarzhasaat foster the legend of her own power. Never again would she treat the desert nomads as less than beasts. Never again would she know that self-destructive pride so familiar to all great empires in decline.

And when the slaughter was finished, Elric of Melniboné slumped in his saddle, sheathing a sated Stormbringer, and he gasped with the demon power which still pulsed through him and he took a great Pearl from his belt and held it to the rising sun.

"They have paid a fair price now, I think."

He tossed the thing into a gutter where a little dog licked congealing blood.

Above, the vultures, called from a thousand miles around by the prospect of memorable feasting, were beginning to drop like a dark cloud upon the beautiful towers and gardens of Quarzhasaat.

Elric's face held no pride in his achievement as he spurred his horse for the West and the place on the road where he had told Anigh to await them with enough Kwani herbs, water, horses and food to cross the Sighing Desert and seek again the more familiar politics and sorceries of the Young Kingdoms.

He did not look back on the city which, in the name of his ancestors, had been conquered at last.

5

An Epilogue
at the Waning
of the Blood Moon

The celebrations at the Silver Flower Oasis had continued long after the news came of Elric's vengeance-taking on those who would have harmed the Holy Girl of the Bauradim. The news was brought by Quarzhasaa-tim, fleeing from the city in an action which had no precedent in all their long history.

Oone the Dreamthief, who had stayed at the Silver Flower Oasis longer than was necessary and who was yet reluctant to leave and go about her proper business, learned of Elric's vengeance without joy. The news saddened her, for she had hoped for something else to happen.

"He serves Chaos as I serve Law," she said to herself. "And who is to say which of us is the worse enslaved?" But she sighed and threw herself into the festivities with a force which was less than spontaneous.

The Bauradim and the other nomad clans did not notice, for their own pleasure was intensified. They were rid of a tyrant, of the only thing in the desert lands that they had ever feared.

"The cactus tears our flesh so that we shall be shown where water is," said Raik Na Seem. "Our troubles were great, but thanks to you, Oone, and Elric of Melniboné, our troubles turned to triumphs. Soon some of us will visit Quarzhasaat and set out the terms on which we intend to trade in future. There will be a welcome equality about the transaction, I think." He was greatly amused. "But we will wait until the dead are decently eaten."

Varadia took Oone's hand and they walked together beside the pools of the great oasis. The Blood Moon was waning and the silver petals of the flowers were shining brighter still. Soon the Blood Moon must wane and the flowers shed their petals and then it would be time for the people of the desert to go their different ways.

"You loved that white-faced man, did you not?" Varadia asked her friend.

"I hardly knew him, child."

"I knew you both very well, not so long ago." Varadia smiled. "And I am growing rapidly, am I not? You said as much yourself."

Oone was forced to agree. "But there was no hope for it, Varadia. We have such different destinies. And I have scant sympathy for the choices he makes."

"He is driven, that one. He has little in the way of ordinary volition." She pushed a strand of honey-coloured hair away from her dark features.

"Perhaps," said Oone. "Yet some of us can refuse the destiny that the Lords of Law and Chaos set out for us and still survive, still create something which the gods are forbidden to touch."

Varadia was sympathetic. "What we create remains a mystery," she said. "It is still hard for me to understand how I made that Pearl, creating the very thing my enemies sought in order to escape them. And then it became real!"

"I have known this to happen," said Oone. "It is those creations that a dreamthief seeks and earns a living from." She laughed. "That Pearl would bring me a good wage for a long time if I took it to market."

"How is it that reality is formed from dreams, Oone?"

Oone paused and looked down into the water which reflected